BEYOND AFFECTION

CALLAGHAN BROTHERS
BOOK 6

ABBIE ZANDERS

Copyright © 2015 by Abbie Zanders
All rights reserved.

Updates: February 2023

Visit my website at https://abbiezandersromance.com
Cover Designer: Graphics by Stacy
Editor: Jovana Shirley, Unforeseen Editing, www.unforeseenediting.com

No part of this book may be reproduced or transmitted in any form or by any means, electronic or mechanical, including photocopying, recording, or by any information storage and retrieval system without the written permission of the author, except for the use of brief quotations in a book review.

This book is a work of fiction. Names, characters, places, and incidents either are products of the author's imagination or are used fictitiously. Any resemblance to actual persons, living or dead, events, or locales is entirely coincidental.

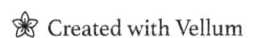

❀ Created with Vellum

BEFORE YOU BEGIN

WARNING: Due to frequent strong language and graphic scenes of a sexual nature, this book is intended for mature (21+) readers only. In addition, this particular story touches upon some very dark, disturbing topics.

It was hard to guess her age; in slumber, she could have passed for one of the undergrads, but his instincts suggested she was more likely in her mid- to late-twenties.

She looked so peaceful; he hated to disturb her. But the elderly custodian had peeked in twice already and was obviously anxious to finish up and go home. The evening class had ended nearly an hour earlier, and besides the cleaning staff, they were the only two people remaining in the building.

"Miss?" he prompted, keeping his tone low and gentle to avoid startling her.

She sighed softly at the sound of his voice, a ghost of a smile playing at the corners of her lips.

"Miss?" he repeated again, reaching over to touch her upper arm.

Her head tilted toward his hand, covering it in silken blonde waves a moment before the warmth of her cheek soaked into his skin. Shane's attempts to wake the woman had somehow resulted in her using his hand as her pillow. The custodian snickered from the doorway.

Shane smiled. He flexed his hand rhythmically but gently, watching with amusement as her head bobbed with the movement. It only took a few moments for her to rouse. Those sleepy eyes opened. He was right—they were a shade of cerulean he'd only seen in the heavens. Bemusement filled them for a moment, and then they landed on him and widened in horrified embarrassment.

"I fell asleep," she murmured with the huskiness that came from deep slumber.

Shane's grin widened. "I must say, I've guest-lectured for Professor Stevens several times, but this is the first time a female student has ever actually drooled over me."

The woman groaned, lifting her head to examine the wetness on his hand. "Oh God," she moaned in mortification as she used the sleeve of her hooded pale-tan sweater to wipe it off with hurried strokes. "I'm so sorry."

Shane wasn't. Mild interest mixed with amusement, as it had from the moment he saw her nodding off halfway through his interactive segment on modern social mores. Most of the time, students found that part particularly interesting, and this class had been no exception. Well, except for her. While hands had shot up all around her, her head had gone down.

"I think this is the part where the earth is supposed to open up and swallow me," she said ruefully. "At least, that's what I'm praying for right now. You might want to take a step back."

He couldn't help it; he laughed. It bubbled up from deep within and felt wonderful. She was embarrassed, yes, but was able to see the humor in the situation. Shane liked a woman who could laugh at herself.

"I guess I don't need to ask what you thought of my lecture."

"I liked it," she said quickly, gathering her books.

Shane arched a brow and inclined his head doubtfully.

"Well," she added with a slightly dimpled smile, "the part I heard anyway. But I haven't been getting enough sleep lately, and your voice is wonderfully warm and soothing and ..." Her eyes widened, and the words cut off suddenly. She dropped her gaze, even as that pretty rose color deepened in her cheeks and spread down the delicate column of her neck. "Oh, God. Open mouth, insert foot. I need to stop talking now."

That only served to draw him in further. He was absolutely enthralled by this adorable, sleepy creature who had just told him she liked the sound of his voice. "Why?"

"Why?" Hands full, she blew a stray section of hair away from where it had fallen over one long-lashed eye. "Because I'm perilously close to dying from self-humiliation, and from what I've heard, it's not a pretty way to go. I'd hate for you to have to witness that. Haunts you for weeks."

Why did he suddenly feel so warm and light inside?

"Why have you not been getting enough sleep?" he clarified before he could stop himself, hoping as he did so that she would not take offense at his curiosity.

"Oh." She hastily tried to stuff her notes into her over-crammed backpack, shooting him a wry smile. The look she gave him—friendly and genuine—pierced him like a bolt of sunlight and did funny things to his insides. "You know, the usual. Too much to do and not enough time to do it." The pack tipped off the desk, and its contents spilled onto the floor. She mumbled a few unintelligible things under her breath.

"Did you just say *fudge buckets*?" he asked, barely suppressing another laugh.

"Yeah, sorry about the potty mouth," she replied but was grinning herself. It hinted at those dimples again.

Shane had a soft spot for dimples.

He knelt beside her and helped her gather her things, skillfully ordering them in her bag so that everything fit.

"You have a gift," she mused in appreciation. "I'm afraid I haven't been blessed with a keen sense of spatial perception. I tend to rely on the stuff-and-cram method myself, but your way works too."

She stood up at the same time he did, her face only inches from his collarbone. At six-two, he was accustomed to women being shorter than him, but she was even smaller than he'd originally thought. Her delicate femininity made him acutely aware of his own masculinity.

"Oh," she exclaimed softly.

He felt the tiny puff of air on his bare skin where he'd loosened his tie and unbuttoned the top of his shirt. He looked down to find her face tilted up toward his, regarding him with those pretty eyes.

That look, Shane thought. He liked that look. It smacked of innocence, surprise, and—dare he say—

desire. He grew taller, larger from it, like a male peacock who wanted to showcase his plumage.

She took a step back, only to stumble on the desk and fall backward. Shane reached out and caught her before she managed to hit anything. His entire body lit up as though someone had flipped a switch, firing up nerve endings in all kinds of interesting places. Her eyes widened, as if she'd felt it too.

"Thanks," she stammered.

If anything, his interest grew, as did the odd warmth that seemed to be coursing through his body. He didn't remove his hands immediately; he let them linger along her upper arms until he was fairly certain she would remain upright and in place.

"Perhaps I should walk you to your car," he suggested.

∽

Lacie smiled weakly, hoping he hadn't heard the small whimper that escaped. It was hard to concentrate on anything with his hands supporting her like that. Her face was only inches from some of the broadest shoulders she'd ever seen. He hadn't looked quite so big when she was sitting down.

She had the most bizarre and powerful urge to lean forward just a hair and *smell* him. That was the G-rated version. The R-rated version had her licking his skin, right there at the hollow of his throat, where a dark shadow was beginning to emerge. As it was, his clean, fresh scent was wrapping around her, making certain parts of her—the most feminine ones—tingle.

She forced herself to look up and then realized her mistake. He was looking down at her, the most beautiful blue eyes she'd ever seen locked on hers, those full, strong lips quirked in amusement. And his breath smelled like chocolate.

That's not fair. He has to look like that and smell like chocolate too?

This man was devastating each and every one of her senses, blowing them away with the force of a nuclear blast. Surely, she was still asleep, dreaming that the sexy prof was actually talking to, walking with, and smiling at her. That was the most logical explanation.

He held open the door for her, while his other hand protectively hovered along her back, its radiating heat contrasting with the crisp night air. She didn't blame him for his caution. So far, she'd fallen asleep in his class, babbled like an idiot, and nearly managed to fall backward over a stationary desk. Of course, walking into the doorway when she glanced back to make sure she *wasn't* dreaming probably didn't do much to convince him otherwise.

"I'm not known for my grace, but I'm not usually this clumsy either," she told him as she rubbed at the now-sore spot on her shoulder.

"You said you're tired," he offered.

She gratefully accepted that small kindness. "Yeah, that must be it."

It certainly couldn't be that a Celtic demigod in human form was walking with her. Speaking with her. Touching her occasionally. It was no secret on campus that when Shane Callaghan guest-lectured in Professor Stevens's Ethics class, it was standing room only. She vaguely wondered where everyone else had gone. Normally, the line to speak with him extended out into the hallway; at least, that was what her younger sister had told her when she took this class last semester.

As they walked along, she realized that not only the classroom was empty, but the entire building as well. She withheld another groan at the thought that everyone must have witnessed her unintentional snooze. Night school was hard enough without adding social ineptitude.

Sparks shot out from the point of contact on her lower back as Shane gently guided her around a piece of statuary that would have done some serious damage to her kneecaps had she walked into it.

"I'm questioning the sanity of letting you get behind the wheel." His deep voice wrapped around her like velvet, filled with obvious amusement.

What he didn't seem to realize was that *he* was the source of her current clumsiness. Shane Callaghan was the human male equivalent of a solar flare, messing up her circuits. She'd walked this path a hundred times and never had an issue. Well, not that anyone saw anyway.

Instead of voicing those thoughts aloud and adding

to her humiliation, however, she simply nodded, hoping to clear away some of the fog while at the same time clinging to it. "You're probably right. Maybe I should grab a coffee first."

"Mind if I join you?"

His words, completely unexpected, had her freezing so suddenly on the spot that Shane took a step beyond her before he realized she'd come to an abrupt halt.

"Why would you do that?" Lacie asked with genuine curiosity.

The light breeze caught his hair—a black so dark and shiny that it looked blue—pushing locks of it into his face. His eyes—a crystalline blue—were like brilliant sapphires in the moonlight. The effect was startling. She sucked in a breath, a conscious effort to remind her temporarily failing autonomic systems that breathing was essential.

He shrugged, offering a boyish grin. "I'm not sure exactly. Maybe because you've made me smile more in the last ten minutes than I have in the last ten days."

It took a few moments for his words to penetrate the haze. *Oh. Comic relief.* She could do that. It was probably the only time she'd ever get a chance like this, so why not?

"You like to live dangerously, don't you?" she said, flashing him a friendly smile. "No, I don't mind, but I'm warning you, you do so at your own risk."

"Duly noted." He chuckled. "But I think I'll take my chances."

CHAPTER TWO

Shane hadn't been entirely honest with her. She did make him smile, that much was true. Heaven knew, he could use more of that these days. Five of his brothers, including his twin, were now happily married, leaving only him and his younger brother, Kieran, feeling somewhat ... lost? Left behind maybe?

They'd always been a close-knit group. For the most part, their adult lives had been a series of dangerous missions, interspersed with Callaghan-centric recharge time. Over the last several years though, the dynamics had changed. They had wives and kids to turn to. They had other places to go. Other things to do.

Not that Shane sat around on the sidelines, twiddling his thumbs, not by any means. As the legal counsel for his family and their vast and lucrative interests, he stayed busy. With himself and Kieran as the only unattached males, they were taking on more assignments, both out of a sense of responsibility and for the sense of purpose it gave them.

But it wasn't the same. Things were changing. Keeping busy wasn't enough anymore. And Shane found himself looking. For what, he wasn't sure. Just ... *something*.

He stole a glance down, catching the illusion of sunshine and moonlight as the old-fashioned streetlamps cast their light upon her golden hair. The sweet, subtle scent of lilies and orchids drifted up to him, wrapping around him like a soft breeze. He filled his lungs with it. Such a light fragrance. Clean. Simple. Pure. Feminine.

Something.

She was being especially cautious now, paying particular attention to where she was walking. Shane bit back a smile. He was being particularly attentive as well. If she stumbled or tripped again, he would catch her. He almost wished she would. It would give him an excuse to touch her again.

The lights of the all-night campus coffee shop glowed welcomingly. Shane stepped forward to open the door for her while performing a quick scan of the room. It was a habit, one that had come from years of special forces work—first for the government and then with his family's "nonexistent" team. Within seconds, the images were locked in his brain. He knew every exit and entry point, the complete layout of the building, and would be able to describe every other occupant in perfect detail.

He extended his hand toward the counter, indicating that she should order first. His curiosity was roused, and this little exercise would provide a chance to study and learn more about her.

He had a natural gift for reading people, for sensing their underlying natures. He could tell when someone was lying or when they were nervous. The ability had served him well over the years, but sometimes he wished he could turn it off. It would be nice to take people at face value occasionally and not know what lay beneath the surface.

The woman with him was slightly anxious, but it was a "good" anxiety, one based on anticipation, as opposed to the kind someone felt if they were afraid or hiding something. Nor was it the blatant, lusty admiration he often picked up from some of the younger coeds, the kind that'd had him turning on his heel and slipping out of the back of the classroom earlier, only to return for his sleeping beauty once the lingerers had left.

Oh, she was interested. The way her cheeks flushed that lovely pink and her pupils dilated every time she looked at him were clear tells. But it was the subtlety of it that made all the difference.

This woman was not the type to throw herself at a man or take the initiative.

That was encouraging.

She had a sense of humor. Her smile lit him up

from the inside out. She smelled like flowers and had what he could only describe as a refreshingly honest interest in him and his company.

His initial analysis was promising indeed.

Personal desire aside, this was also an exercise in the study of human nature. Would she defer to him or order for herself? Would she select something she actually wanted, or would she be more worried about what he might think?

"Medium hazelnut, extra cream and sugar, and, um, let me see ... how about one of those cream-filled doughnuts with the chocolate icing, please?"

Shane smiled broadly and then doubled her order. She grinned right back at him.

By the time she dug down into the front pocket of her blue jeans and extracted a handful of crumpled bills, Shane had already paid.

He picked up the tray and guided her back to the most private booth in the place. The on-campus café wasn't overly crowded at this time of night, but there were a few tables occupied.

"Thank you," she said the moment they sat down. "You didn't have to pay."

Shane shrugged, an easy lift of his shoulders. "It's the least I could do," he said. "I'm the one who put you to sleep."

She flushed a very pretty shade of rose. He couldn't help but wonder how far down that color extended.

"I'm just glad you were kind enough to wake me," she said, taking a sip of her coffee. "I can imagine waking up at midnight with the wood grain of the desk ingrained in my cheek and being locked in for the night."

Shane laughed again. "Now, there's a visual. I'm glad I could help." He took a sip of his coffee. "I seem to be at a disadvantage here. I don't know your name."

"Lacie," she said, extending her hand over the table. "Lacie McCain."

"It's a pleasure, Lacie McCain," he said sincerely as he took her hand. He briefly considered bringing it up to his lips, but he refrained, choosing instead to let the soft weight of her hand rest in his, pleasantly warm and firm.

The contact lasted longer than it would have had it been anyone else's, but he didn't want to let go. On the contrary, he wanted to pull her over to his side of the booth, so she would be closer to him. The urge was so unexpected and powerful that it took him a moment to process. That had never happened to him before. Being the intellectual that he was, it definitely warranted further study.

"Shane Callaghan."

"I know who you are," she said, amused.

Of course she knew who he was; he had guest-lectured her class. Shane offered a slightly embarrassed grin, reluctantly releasing her hand. She let it linger a moment more before reclaiming it to break off a bite-sized piece of doughnut.

Her next words surprised him. "I recognized you earlier. You spoke at Maggie Flynn's rezoning meeting a while back. You were wonderful, by the way. Very eloquent."

Her words had been spoken with no trace of flirtatious flattery. Shane's mind flew back to that night, his photographic memory allowing him to review the room section by section. Ah, there she was, sitting left of center, halfway back. He remembered his eyes had lingered on her then, too, but had turned away when the man she was sitting next to draped his arm around her shoulders and cast a possessive glance in his direction.

"I remember," he said without thinking, which was something very out of character for him. "You were with someone. Tall guy, short-cropped hair, ex-military."

Lacie's eyes opened wide. "How could you possibly remember that?"

Shane shrugged, realizing his mistake. "Blessed with a good memory, I guess."

Some people were put off by his ability to remember and recall things at will; it was not something he shared often. His brothers knew, and that was enough. If this woman was who he was beginning to suspect she was, it wouldn't matter, but he wasn't about to take any unnecessary chances until he was certain. He was a cautious man by nature.

Lacie, however, was as astute as she was attractive. "Better than good, I'd guess. Photographic?"

Shane nodded cautiously, but once again, his instincts had been correct.

Lacie's grin grew. "And you're modest too. You are not at all what I expected, Mr. Callaghan."

"Shane, please," he insisted. He was on the verge of asking her exactly what she had expected, which would have been followed closely by inquiring just when and for how long she had been thinking of him in any regard, but decided against it.

"So, you were there to speak on Maggie's behalf?"

"Yes. Maggie is amazing. My parents used to take me and my brother and sister up there back when Maggie's grandparents were still alive to pick apples and pumpkins and go on the hayrides. We made such wonderful memories. Now, I take my kids there. They love it."

Shane's chest constricted; his focus snapped back to the woman across from him, the memory of that man's arm around her shoulders flashing in his mind's eye again. "You have children?"

Lacie's shy smile lit the whole room. "Not technically, no. I teach kindergarten. I refer to my students that way. For a few hours each day at least, they are mine."

The tightening in his chest eased. He could easily picture her in a room full of little ones, sitting on the floor with them surrounding her as she read from a book of fairy tales. Even with his talent for detailed imagery, this one was particularly clear.

"You're not married then?" he fished. He'd already noticed she wore no ring on her finger, nor was there any indentation or tan line, but he would rather hear the confirmation from her lips.

A light-pink blush suffused her cheeks. "No."

"Seeing anyone?" He tried to keep his expression neutral, but he could not keep the glimmer of hope from his eyes.

"Not unless you count this," she teased. "You?"

The neutral expression vanished; a genuine grin took its place. "Present company excluded? No."

The next few hours flew by. Shane learned that in addition to teaching morning and afternoon kindergarten classes at Pine Ridge Elementary School, she was also working toward her master's degree in education, one night class at a time, ruefully noting how long it would take her to finish the program.

She had one older brother, Brian, who was in the service—Army. He'd gone missing nearly three years earlier while stationed in Afghanistan. From the way she spoke of him, Shane could tell that they were very close. Lacie believed that he was alive and would return, saying with absolute conviction that if Brian were gone, she would *know*. He didn't immediately discount her claim. He had similar connections with his brothers, often instinctively sensing when one was in trouble.

She also had a younger sister, Corinne, who was a full-time undergrad at the university. It was Corinne, he learned, who had recommended Professor Stevens's Ethics course to her sister to fulfill one of her optional humanity requirements. Shane was profoundly grateful she had.

Lacie had an apartment in town—a property owned and managed by the Callaghan family, he noted—where she could be close to both the elementary school and the university. She had no roommates, but sometimes her sister crashed with Lacie, especially when she had early morning classes.

He wasn't the only one probing for intel. Lacie was curious about him too. Shane obviously couldn't tell her everything about himself, but he did mention that he had a law degree and dabbled in real estate. She knew of the pub his brothers Jake and Ian ran together, which was not surprising since Pine Ridge was a small community, though she admitted she'd never actually been inside. She also knew of the garage his twin, Sean, owned and operated. She had heard that Maggie had married a Callaghan, a doctor whose name she could not quite recall until Shane told her, and that Kieran ran the popular fitness center, BodyWorks, downtown.

When Lacie's cell phone chimed with a pleasant, classical melody, she gasped at the time. "I'm sorry, I should take this," she said to Shane.

"Go right ahead," he replied, curious as to who was calling her at that hour.

She accepted the call and raised the device to her ear.

"Where the hell are you? Is everything all right?"

Lacie immediately held the phone away from her

ear, wincing. Shane had no trouble hearing the agitated male voice projecting through the tiny speaker. Inwardly, he tensed.

"I'm fine," Lacie said when the shouting stopped, shooting an apologetic glance at Shane. "Just lost track of time."

The caller fired off another series of questions in rapid succession. "What are you doing? Are you still at the university? It's too late to be out. Tell me where you are. I'll come get you and bring you home."

Lacie responded with practiced patience; Shane had the distinct impression that this was a common occurrence and something she was accustomed to. He, however, was not and found it gratingly irritating.

"Coffee. I'm having coffee. Yes, I'm still on campus. No, I don't want you to come and get me. I'm perfectly capable of getting myself home."

There was a brief pause and then, "You're not alone, are you? Who's with you, Lacie?"

Shane heard the man clearly and bristled at the possessive tone in his voice. His mind brought up the image from the rezoning hearing, and somehow, he knew it was the same man.

"That's really none of your business," Lacie said politely but firmly. Her cheeks pinked in either embarrassment or annoyance—maybe a little of each. "And I'll be fine. Go to bed, Craig. I'll talk to you tomorrow." She disconnected the call and sighed.

"I'm sorry," she said to Shane as she began to pile the remains of the sugar packets and creamers on the tray. "I didn't realize it was so late. I should be going. Thanks for the coffee and the doughnut as well as your company. This was really nice."

He didn't like the shadow that darkened her pretty face. "Everything okay?"

"Yeah." She smiled unconvincingly.

"An ex?" he prompted. Normally, he was not one to push, but he couldn't help himself.

"No," she said quickly. "Nothing like that. More like an overprotective big brother."

Maybe to her, Shane thought, but his instincts told him the caller saw things differently.

It was something that would have to be investigated in greater detail, but that was for a later time. One when she wasn't looking at him with those big blue eyes and their time together was drawing to such a swift and unwelcome close.

"You're safe with me," he said softly.

Oh, the look she gave him! Hope mixed with a touch of wonder. Anticipation and something else—something strong and feral—bubbled in his veins.

"Yes." A simple affirmation but one that he felt all through his body.

Does she feel it too? he wondered. That invisible connection that was already forming between them?

He smiled, forcing his hands into his pockets to keep from sliding his fingers into that silken mass and kissing her, erasing every other man from her memory. "I can't remember the last time I enjoyed an evening so much," he told her truthfully.

"Doesn't say much for your social life," she teased, but he could tell that she was pleased.

"I can say the same of yours," he countered.

"I don't know," she mused. "I think I definitely got the better end of the deal."

She stood, tossing her backpack over one shoulder. Shane picked up the tray and followed her toward the door, falling into step beside her as they walked toward the commuter parking lot. Perhaps he should have asked if she minded the escort, but it didn't matter. He wasn't about to let her walk through the campus alone this late at night.

She stopped at a silvery-blue VW Passat, not one of the later models, but in relatively good condition. Shane opened the door for her and glanced inside. The interior was clean but untidy.

"I know what you're thinking," she said, following his gaze to the piles of paperwork and boxes of arts and crafts supplies. "But believe it or not, I know where everything is. Every time I try to organize things, I lose them indefinitely."

His lips curled into a smile. "Fair enough."

By nature, he was a very neat, organized person. He could use a little disorder in his life, especially if it came in the form of a certain blonde schoolteacher who smelled like spring flowers.

"May I call you sometime?" he asked, leaning against the car as she fastened her seat belt.

Her grin lit a fire in his chest. "I'd like that."

A straightforward, honest answer, he noted with

approval. So much of his life was based on secrets and deception, word games, and acts meant to hide the truth.

He glanced again at her eyes, sweeping across her facial expression. Her body language was somewhat relaxed, comfortable, but he couldn't help but notice the tap of her finger against the steering wheel. Not nervous, but ... a little excited perhaps? Yeah, he'd take that.

She recited her mobile number, thanked him again, and wished him a good night.

CHAPTER THREE

Lacie drove home with a pleasantly warm, tingling feeling throughout her body and a contented smile on her face. Though it had started off badly, it'd ended up being a fine evening. Shane had been wonderful company. It was easily the best date she'd ever had even though it wasn't really a date. More like an unplanned, fortuitous encounter. They'd done nothing more than talk over coffee.

He wasn't anything like she'd expected. Usually, men who looked like he did had egos the size of Texas, but he was down-to-earth and easy to talk to. More interested in talking about her than himself.

He'd seemed to enjoy himself, too, though since she could count the number of dates she'd had on one hand, she was no expert. She'd never felt so instantly at ease with anyone before. Well, perhaps *at ease* wasn't the proper phrase. There were parts of her that had flared to life and remained fired up throughout the evening.

Besides being extremely handsome, he was also smart, funny, attentive, and a perfect gentleman. He hadn't even attempted to kiss her good night.

She had mixed feelings about that. Her cautious nature appreciated his self-restraint, but there were other parts that were curious about what it would be like to kiss him. It had been impossible *not* to think about it while sitting across from him, looking into his beautiful, masculine face, listening to that velvety voice, and smelling the clean, sexy scent that clung to his body.

Lacie shook her head and focused on the road. What the heck was wrong with her? She wasn't the crushing type. She didn't gawk over good-looking men —okay, maybe sometimes, she did but only discreetly —and was a firm believer in establishing compatibility before even thinking about progressing to something more.

Shane Callaghan, apparently, was a glaring exception to her usual rules because she *was* crushing. They were obviously compatible, and she was thinking some very physical thoughts.

It was a constant battle back and forth for the five-mile drive, but her propriety eventually won out. By the time she pulled into her complex, she decided she was glad he hadn't tried to kiss her. Not only had it indicated that he was a gentleman, but it'd also hinted that he might be interested in something more than a good time. Not to mention, it was already increasing her anticipation for when he did eventually kiss her—assuming that things did progress to that point, of course.

She tried not to get her hopes up. Yes, he had asked for her number, but that didn't mean he would call. She hoped he did though. After only a few hours with him, she knew she would be terribly disappointed if he didn't.

"Lacie." The voice startled her, making her jump.

She whipped around, accidentally pushing the car door closed before she could get her hand completely out of the way. She bit back a cry and extracted her hand, flexing it experimentally. Nothing seemed to be broken, but it would be sore tomorrow, and she'd probably have to tape it up. It wouldn't be the first time.

"Craig, you scared me half to death! What are you doing out here?"

"Making sure you got home safely," he said without apology. His eyes scanned her head to toe. Though he was no longer in the Army, he chose to keep his blond hair shaved close to the scalp in military fashion and still wore his tags beneath the army-green tee stretched across his muscular frame. "Let me see your hand."

She ignored his request, reaching in the car with her other hand to grab her backpack. He took it from her, carelessly tossing it to the ground while grasping her forearm. She pulled away, irritated.

Ever since he'd come back from overseas, he'd been especially protective. Brian had always looked out for her as her big brother, and as Brian's best friend, Craig had been right there with him, so it hadn't been a total surprise when Craig simply picked up where he'd left off. Maybe it was his way of dealing with Brian's MIA status, too, which was understandable, but at the moment, it was pissing her off. They weren't kids anymore, and she didn't need a keeper.

"Come on. Let me take care of that for you," he said, reaching out again.

"I'm fine," she said through clenched teeth, partly out of annoyance and partly from the painful throb along the back of her hand. She pulled it back out of his grasp, sucking air at the sudden stab that resulted from it.

"Stop being so stubborn. We need to ice that up before it swells."

"No." She picked up her bag and pushed past him. "That's what *I* need to do. *You* need to go back to your own apartment and stop treating me like a child."

He trailed closely behind, invading her personal space. "I will when you stop acting like one."

She increased her pace, not stopping until she reached her door. Craig snatched the keys from her hand to unlock it. Ignoring her protests, he followed her inside and went right to the freezer. He pulled out a bag of frozen peas and put it on her hand.

Lacie sighed, too tired to fight. In their lifetimes, they'd replayed some version of this scenario a hundred times, and he always won. Besides, she was in too good of a mood to let Craig's antics dampen her spirits.

"Who was he?" Craig asked, pulling open the cabinet that was so well stocked with medical supplies.

As a joke, everyone in her family had bought her first aid kits for her last birthday, given her proclivity toward accidents. It was proving to be more practical than she would have liked, especially since Craig had moved into the apartment across the hall.

"Who?" It was immature on her part perhaps, but if he was going to accuse her of acting like a child, then she would oblige him.

He shot her a look that told her without a doubt that he was not amused. "Don't make me have to find out on my own, Lacie, because I will."

Yes, he probably would, she thought, and he wouldn't be subtle about it.

Craig knew everyone in town and had a way of ferreting out information that was downright scary sometimes. By telling him herself, she might avoid being the topic of a few local inquiries.

"Shane Callaghan," she said, wincing when he pulled the tape tight around her hand.

The name struck a chord, judging by the way her hand was folding inside his strong grip. The slight ache turned into a sharp pain; she made a noise of protest until he let up.

"What the hell were you doing with him?"

"Having coffee," she answered with a scowl,

snatching back her hand and trying unsuccessfully to flex it. "He guest-lectured for Professor Stevens tonight. I fell asleep in his class."

Despite his ire, one side of Craig's mouth twitched. "You fell asleep in his class? Did you drool on the desk too?"

"Afraid so. He had a heck of a time waking me up. Apparently, I slept well past the end of the lecture, and the janitor was about to lock me in."

Some of the tension drained from Craig's face and he cracked a tiny smile.

"He asked me if I was okay to drive, I said I was going to grab some coffee, and he said that sounded like a good idea. End of story."

She didn't go into any more detail than that, shrugging it off as if it meant nothing. To admit to anything more would get Craig's protective hackles up. Besides, she didn't know if it would amount to anything. She certainly hoped it did, and if so, she would deal with Craig then. She'd learned to pick her battles with him.

"That's it?" he asked, finishing up the wrap and stepping back.

"That's it. Satisfied?"

He stared at her for a long minute, as if trying to decide if she was telling him the truth, and then nodded. "I worry about you, Lace. You're too trusting. Any number of guys would take advantage of that."

She nodded, though she disagreed. She didn't consider herself unreasonably trusting, nor did she think Shane Callaghan was the type of man to take advantage of anyone, but she held her tongue. Craig was finally calming down, and she didn't want to get him riled again.

"Thanks, Craig," she said, stifling a yawn. "But I'm beat, and I'm afraid that caffeine rush is over. I've got school tomorrow."

"All right, babe. I'm out of here. Lock the door behind me, yeah?"

"I will."

"Night, Lace."

"Good night, Craig."

With a sigh of relief, Lacie closed the door behind him and then engaged the dead bolt as well as the chain. She exchanged the thawing bag of peas for a wraparound ice pack and shuffled toward the bedroom, where she peeled off her clothes and slipped between the sheets, not even bothering with the effort of pajamas. Her head barely hit the pillow when her cell chimed softly. She looked at the display, frowning when the caller ID showed up as *Withheld*.

Who the heck is calling at this hour?

Curiosity got the best of her. "Hello?"

"Lacie? Did I wake you?" Shane's voice flowed fluidly through the phone and into her skin. It had been bad enough when she was fully clothed and in a public café, but now that she was naked between her sheets in the darkness, it was downright erotic.

"No, I was just crawling into bed."

There was a momentary pause before he asked, "I

suppose it would be improper for me to ask what you're wearing?"

If anyone else had said those words to her after knowing her for only a few hours, she would have made a rude comment and hung up on them. But this was Shane, and she could hear the teasing in his voice. Once again, he was an exception to her usual rules.

She chuckled. "Very."

"Right. I'll just use my imagination then."

"You do that."

He laughed, confirming her belief that he was having fun with her and was not a complete pervert.

"I know there's some protocol for exactly how long a man should wait before calling when a woman gives him her number, but I'll readily admit to being woefully ignorant of such things and hope that you find my confession adorably honest enough to let me slide. Would you please have dinner with me this Friday, Lacie?"

The warmth that had sparked at the first sound of his voice now blossomed from the very core of her being, filling her with a sensation she found both intensely pleasing and exciting. "I would very much like to have dinner with you this Friday, Shane," she said without hesitation.

She could practically hear the smile in his voice. "Excellent. Wear something nice, elegant but not too formal. I'll pick you up at seven."

"Sounds good."

"Lacie?"

"Yes?"

"Pleasant dreams."

With Shane's velvety voice echoing in her head and the promise of seeing him again in three days, that was a given.

CHAPTER FOUR

Lacie was a patient person by nature, but anticipation rode her hard for the next few days. It was a good thing her kids kept her so busy. There were only a couple of weeks left in the school year, and there was still so much to do.

During the daytime hours, her mind was sufficiently occupied with word walls, story time, and other things to keep a room of twenty five-year-olds focused and busy. Not so in the evenings, when her thoughts were decidedly more adult-oriented. More than once, she'd had to pull herself back from daydreaming about her upcoming date with Shane while grading papers or planning out the next day's lessons.

Shane hadn't provided much in the way of hints, so her active imagination was working overtime, conjuring all sorts of images. She knew they were going to dinner and that it would be a nice place. That left a lot of room for supposition.

Where were they going? Would there be that same inexplicable, instant attraction between them, and if so, would it be as strong as it had been the first time? Would she be able to make it through the night without tripping or walking into something or knocking something over? If it went well, would he attempt to kiss her good night this time?

That last thought sent yet another delicious tingle of anticipation through her. Of all the things she'd been thinking of, kissing Shane was one of her favorites. In her private, late-night fantasies, Shane Callaghan was an exceptional kisser.

"So, who's the hottie?" her younger sister, Corinne, asked, sprawled across Lacie's bed as Lacie tried on her seventh dress.

"Who says he's hot?" Lacie asked, turning in the mirror and frowning at her backside. *Time to start working out again*, she thought, having lost the motivation to exercise every day like she once had.

"He must be for you to give him the time of day," Corinne quipped, sliding gracefully to her feet and selecting a black sheath from Lacie's closet. "We all know how particular you are."

Lacie took the dress and slipped it on. It was perfect. Conservative but flattering. Subtle but sexy.

"I'm not that particular. It's just that very few men ask me out."

That was true. Enough had shown interest, but for some reason, things never seemed to progress beyond that.

"That's because Craig scares them off." Corinne's tone was less than cordial.

"You think so?" Lacie frowned. "How would you even know that?"

"Duh," her sister said. "He's like white on rice, Lace. You being the rice."

Lacie laughed, but inside, she squirmed. Craig *was* attentive, and he did seem to be around a lot. Lacie chalked it up to having too much time on his hands and too few outside interests. He was lost without his wife, lost without Brian. As she was Brian's sister and his wife, Mikaela's, best friend, maybe he saw a bit of both of them in her and clung to that.

"He's a little overprotective, I admit, but it's not like he's a stalker or anything."

Corinne snorted but thankfully let it go. There were more important issues at stake here. "So ... a name?"

Lacie's grin was brilliant, her unease dissipating instantly as visions of blue eyes and a sexy grin filled her mind. "Shane Callaghan."

Corinne, rooting through Lacie's limited jewelry collection, whirled around in shock. "*Really?*"

"Really," confirmed Lacie, pleased with her sister's response.

"Oh. My. God. He is the epitome of hot. How'd you manage that?" Corinne handed her an antique silver bracelet with tiny blue sapphires and a matching necklace and then plopped down on the bed. "*Dish.*" Cross-legged, eagerly leaning forward with her elbows on her knees, she demanded information.

Lacie obliged, relaying the story of how they'd met, while Corinne stared, openmouthed.

"You fell asleep in his class, drooled on his hand, fell over a desk, and walked into a doorway?"

"Pretty much."

"Hmm. Unconventional but clearly effective. Think it would work for me?"

Lacie laughed. "Like you could ever be anything less than graceful, Rinn. Syrup doesn't move as fluidly as you do."

"So true," Corinne admitted without a trace of vanity. She'd been taking ballet and gymnastics since she was a toddler. She didn't walk as much as *flowed*.

She pointed at the tape covering Lacie's hand. It stood out like an eyesore against the elegant black dress. "We need to do something about that though," she remarked. "Do you need it?"

Lacie looked at her hand. It still hurt if she moved a certain way, making her think that she might have fractured a few bones after all. She'd meant to go down to the nearest urgent care and get it X-rayed, but it had been a busy week.

"No, I think I'll be all right." She held out her hand for Corinne to cut the wrap with a pair of cuticle scissors. As long as she didn't move it too much, she'd be okay for a couple of hours. She'd just make sure she didn't order a meal that required a two-handed maneuver, like cutting.

Lacie was just about finished dressing when Corinne glanced out the window.

"Uh-oh. Don't look now, but here comes Craig and Shelly with a pizza."

A stab of guilt shot through Lacie. "It's Friday night," she said, hoping Corinne didn't catch the forced casualness in her voice.

As part of a joint custody agreement with his in-laws, Craig had his daughter on the weekends. Craig's wife—Shelly's mother—had died tragically in a car crash two years earlier. Fortunately, Shelly had been too young to fully comprehend what had happened.

Lacie thought the world of the little girl. Shelly was in Lacie's morning class and was such a sweet child. Ever since Craig had moved into the apartment across the hall six months earlier, it had become a tradition to order takeout and watch movies together on the weekend. It had never been an issue before; Lacie rarely had other plans.

Corinne pinned her older sister with a look. "He doesn't know you've got a date, does he?"

Lacie didn't meet her eyes, focusing on sliding on the thigh-high stockings instead. "It didn't come up."

"Oh, Lace. It's getting worse, isn't it?"

"Yes," Lacie breathed.

She didn't bother lying to her sister; Corinne would see right through it.

Corinne had been the first one to say something to Lacie when Craig's interest seemed to go beyond what might be considered reasonable, but Lacie had rationalized his behavior. They'd grown up together. Craig was like a second brother who felt an added responsibility since Brian had gone missing. Corinne pointed out that those same reasons could be applied to her as well, but Craig's obsession only seemed to extend to Lacie. Over the last few months, Lacie had found herself agreeing with Corinne more and more, though she would not admit it—not yet. She was getting close though. Maybe it was because he was living right across the hall, but the overall effect now bordered on smothering.

"Have you tried talking to him about it?"

"Yes. Hasn't helped much though. And afterward, I feel bad, you know? Like I kicked a puppy or something."

"This is serious, Lace. You need to talk to Dad."

"And say what exactly? Craig's looking out for me too much? He makes sure I get home safely every night? Calls me every day to see if I need anything? Insists on repairing every little leak and squeak for me? Jeez, Rinn, Dad's more likely to pat him on the back than tell him to back off. He had a barbecue in celebration when Craig informed him the place across the hall from me opened up and he was taking it."

Corinne bit her lip. "Well, when you put it like that, I can see your point. But I don't know, Lace. I know Craig has had a really hard time of it and all, and Shelly is, like, the sweetest little girl ever, but he gives me the creeps. Have you seen the way he looks at you sometimes? There's nothing brotherly about it."

"You're overreacting," she said, but inwardly, Lacie suppressed a shudder.

"Oh, fuck me," Corinne breathed, slicing into Lacie's thoughts.

Lacie was just about to admonish her for her vulgarity when she joined her at the window to see what had commanded such an exclamation. For a few moments, her heart stopped beating, and she found the same phrase echoing in her own mind. Shane Callaghan had just pulled up to the apartment building in a sleek black Lexus. He was beyond devastating in a black suit, white shirt, and silvery-blue-gray tie.

"Any chance you're feeling ill and you need me to cover for you?" Corinne asked hopefully.

"Not a prayer," Lacie breathed, forgetting her injured hand as she wiped her suddenly sweaty palms on her dress. A nauseating pain echoed up her arm and right into the pit of her stomach. She'd have to remember not to do that.

Corinne could barely contain her excitement when Shane knocked on the door a short time later. She opened it, grinning from ear to ear like a Cheshire cat.

"Come on in," she said. "My sister's almost ready."

∽

SHANE STEPPED INTO THE APARTMENT, allowing her to close the door behind him. The young woman who greeted him had the same honeyed hair and similarly unusual shade of blue eyes as Lacie. She was smiling broadly, not even trying to hide the fact that she was checking him out from the back as well as the front.

"You must be Corinne," he said smoothly. "Lacie's younger sister."

"Not that much younger." She grinned suggestively, but it was done with such good humor that he smiled right along with her.

"Rinn!" Lacie admonished, entering the room. "Ignore her," she said to Shane. "She hasn't quite mastered her hormones yet."

Corinne snorted indignantly in response, but Shane barely heard it. His smile faded as he got his first good look at Lacie.

"You look ... stunning," he said.

Gone was the adorable klutz in jeans and a hoodie, who had fallen asleep in his class. In her place was a gloriously sexy, curvaceous woman, sheathed in black, her bare skin glowing with a natural radiance that made him want to lick his lips. Her blonde mane had been tamed into an updo that left small strands framing a face perfectly done with the slightest hint of makeup.

"She does, doesn't she?" Corinne said smugly, openly taking credit for the makeover. "All my doing, of course. Hey, you guys match."

They did. *Perfectly*, he thought. Their clothes went together well too.

"Shall I put those in some water?" Corinne prompted, a mischievous glint in her eye as she pointed to the bouquet of flowers Shane held in his hand.

He and Lacie seemed to have been frozen, staring at each other like star-crossed lovers.

Shane blinked, remembering the gift he'd brought. "Of course." He grinned and held the flowers out to Lacie. "For you."

She took them, bowing her head to inhale their sweet scent. "They're beautiful, Shane. Thank you."

"Hey, Lace, do you have a vase around here somewhere?" Corinne called from the kitchen area. "No, of course not," she mumbled a few seconds later when no response was forthcoming. "Why would you?" She gave up and filled a glass pitcher sporting pictures of lemon slices along the sides with water, lifting the flowers from Lacie's hand and placing them in the makeshift vase.

"Oh, for heaven's sake," Corinne said, rolling her eyes. "Are you guys going out to dinner, or are you going to stand here, making googly eyes at each other all night?"

Lacie flushed a dark pink, but Shane laughed.

"Dinner first, googly eyes later. What do you think?"

"I'll try, but no promises. You're gorgeous."

Shane's grin grew. "Thank you."

Lacie seemed confused until Corinne leaned over and whispered loudly, "You said that out loud, sis."

"Ah fudge," Lacie murmured, her cheeks growing even pinker.

Shane held out his hand. "Shall we?"

"Have fun, kids," Corinne said as she closed the door behind them. "Midnight curfew, Cinderella. Charming, behave yourself."

Lacie started apologizing for her sister when the door across the hall suddenly opened and a male form filled the doorway. The guy took one look at Lacie and Shane, a flash of barely contained fury washing over his features before he hid it carefully beneath a mask. Shane caught it, recognizing him as the man who'd been with Lacie at the rezoning meeting.

"Lacie!" said the tiny urchin scooting through Craig's legs to hug her. "You look like a princess! Who's your friend?"

Lacie's features softened; she obviously adored the little girl. "Shelly, this is Shane. Shane, this is Shelly and her dad, Craig Davidson."

The men nodded tightly to each other. Shane smiled and said hi to the little girl.

"You look really pretty," the little girl continued, reaching out to touch the bracelet on Lacie's wrist. "Are you and your friend going to watch movies with us tonight?"

Lacie smiled. "Not tonight, sweetie."

Shelly frowned. "Whatcha gonna do?"

"Go out to dinner."

"Will you come over later?"

"No, you'll probably be in bed by the time we get back. But I'll see you tomorrow."

"Good. Daddy's making pancakes. You love Daddy's pancakes."

Shane didn't like the way Davidson's chest puffed out at the child's statement; there was something far too possessive in the action for his taste, and it was clearly making Lacie uncomfortable. He put his hand to Lacie's lower back, pleased with the way she unconsciously shifted her weight into it. Davidson's eyes filled with fire as he zeroed in on Shane's hand.

Lacie wished them a good night. As they walked away, Shane could feel Davidson's glare almost as tangibly as he felt the tension coiling in the woman beside him.

He expected Lacie to say something about Davidson and his little girl, but she didn't. Her sudden uneasiness worried him. He helped her into the car, then slid into the driver's seat. "Are you okay?"

She looked at him and smiled. "Yes. I'm sorry about that."

He pulled out of the lot. "Don't be. The little girl really seems to like you."

"She's a good kid," Lacie said. "Her mom was a friend of mine."

"Was?"

"She died in a car accident two years ago."

"I'm sorry."

"Thanks. It was a difficult time. Craig had only just been sent home from Afghanistan, not sure if he'd ever walk again and blaming himself for Brian's disappearance. Shelly was just three, too young to realize what was going on, but maybe that's a blessing."

"Davidson was with your brother?"

"Yes. They were good friends. They did everything together, including enlisting. It was like having two big brothers instead of just one."

Shane had seen the look in the man's eyes, and it reinforced his earlier impression that Davidson's feelings for Lacie went beyond brotherly affection. He'd have to step carefully until he learned more about what was between them. If he shared his gut feelings with Lacie at this point, she might not take it kindly. Until he had a chance to further explore this compelling attraction he felt for her, he didn't want to do anything that might push her away.

"He seems rather protective of you," he said instead, keeping his tone conversational and only mildly curious.

"He is," Lacie admitted, frowning.

"Does it bother you?"

"Sometimes," she exhaled. "I don't know. He's been different ever since he came back, you know? Something happened over there, something that changed him."

"War can have that effect on people." He spoke the words with the heaviness of someone who understood all too well how combat could change a man, how the need to commit unspeakable acts in the name of God and country and freedom could damage his soul.

"Were you in the service?" Lacie's attention was on him now.

"Yes."

"Not the Army?"

"SEALs."

"Do you ever talk about it?" she asked quietly. "What you've seen? Where you've been? What you've done?"

Shane cast her a sideways glance. She was looking at him with those big blue eyes, not with morbid curiosity, not with sympathy or pity, but because she was trying to understand something that was beyond her comprehension, past any frame of reference she might employ. Whether it had been her intent or not, she was reaching into a part of him that he kept tightly locked away.

"No."

"Why not?"

Shane slowed the vehicle and then stopped as the traffic light turned red. Turning his blue eyes on her, he said, "Because there are some things in this world that should never be spoken of."

He wasn't sure how she would respond to that; the conversation had taken an unexpected and dark turn. She seemed to give his answer some serious thought. Finally, she nodded, placing her small hand over his, where it rested on the gearshift. She got it, and she accepted it. He felt one of his internal tumblers moving slowly into place, the first in a series that would unlock his heart completely.

"It's different for me though," he continued. "I have six brothers and a father who were SEALs as well. I grew up with it, and I was constantly surrounded by men who understood exactly what I was going through because they'd gone through it themselves. We've always been there for one another even if we don't talk about it much."

Lacie smiled, a gentle, caring smile that warmed him. "I've heard you are very close."

"We are," he confirmed. The light changed, and he moved forward, turning off onto the road that would take them out of Pine Ridge proper and up the mountain.

"Brian and I are close too," she told him.

Shane shifted and curled his fingers around hers. It felt natural to do so.

"That's how I know he's still alive, waiting for someone to find him." She paused, taking a breath. "Corinne and I are pretty tight, too, but as you've already seen, she's insane."

Shane smiled. "I like her."

"Oh God, don't tell her that. She'll camp out on your doorstep, and you'll never get rid of her."

"You'll have to protect me then."

She squeezed his hand and winked. "Don't worry. I've got your six."

CHAPTER FIVE

Much to Lacie's delight and surprise, Shane had reservations at the Celtic Goddess, an exclusive five-star restaurant built into the mountainside just outside of Pine Ridge. From the moment they pulled up in front of the signature Greek-columned entrance, her eyes went wide and stayed that way. She stared in wonder at the opulent decor as they entered the lobby. More columns. Gleaming marble flooring. Elegant, sculpted statues and a proliferation of lush greenery.

Shane gave his name to the tuxedoed man behind the ornately carved podium, and they were led to a secluded table for two in a balconied alcove overlooking the valley.

"This is for us?" she whispered quietly, sure that the maître d' had made a mistake.

"Yes." Shane grinned, accepting the bottle of champagne.

The tablecloth was an ivory linen trimmed in gold. The place settings were elegant china; she was sure that the utensils were *real* silver.

As if all that wasn't enough, the meal was an event in itself. Seven courses of the most delicious food she'd ever tasted. By the time dessert arrived—twelve paper-thin layers of a heavenly hazelnut chocolate torte—her sensory systems were in a state of blissful shock.

"Dance with me," Shane said, rising from the table and holding out his hand.

Lovely music flowed softly from hidden speakers all around them. The dishes had been cleared away, nothing between them but soft candlelight and the fresh flowers that comprised the small, tastefully done centerpiece.

She blinked. "Here? Now?"

It was only the two of them in their own romantic little world, set apart from everyone and everything else. In truth though, it wouldn't have mattered if they had been placed dead center in a room amid thousands of others. Tonight, there was no one in her universe but Shane.

"Yes." He grinned, and her heart skipped a few beats.

Not even the grandeur of the Celtic Goddess or the breathtaking view could take away from his presence. He was, quite simply, the most beautiful man she had ever met. His features were as stunning as the hand-carved Greek statues around them—strong and masculine yet tempered with intelligence and depth.

Against the contrast of his black suit, his eyes blazed a luminous blue, and throughout the evening, they had been pinned solely on her.

"Aren't you afraid I'll trip and send us both crashing through the window?"

He tugged lightly on her hand. "I won't let anything happen to you, Lacie."

How could she resist when he said things like that? The past few hours had been spent in the perfect place, with the perfect man. To be held in his arms while they danced alone beneath the stars with the entire valley spread out below? She'd never forgive herself if she didn't.

Stepping into his arms was like coming home. Her body molded itself to his. Every curve, every dip, every line fit together, as if crafted by a master artisan. They moved together as if they had been doing so all their lives. Shane was smooth and graceful, and for the first time in her life, Lacie felt that way too. At least until Shane gave her injured hand a slight squeeze. She uttered a little cry before she could stop herself.

Shane stepped back immediately and examined her hand. "What happened?"

"It's nothing," she told him. "I caught my hand in the car door. It was an accident."

He cast a look from beneath thick, dark lashes that were practically sinful on a man. "I would certainly hope you didn't do it on purpose." His fingers brushed lightly over the back, skimming along the knuckles and tapping her fingers. "When did this happen?"

SHANE SENSED HER HESITATION; she didn't want to tell him.

"Tuesday night," she finally mumbled.

That had been days ago. The night he'd guest-lectured at the university. Shane took a discreet, calming breath.

"Tuesday?"

"Yes." She bit her lip, glancing down at where his hand now gently held hers, as if it would break. "It happened when I was getting out of my car."

Shane prayed for patience. The thought that she was injured did not sit well with him. The fact that she had suffered all week was even less appealing. "You didn't mention it."

"No, I didn't."

There was no mistaking the hint of defiance in her tone, telling him clearly that she didn't feel the need to share everything. It bothered him, and he was somewhat taken aback by the fierce, protective urges taking root. At the same time, he sensed that pushing her too hard, too soon wouldn't be beneficial to his interests. The more time he spent with her, the stronger that compelling interest became.

When he spoke again, it was with less demand and more concern. "Did you get this X-rayed?"

The defiance faded quickly, followed by something almost apologetic. It made those protective urges surge again.

"Not yet. I didn't think it was that bad."

Shane lightly flicked a finger beneath hers, receiving a wince in response. He hadn't meant to hurt her; it was barely a brush, which meant it was worse than she was letting on.

"Really?" he said, his disbelief apparent. "At the very least, you should have this taped."

"I did. That's probably why it didn't bother me much."

He arched a brow. "It's not taped now."

Her lashes lowered, and she averted her eyes. "It didn't look good with my dress," she said softly.

He lifted her chin and pinned her with his eyes. He hadn't figured her to be one who would forego common sense for something so superficial.

The answer came a moment later, a softly spoken confession from beneath shuttered eyes. "I wanted to look pretty for you."

Another click snicked deep within. That she would go to such lengths for him had his heart swelling until it consumed every available space in his chest.

"I've never seen a woman look more beautiful than you do tonight. But don't ever do anything like this for my benefit again," he chastised. "Now, will you promise me you will have this taken care of tomorrow, or should we stop at the ER on our way back tonight?"

She blinked away a sheen of moisture. "I'll go tomorrow," she promised.

After a few more dances, Shane reluctantly took her home. Lacie allowed him to temporarily bind her hand from the first aid kit he kept in his trunk. He would have preferred to have his brother Michael check it over, but he trusted Lacie to keep her word, and he didn't want her to have any unpleasant memories of this night. If she had managed to make it through the week with a full schedule, one more night wasn't unreasonable.

"Did you have a good time tonight?" he asked, opening the door for her.

She didn't answer him at first. When she did finally speak, she did so as if choosing each word carefully. "If I took every dream I ever had of the perfect romantic date and put them together, it still couldn't compare to what you've given me tonight."

Shane wondered at the pure pleasure her words gave him. "That's a yes then?"

"That's most definitely a yes. But ..."

Shane's brows drew together. There was a *but*? He had planned everything down to the minutest detail, and the evening had gone off without a hitch. Granted, getting a private balcony table at the Celtic Goddess on such short notice had been made easier by the fact that his sister-in-law was the head chef and co-owner, but he thought he'd done pretty well.

"But?"

She looked at him shyly from beneath thick lashes. "As wonderful as it was, it wasn't because of the restaurant or the food or the music. That was nice and all, but the night was wonderful because I was with you."

Shane felt a fist curl around his heart and squeeze.

There went another tumbler as his heart clicked one step closer to completely opening for her.

"So, if our next date is hot dogs and beer at a baseball game, you'd be okay with that?" he teased.

"Actually, I would love that." She laughed. "But just so you know, I'm more of a soft-pretzel girl."

"I'll remember that."

∼

Shane walked her to her door. His hand rested lightly on her lower back in a simple, gentlemanly gesture. He probably didn't realize the thrill it gave her or the desire it incited, the same desire now curling around deep in her center.

She hesitated, wondering if she should ask him in. She wanted to, but she couldn't quite form the words. It was only their first real date after all—second, if she counted the coffee—and even though no man had ever made her feel quite so ... needy ... she didn't want him to think she was easy. If she asked him in and he accepted, there was no doubt in her mind where they would end up, no matter how good her intentions.

As it turned out, Shane made the decision for her. "I had a wonderful time tonight," he said, lifting her uninjured hand to his lips. He pressed a soft kiss to the back of it and then stepped back. "May I call you again?"

"Yes," she said, her voice breathy. "Please do."

He waited while she unlocked the door, making sure she was safely inside. "Good night, Lacie."

"Good night, Shane."

And then he was gone.

Resisting the urge to lean against the door and sigh, she hurried to her window, peering out to see Shane get into his black car and pull away. Only then did she allow the full-body sigh.

"So ... how was it?" Corinne's unexpected voice nearly gave her a stroke.

"Corinne!" Lacie exclaimed, clutching her chest and willing her heart to stop pounding like a jackhammer.

"Come on, sister." Corinne grinned unrepentantly. "I made popcorn. I want to hear every last detail."

Lacie obliged, painting a highly accurate and detailed account of their evening as she changed out of her clothes and slipped into soft flannel PJs. Corinne hung on every word, her mouth opening and closing several times as she made Lacie repeat the best parts.

Two hours later, they lay side by side in Lacie's queen-size bed, just as they had when they were teenagers. "I'm glad you're here," Lacie confided in the dark. "I think if I'd had to wait until tomorrow to tell you, I would have exploded."

Corinne laughed. "I'm still not sure I believe that really happened. It's just too good to be true."

"Believe it. Now that you know everything, why don't you tell me what's bothering you?"

Corinne had been listening with rapt attention, but

Lacie always knew when something was on her younger sister's mind. Even if she hadn't picked up on it, the telltale twisting of the hair tie in Corinne's hands would have clued her in.

Corinne exhaled heavily, not bothering to deny it. "Tomorrow, okay? Let's just bask in the afterglow of your perfect date tonight. You can keep replaying it in your head, and I'll do the same, pretending it was me instead of you."

"Okay." Lacie chuckled, setting her worries aside for a little while longer.

CHAPTER SIX

The next morning, Corinne seemed even more preoccupied. She brooded over two cups of coffee and munched down some granola at Lacie's insistence before finally raising the white flag.

"All right!" she said. "I'll tell you. But promise me you'll listen and not jump down my throat and say I'm just being paranoid, okay?"

The somber look on Corinne's face was worrisome. For as much as Lacie teased her younger sister about overreacting, she knew that when she got *that* look, it was serious.

Lacie slid into the chair next to her and gave Corinne her full and undivided attention. "Okay, I promise."

"I caught Craig sneaking into your apartment last night," Corinne blurted out.

"What?!"

"He had a key. Did you give him a key?" Corinne looked at her accusingly.

"Well, yes, but it's only for emergencies," Lacie admitted, slightly shaken. "I have one to his place, too, but I've never used it. What did he want?"

"He said he was looking for some chamomile tea because Shelly had an upset stomach from eating too much pizza."

The tone of Corinne's voice revealed her thoughts on the matter more clearly than her words.

Lacie caught the reflexive defense on the tip of her tongue, remembering her promise. "You don't believe him."

"No," Corinne confirmed. "Before he realized I was here, I saw him going through your desk. You don't keep chamomile in your desk, do you?"

Lacie shook her head, disturbed by Corinne's reveal. Her hands gripped harder around her oversize *Teaching Is Heart Work* mug.

"Whatever he was looking for, I don't think he found it. I made some noise to make it sound like I was coming out of your bathroom, and when I came back out, he was in the kitchen, getting the tea."

A shiver went down Lacie's spine. Craig had been in her apartment hundreds of times, enough to know where everything was. Why did that suddenly seem overly intrusive?

"That's why you stayed."

"Partly. I really did want to hear about your date with Shane. But, yeah, I was afraid if I didn't, he'd be waiting for you when you got home. I don't think he was very happy about you going out, Lace."

No, he'd made that obvious. The look in his eyes when they'd been leaving was quite telling. Thankfully, Shelly had been there. If she hadn't, Craig would have been far more vocal in expressing his opinions.Thanks, Rinn." Lacie gave her sister a hug and moved over to the desk.

What in the world would be of interest to Craig? Bills, her planner, a few articles. At first glance, she didn't notice anything out of the ordinary. Papers were strewn in what looked to be haphazard, random stacks, but Lacie knew what to look for.

Corinne stepped up quietly beside her. "See anything amiss?"

"Yeah. My file on Brian. It's not where I left it."

She spotted it a few inches to the left and then picked it up to examine it. The papers inside were out of order, as if someone had been rifling through them and hastily shoved them back. In the nearly three years that Brian had been missing, Lacie hadn't given up hope, ceaselessly writing letters, making phone calls, and ensuring that no one forgot that he was still out there somewhere. She'd carefully documented everything in that file.

"Is there anything missing?"

Lacie went through everything twice more before she answered. "It doesn't look like it, but something's not right." She held up an aerial photo, an enhanced view of something that looked like it might have come from Google Earth. "This looks different to me."

"Different how?" Corinne asked, squinting. "It looks like a rocky desert to me."

"I can't put my finger on it," Lacie said, but she knew something was off. At that moment, she wished she had Shane's photographic memory. "This is a satellite photo of the area where Brian's unit was attacked."

Corinne sucked in a breath. "How did you get that?"

"Don't ask. I'm not sure it's entirely legal."

"Oh, Lace."

Lacie set her shoulders and gave her a determined look. "Hey, if it helps bring Brian home, it's worth it."

"Do you think Craig switched the photos?" Corinne asked, tapping her teeth like she always did when pondering something. "But why would he do that? For what purpose? I know I said I think Craig's a little"—she swirled an index finger in a tiny circle next to her temple—"but that seems farfetched, doesn't it?"

"Maybe he thinks he can use it somehow, and he doesn't want me involved. He's forever telling me I'm going to tick off the wrong people one of these days and warning me to let him handle it."

"Maybe he's right, Lace. He knows a lot more about how the Army works than you do."

"I know. But I just can't sit back and do nothing. Brian is still out there ..." Lacie's voice cracked.

"I know," Corinne said, hugging her. "I miss him too. And we *will* get him home. But promise me you won't say anything to Craig about this, okay? He doesn't know I saw him outside of the kitchen last night, and I've got a bad feeling about this. I know I've said this before, but he creeps me out."

Lacie promised, and Corinne left shortly thereafter.

Lacie took a long, hot shower, pushing thoughts of Craig and whatever he was up to out of her mind, preferring to relive her amazing date with Shane over and over instead and wondering when he would call. Her phone rang as she was towel-drying her hair. She lunged for it, thinking it might be him.

"Lacie?" a little girl's voice said over the phone.

"Shelly?"

"Um, yeah. Um, we're going to start the pancakes. Daddy says you need to bring the whipped cream."

"Okay," Lacie said, cursing herself for having forgotten. "Give me five minutes, and I'll be over, okay? Do you want fresh strawberries too?"

Shelly squealed in affirmation before Lacie disconnected the call. She rushed around, hurriedly pulling on a clean pair of jeans and a long-sleeved cotton tee, running a brush through her damp hair, and gathering the supplies from her fridge. She had completely forgotten about their weekly breakfast date, her mind distracted by a gorgeous Irishman with silky black hair and blue eyes that sent electricity into her most sensitive parts every time they landed on her.

She didn't bother with shoes; she was only going

across the hall. Her own door had barely closed when Craig's opened up.

"Here, let me help you with that," Craig said, taking the bowl of fresh berries and the can of whipped cream. His expression was dark, and there was a slight edge to his voice.

Yep, he was displeased.

"Thanks," she said, stepping into his place as if she hadn't noticed.

Shelly kept up a steady stream of conversation while they made and ate pancakes, finger-painting them with whipped cream and adding features with chocolate chips and strawberries. Craig continued to eye Lacie closely but said little. Lacie had the distinct impression he was brooding.

When they had their fill, Lacie began to clean up. Craig noticed she was only using one hand.

"Is your hand still bothering you?"

"A little. I was thinking I might head down to the ER and get it X-rayed later."

Craig looked as though he was about to protest and then thought better of it. "All right. Shelly and I will drive you over."

"No." Lacie shook her head. "I don't want Shelly in the ER. It will scare her. I already have a ride lined up."

"Is it Callaghan?" Craig hissed with enough vehemence that Lacie took a step back.

"No," she said, eyeing him warily. "Corinne is going with me. We're going to do some shopping afterward."

Craig visibly relaxed.

"What is it you've got against him anyway?"

Lacie recalled Corinne's theory that Craig was the reason so few men asked her out. He *was* intimidating. She hoped Shane wouldn't be deterred and then dismissed that thought entirely. As gentle as he had been with her, she had sensed something dangerous lurking beneath the surface. Shane didn't give the impression of a man who scared easily.

"He's sniffing around you—that's what," Craig said decisively, casting a quick glance into the living room, where Shelly was happily coloring in front of the television. "What do you see in him anyway?"

"Honestly, Craig, I don't pry into your sex life." Lacie moved away from the sink to gather the last of the dishes from the table.

"*You're having sex with him*?!" Craig reached out and grabbed her by her injured hand, forcing her to face him.

"Of course not!" Lacie hissed, fighting the pain, which was overshadowed by her mortification of having this conversation with him. "It's an expression! God, Craig, you've known me my whole life! I would think you'd know better than that."

His grip loosened, but he did not release her until she pushed at his arm. "I do know you, babe, which is how I know that you are in way over your head with this one."

"I beg your pardon?" She forced herself to take even breaths as the pain seared up her forearm. Craig was too worked up to notice.

"These Callaghans, they're like wolves, prowling around, looking for innocent little lambs. They sink their fangs into you, rip you to shreds, and then stalk back into the woods to wait for their next victim, leaving you to stitch yourself back together."

That was a rather ironic analogy, she thought, coming from the man who currently looked like he was ready to lay waste to everything within a five-mile radius.

She couldn't imagine the same wild look on Shane's face; she instinctively knew he would always be in complete command of himself.

Feeling the need to defend both Shane and his family, she said, "Five of them are happily married and utterly devoted to their wives and children."

Her words only seemed to inflame him more. "Not your man, Lace. What does that tell you?"

Her chin tilted upward. "That he hasn't met the right one yet."

"Jesus Christ, look at the stars in your eyes!" he said in disbelief. "You think it might be you, don't you?"

"I don't think anything, you big idiot," she said through clenched teeth, her voice an angry whisper. "We've only seen each other a couple of times."

He nodded, as if she had just proven his point. "Ah, but the Callaghan men say they recognize their soul mates right away. If it were you, you'd already know."

They believed in love at first sight? That was news to her. She refused to read anything into it. For all she knew, that statement was as biased and fabricated as Craig's wolf-lamb analogy.

"Where did you hear that?"

"Doesn't matter, does it? It's true. Do yourself a favor, Lacie, and forget this guy before he breaks your heart and I have to clean up what's left."

Her irritation swelled suddenly into an uncharacteristic rage. "Why don't you do me a favor and stay the fuck out of my business?!"

Craig's eyes opened wide as Lacie's hand flew up to her mouth. Lacie had never cursed at him; she was every bit as shocked as he was. She never used the F-word, not to anyone.

Lacie was out the door and back in her own apartment before he could respond.

CHAPTER SEVEN

Shane palmed the small mobile device, flipping it over and over in his hand, fighting the urge to call Lacie. It had been exactly seventeen hours and thirty-seven minutes since he'd done the honorable thing and left Lacie at her doorstep with naught but a brushed kiss across the back of her hand.

What he had wanted to do, what his body had begged him to do, was sweep her into his arms and carry her to her bed, where he would have spent the night making mad, passionate love to her. His entire body ached with want; just the image of her in that little black dress had him tight with desire, unable to sit still. It was such an unusual state for him that he wasn't quite sure how to handle it.

Shane flexed his hands in frustration. It wasn't as if he'd never been sexually attracted to a woman before. But this—what he was feeling for Lacie—went way beyond simple desire. This was a burning deep in his gut, a soul-deep need to take her and make her his own.

He froze in sudden realization. Lacie was his *croie*. His heart.

It was a stunning revelation. On some level, he might have suspected, given the instant and powerful connection between the two of them. He'd seen the same thing happen to five of his brothers over the past few years.

Had it been like this for them too? Had they experienced this sudden shift in their universes, where everything fell into place? As if, up to that point, it had all been a little off and they'd never realized it?

When his mind came back online, things were crystal clear. His senses were more acute than they had ever been. Even physically, he felt a change. Every part of him now had a single, united purpose—to join in mind, body, and soul with Lacie.

Absently rubbing his chest over the spot where his heart beat with renewed vigor, he wondered if it was like this for Lacie too. According to Taryn, his brother Jake's wife, she had experienced something similar. His other sisters by marriage—Lexi, Maggie, Nicki, and Rebecca—had said the same.

Did that mean Lacie was thinking of him right now, wishing she were with him until her heart ached? Was she reliving their date over and over in her mind, relishing every look, touch, scent, sound, and taste? Was her body a prison of stark, raw need?

He'd planned on taking things slow with Lacie and

seeing where they led. Courting her with traditional methods that had proven successful over time—flowers, candlelight dinners, fun outings. But that no longer seemed possible. Now, there was an urgency that hadn't been there before.

His mission was clear; there was no question where things would lead. They were destined to be together, and getting to that point gradually didn't seem as appealing anymore. The challenge now would be to progress as quickly as possible without doing any damage. *Croie* or not, they had met less than a week earlier, and Lacie was a respectable schoolteacher with a clear sense of propriety. Hopping into her bed and declaring her his for the rest of their lives was not part of any romantic hearts-and-flowers package that he was aware of.

Shane was, by nature, a cautious man, and Lacie was a romantic at heart. He had known that from the moment he met her. Little things, like holding the door open for her and bringing her flowers, had thrilled her, and he was only too happy to comply. Oh, she'd liked their date at the Goddess. His intention had been to impress her, and he felt that he had accomplished that several times over. But what had really made him happy was when Lacie told him that just being with him was what made the evening so special.

His gift for reading people told him that beyond a shadow of a doubt, when Lacie had spoken those words to him, she *meant* them.

He loved that about her. There was a purity, an

innocence around her that he had rarely seen. She was a woman who cared deeply for others, lived her life simply, and believed in everything she said and did with both passion and compassion.

She was perfect.

If there was one thing that worried him though, it was that she might be *too* compassionate, especially where one particular former GI was concerned. Shane hadn't liked Craig Davidson from the moment he'd laid eyes on him, and each subsequent encounter had only deepened his sense that something was not right with the guy. Even Lacie seemed to realize it; Shane hadn't failed to notice the edge in her voice and the shadows that darkened her eyes when she spoke of him, but she seemed loyal to him for some reason.

One thing was certain: Shane would not share Lacie, not with anyone, but especially not with Davidson. The guy was a step off, and the brief encounters Shane had witnessed raised some red flags. There was a lot of history there, so he'd have to tread carefully, for fear of alienating Lacie if he voiced his concerns too vehemently at this stage. Now that he knew for certain that Lacie was his *croie*, it was more important than ever that he understood exactly what he was dealing with.

And he knew just where to begin.

"What do you know about Craig Davidson?" Shane asked his older brother, perched on a stool at Jake's Irish Pub.

The public bar was on the first floor, with living

quarters on the second and third floors. At one time, all the Callaghan men had called the place home, but marriage and children had changed that, though they all kept space there.

Jake glanced up from the fresh keg he was tapping. "The ex-Army guy?"

"Yeah, that's the one."

"Not a hell of a lot." Jake shrugged. "I think he joined up right after high school. Came home a few years ago, sliced and diced up, but he was luckier than most. No one else in his unit did. Most of them came home in pieces with a flag draped over the box that held them. A couple are still MIA, from what I hear."

Ian emerged from the back, carrying several stacked trays of clean glasses. "I heard about that. Total assfuck all around."

"What are we talking about?" asked Michael, coming from the private living quarters, where he had just left his wife Maggie and their son, Ryan, with the other wives and kids.

Jake poured him a beer.

Shane felt a familiar humming in the pit of his stomach. Unless he was mistaken—and he rarely was—his brothers would be coming together instinctively, as they always somehow managed when they were needed.

"The shitstorm that took a couple of local boys down a few years ago," Ian answered.

Michael's brows drew together. "Lone survivor, right? Craig something."

"Davidson," Shane supplied. "Craig Davidson."

"Yeah, that guy was a mess," Michael confirmed. "Demolitions man. One of his own detonations blew him clear off the zone, tearing him up pretty good in the process."

"Ended up saving his life though, didn't it?" Jake commented. Something in Jake's tone had Shane looking up sharply. "Why the sudden interest in Davidson, Shane?"

"Davidson?" Kieran piped up, joining them as he tossed his bag behind the bar, returning from his latest mission. The humming in Shane's gut increased in pitch. "Craig Davidson?" When Shane nodded, Kieran said, "The guy's a total douche bag."

"You know him?"

"Yeah, he comes into the gym every day. I'm thinking of canceling his membership; he's an asshole. Why?"

"Friend of a friend."

"A female friend?" Jake asked knowingly.

"Maybe."

Kieran leaned forward in interest. As Shane was the only other unclaimed Callaghan male, he was intrigued. "Do tell."

"Fuck off."

Kieran laughed.

Ian looked at Shane long and hard. "Wouldn't be Lacie McCain by any chance, would it?" he asked quietly.

"Might be," Shane said carefully. "Why?"

"Lacie McCain. She's that cute schoolteacher, right?" Sean asked, striding across the bar. At his twin's arched brow, he added, "What? She brings her Passat into the shop for maintenance. She's nice. Nicki loves her. Said she helps out at the shelter. Donates a lot of books and stuff, has crafts and activities she does with the smaller kids."

Shane had no trouble believing that. Lacie was meant to be around kids. If he had his way, he'd give her a houseful. The very thought had him throbbing painfully again. Thankfully, no one else seemed to notice.

"McCain. Why does that name sound familiar?" Kane added, startling everyone. For as huge as he was, he moved as silently as the grave.

The fact that they had all gathered here without premeditation was not lost on any of them. They sensed a mission.

"Brian McCain is one of those still listed as missing," Sean said soberly.

As men who had spent time in hell, they knew more than most what that probably meant.

"Lacie's brother." Kieran nodded. "I remember him. *He's* a good guy."

"And Davidson's best friend. At least, in theory," Ian mused.

Shane's spine stiffened. "What does that mean?"

Ian leaned in closer. "It means that McCain and Davidson were tight until Davidson started getting a hard-on for McCain's little sister. Big brother wasn't too keen on the idea, apparently."

"Wait," Shane said, shaking his head. "Davidson was married; he has a kid."

"Ever hear of a shotgun wedding?" Ian smirked. "Davidson wanted McCain's sister, but that didn't stop him from fucking other women, especially those who bore a striking resemblance to her. Word is that while Lacie wasn't interested, her best friend *was*, and Davidson took advantage of that. Got her pregnant. Her daddy, Pine Ridge's very own Mayor Daniels, wasn't happy. He forced them to get married."

"Wasn't she killed in a car accident a couple of years ago?" Michael asked.

"She was killed in a car *crash*," Sean corrected, "not too long after Davidson left the service and was home for good."

The silence was thick and heavy until Shane asked the question they were all thinking, "You don't think it was an accident?"

"Didn't say that, did I?" Sean shrugged, but Shane knew his identical twin well enough to know that was exactly what he thought.

It did absolutely nothing to soothe Shane's worry that Craig Davidson was too close to Lacie.

Before he could ask anything more, Shane's private cell rang. He took one look at the number and excused himself, walking to a quiet corner of the pub, where he could speak in private.

"Lacie?" he said, accepting the call.

It wasn't Lacie's voice that answered.

"No, this is her sister, Corinne. Is this Shane?"

"Yes. Is Lacie all right?"

"Yeah, sort of. I'm here at the hospital with her now."

"Her hand?" he guessed.

"Yeah. It was broken, and some of the bones already started fusing incorrectly. They had to re-break it to make things right. They shot her up pretty good with pain meds."

"Jesus."

"Hey," she said hesitantly. "I'm not sure if I should even be asking you this, but you seem to care for her, and I was hoping that maybe you could do something. I didn't know who else to call."

"Anything." He was already reaching for his jacket, pulling out his keys.

"They're going to release her soon, but I don't think she should be alone tonight with the meds and all. I'm supposed to drive our parents down to Philly tonight; they're going on an anniversary cruise. They don't know about Lacie's hand; she made me promise not to say anything because she thinks they'll cancel their trip if they know. Would you consider coming over and keeping an eye on her until I get back?"

He didn't hesitate. "I'm there. What time?"

"Six? I should have her settled by then. She'll probably sleep most of the night, but I'd feel better if she wasn't alone."

"I'll be there."

"Thanks," Corinne said, breathing a sigh of relief. "And, Shane?"

"Yes?"

Corinne spoke slowly, as if choosing her words carefully, "It might be a good idea if you came in the back way."

He was silent for a moment, hearing what she wasn't saying. "Got it."

"I knew I was right about you." She hung up before he could respond.

CHAPTER EIGHT

Corinne stared out the window, awaiting Shane's arrival. Other than a nondescript silver sedan that disappeared around the block, there hadn't been any traffic on the small side street. She checked her watch again. She hoped he remembered not to come in through the front. If Craig spotted him, it would just make things more difficult.

A quiet knock on the back door startled her. She peeked through the peephole and gasped.

"How did you do that?" she asked, opening the door.

Shane grinned as he slipped noiselessly inside but didn't answer her.

"Right," she murmured.

She'd heard the same rumors that everyone else had—that the Callaghans were a lot more than they seemed. It was impossible to live in Pine Ridge and not hear them. They all had this quiet air of danger about them, but it was said that they were good men, fiercely loyal and incredibly protective of their family and friends. Corinne withheld a shiver from the waves of intensity rolling off of Shane and was glad her sister was now included among that inner circle.

"Thanks for coming so quickly. I've got to haul ass, or my parents are going to miss their flight. Lacie's sleeping, out cold. Here." She thrust a pill bottle into his hand. "These are her pain meds. Give her one with some crackers and water or ginger ale if she wakes up. Here's my cell number, and I've written down the flight numbers and schedule and stuff. If everything's on time, I should be back around three a.m. or so."

Shane leveled those intense blue eyes at her. "Take your time. I'm not going anywhere."

Corinne glanced down at the small black bag he carried with him and grinned. "Gotta love a man who's prepared."

His eyes sparkled.

"So, listen"—she dropped her voice even further and leaned toward him—"I don't know how much you know about things, but you strike me as the type of guy who catches on pretty quick. Craig's across the hall. He wasn't here when we got back from the hospital, so he doesn't know about any of this. Let's try to keep it that way for a bit longer, okay? If he realizes he broke her hand, he's going to freak out and make things really uncomfortable for Lace."

Shane's entire body tensed, his face hardened, and

his eyes grew cold. "Davidson did this? Lacie told me she caught it in a car door."

This time, Corinne couldn't withhold her shiver at the sound of his voice, glad that such barely-leashed vehemence was directed at someone else, and she knew that she had done the right thing in calling Shane. He wouldn't let anything happen to Lacie, and she could already tell that he would be a valuable ally. For this reason and several more of her own, she had no trouble telling him the rest.

"That's what she told me too. But the doc pulled me aside later—I used to babysit for him and his wife, so I know him pretty well—and he said the fractures came from compression along the sides, like someone had squeezed her hand too hard, although there was some bruising on the back that he said was consistent with catching a hand in a car door, like she'd said."

"You think it was Davidson?"

She nodded. "I know it was. I'll bet anything that he was waiting for her when she got home that night she had coffee with you. He tends to be a bit ... possessive with Lacie."

Shane flicked a glance toward the bedroom. "He does that often?"

"Too often. He thinks he owns her or something."

"Why does she allow it?"

Corinne snorted, gathering her bag. "You don't know Craig. He's a born manipulator, and he knows her soft spots. She's tried to talk to him about it, but he twists everything around until she feels bad for saying anything."

She hefted the bag over her shoulder and put her hand on the door. "Shane, I know you guys are just getting started and all. I'm sorry if I'm expecting too much or reading too much into it. I just thought ..."

She let the sentence hang, unsure of how to express what she suspected was going on between them. It was hard to misinterpret the look Lacie had in her eyes when she spoke of him, and Corinne had seen the same in Shane's when he looked at Lacie. There was certainly no mistaking the almost-feral intensity surrounding him now, something starkly male and protective that sent a twinge of envy through her.

"You thought right," Shane said, putting her fears to rest. "I'm glad you called. I'll take good care of her."

Corinne smiled, a mischievous glint in her eye. It was always nice to be proven right. "So ... if I'm too tired to drive back tonight and I don't make it here till around noon tomorrow, that would be okay?"

With a devastating grin, Shane assured her it would.

∼

SHANE SILENTLY MADE his way toward Lacie's bedroom, not wanting to wake her. She was tucked beneath a hand-stitched ivory-and-blue quilt, the top edge barely covering her breasts. Her chest rose and fell with the rhythmic breaths of deep slumber; her now-casted hand lay atop the covers, the plaster extending from the middle of her fingers to slightly beyond her wrist. The corners of his lips quirked. Her cast was a soft pink color that matched her nightshirt. Corinne had already signed it with a flourish of curls and hearts.

He watched her for a while, remembering that the first time he had seen her, she'd been asleep too. Her long lashes created perfect crescents against her smooth skin. Strands of her lighter-blonde hair fell wantonly across her forehead, the rest bunched into a halo of soft, tousled curls where her head rested on the pillow. Shane felt what was becoming a familiar pang shoot across his chest. There was no doubt about it. She was his.

His eyes flicked back to her hand, the slow burn of rage beginning all over again. Lacie was his to love, care for, and protect.

And Craig Davidson was a dead man.

Shane also remembered the phone call that had signaled the end of their time together that night, Davidson's enraged voice clearly audible across the table they shared. He should have realized what might happen. Why had he not followed Lacie home that night? And why hadn't she said anything?

Corinne's words replayed in his head. *"He thinks he owns her or something."*

Shane would make sure that misconception got cleared up very quickly. Lacie belonged to no one. Except him. But that would be because she wanted to, and as his *croie*, she would. She might look like an adorable bit of fluff, but she had a strong, clever spirit.

As if she sensed his presence, Lacie's eyes flickered open and went right to him, though she was having trouble focusing. "Shane?" Her voice, husky with sleep and thick from the pain meds, wrapped around him and pulled him closer.

"Hi, Lacie. Yes, I'm here." Very gently, he took her good hand in his, bringing it to his lips to brush a light kiss upon it.

"Am I dreaming? It's the drugs, isn't it? Man, that's some good stuff."

Shane chuckled. "You're not dreaming, Lacie. Corinne called me to keep an eye on you while she drove your parents to the airport."

"She worries too much."

"She loves you."

"I know." Her eyes closed for a long moment, and he thought she'd dropped off again. "I'm sorry, Shane. I'm afraid I'm not going to be very good company. These pills make me so sleepy."

"Don't be," he said, brushing the hair from her face. "Instead of sitting at my place all night, thinking about you, I get to be here, taking care of you."

She gifted him with a tiny but genuine smile. "Just how you wanted to spend your Saturday night, right?"

"Sweetheart," he said quietly, running the backs of his fingers over her cheek, "there is no place I would rather be."

She sighed softly. "Now I know I'm dreaming

because I've had this one a couple of times already this week." Her words were slightly slurred, her eyes fighting to remain open. "The next part's really awesome, but I'm just so tired ..."

God help him, if she admitted anything more about her fantasies, he was going to crawl into bed with her and make them all too real. What she needed now was rest. There would be time enough for his selfish desires later.

"Go back to sleep, Lacie."

"You'll stay?" she murmured, her eyes already half-closed.

"I'm not going anywhere." He pressed a kissed to her forehead, smiled at the barely audible moan she'd uttered, and felt the final lock in his heart break open as she drifted back into the land of medication-induced dreams.

He stayed with her for a while until he was certain she was comfortable and deeply asleep. The pain pills would have her out for several hours. To pass the time, and because Shane was curious about the woman he now knew without a doubt he was going to marry, he decided to have a look around.

Overall, her apartment was clean but, like her car, untidy. There seemed to be no obvious method to her placement and storage of things, but he suspected there was some underlying rationale behind it. After a bit of time and thought, he began to see a pattern emerging, and he smiled. Lacie had a different way of thinking about things, but once he saw it, it made perfect sense.

It was her desk that interested him most. There were lesson books, planners, and a list of accounts and financial statements. Whereas he would have had them in neat and labeled files, Lacie kept hers in specific piles across the desktop. Looking more closely, he saw that the stacks were arranged in a vague semi-circular pattern, leaving her a small workspace in the center. Those to the left were time-sensitive, like bills, policies, and renewals; those to the right were not.

In addition, rather than being stacked neatly, each pile had sections that fanned out. That was how she distinguished the various accounts from one another. Among each "fan blade," there were individual papers that stuck out at odd angles. His fingers itched to tidy them, but he realized upon closer inspection that the incongruous pages were remittance forms. All she would have to do when she sat down to pay her bills was pull out the offset pages, working bottom to top, left to right.

It wasn't how he would have done it, but he had to admit, it was effective. After they were married, however, he would try to persuade her to let him handle their accounts.

When he was satisfied that he had decoded her system, his eyes were drawn to a thick stack located at the center of the half-circle. The folder perched on top caught his attention. It was simply labeled *Brian*.

After checking on Lacie and finding her still fast

asleep, Shane settled down in the comfortable recliner with the file, positioning himself so that he could keep an eye on her through the partially open door. Shane found organized lists of names, dates, and printed emails. Notes she'd made from various phone calls, copies of letters and official correspondence. Aerial photos, some of which she had lightly marked with a fine black Sharpie.

Lacie was trying to find out what had happened to her brother. He whistled softly, impressed by some of the names she'd contacted. He also recognized the all-too-standard runarounds in the replies she'd received. The amount of information and detail she had managed to acquire was substantial, especially considering she was a kindergarten teacher from Pine Ridge. His *croie* was clever and resourceful. A feeling of pride welled in his chest at the thought.

As he read each page, he committed it to memory. When he got back to the pub, he was going to talk to Ian. His brother was a certified master at gathering information. If anyone could find out what had happened to Brian McCain and the others, Ian could.

He wouldn't mention anything to Lacie just yet though. He didn't want to get her hopes up, and chances were that after almost three years, the news wouldn't be good. If nothing else, he might be able to at least give her closure.

Shane was careful to put everything back where he'd found it before allowing himself one last look at Lacie. She was resting peacefully, the ghost of a smile playing about her lips, and he wondered if she was dreaming of him. The thought pleased him greatly.

He forced himself out of Lacie's room and back into the living area, taking comfort in the hint of messiness. It was so unlike his room at the pub. There, everything was done in monochromatic shades; the furniture had clean, sleek lines, and the only personal items were some framed pictures he'd hung in a perfectly spaced geometric pattern over his desk.

In contrast, Lacie's furniture was comfortable, an eclectic collection of pieces that spanned a multitude of styles but each was uniquely appealing. There were photos and personal mementos everywhere, including handmade gifts from her students. It looked as though Lacie had kept every one of them, for they now overran the shelving space she'd allotted. There were several scrapbook albums of hand-drawn pictures and notes as well, each written from small hands and big hearts.

It was easy to get a clear picture of Lacie's life from the photos alone; they were everywhere. There was a lot of her with her family—her mom and dad, Corinne, and a male who could only be her brother, Brian. They shared similar features. Brian had the same easygoing smile, same blue eyes and blond hair. The love they had for each other came through the still shots clearly. The last one must have been taken just before Brian was deployed. It showed him and Davidson, both dressed in fatigues with fresh buzz cuts, standing proudly with Lacie between them.

The mere sight of Davidson so close to Lacie made

the small hairs on the back of Shane's neck stand on end. The man was in a lot of the pictures, spanning most of her life. And in all of them, Shane noted, he was looking at Lacie or touching her in some way. There was no doubt in his mind that Davidson was in love with her and probably had been for some time, but he had hidden it well. Only a man trained to notice such things—or a man who planned on devoting the rest of his life to his *croie*—would spot the subtle body language and the possessive gleam in Davidson's eye.

CHAPTER NINE

Shane must have dozed off at some point. The next thing he knew, the morning sun was streaming through the window, and Lacie was tucking a soft blanket around him.

"You're supposed to be in bed," he said, greedily breathing in her light, floral scent and something minty, like toothpaste or mouthwash.

The smile she gave him took his breath away. "I was, but I think fourteen hours is enough, don't you?"

"What time is it?"

"Around eight."

Shane sat up and gently tugged Lacie onto the sofa with him, mindful of her injured hand. Lacie offered no protest, joining him easily. There was plenty of room, but Lacie's body was nice and snug against his side as he slipped an arm around her shoulders.

"Thanks for hanging out," she said into his shoulder.

"My pleasure," he said, meaning it. "How's the hand?"

～

"Sore but manageable. I think I'm going to stick with the over-the-counter stuff today though. I prefer to be lucid." *And not miss another minute with you.* "I guess Corinne told you what happened, huh?"

Shane stroked her upper arm with lazy movements that had her nestling closer. It was impossible to get close enough to him and an effort not to climb onto his lap. Thankfully, she managed to control her baser impulses, and he didn't seem to mind the invasion of his personal space.

"Yes. I'm sorry you had to go through that."

She smiled against his collarbone, discreetly drawing his scent into her lungs. It was clean and fresh and slightly musky; he was the best-smelling man she'd ever come across, hands down.

"At least you're not giving me a lecture about not having it taken care of sooner. You'd swear Corinne was the one getting her bones re-broken with the way she carried on."

"Sometimes, seeing someone you care for hurting is worse than feeling it yourself."

The deep tone of his voice and the depth of feeling went past her ears and well into her heart, making her sigh. Shane Callaghan had a way of doing that to her.

She was falling hard and fast for him, she realized.

She would have to be careful before she made a complete fool out of herself. The last thing she wanted to do was scare him off. Heck, she was scaring herself a little with these powerful urges and feelings.

"You're right. I would have been worse if our places had been reversed," she agreed and then asked suddenly, "Are you hungry? You've been babysitting all night, cramming yourself into a sofa that was not designed for anyone over five-ten, and been an all-around good sport. The least I can do is make you breakfast. You strike me as a waffle kind of guy. Am I right?"

Shane looked down at her, amusement dancing in his eyes. "I love waffles, and I'm quite skilled at making them, so I will be doing the cooking this morning while you rest that hand. This sofa is actually pretty comfortable, though I must say, I'm enjoying it much more with you here than I did alone. And I was not babysitting. I was caring for someone I seem to have become especially fond of in a very short amount of time."

The man knew exactly what to say to make her melt. His blue eyes sparkled with intensity, and the corners of his lips turned up in a challenging grin. A dark shadow crept over his jawline. When matched with his slightly mussed hair, it gave him a roguish, bad-boy look that had her core temperature shooting up at a record pace.

"Yeah?" she asked, her eloquence fleeing as quickly as her sense of propriety.

"Yeah."

He was staring at her lips, which made her gaze drop to his. So full. So firm. So male. So close ...

As if reading her mind, Shane leaned forward and touched his lips to hers. A hint of cinnamon and mint teased her senses, mixed with something decadently rich and uniquely Shane. She'd never tasted anything like it, but she found herself instantly addicted.

Her initial shock quickly gave way to something much better. She softened beneath him in surrender, parting her lips at his tender insistence. He was a superb kisser; he knew how much pressure to apply, where and when to use his wicked tongue, and how to make her forget everything else until her entire universe was reduced to the space within his arms.

Minutes, hours, days later, Shane finally pulled away, breathing almost as heavily as she was. He rested his forehead upon hers. "What were we talking about?" he asked, his voice low and husky.

Lacie blinked. Once. Twice. Her mind was a jumble of images, scents, and sensations. "I have no idea."

The timely rumbling in Lacie's belly reminded them about breakfast. Reluctantly, she allowed him to tug her to her feet and lead her into the kitchen.

Shane was stubbornly adamant about making waffles but was willing to allow Lacie to help. Lifting her easily, he placed her on the counter next to where he'd be. Her job, he informed her, was to tell him where everything was. She could assist with those tasks requiring only one hand under his strict supervision.

"Are you always this bossy?" she asked, amusement lacing her voice. She would allow him this moment of male dominance in her kitchen but only because her lips were still tingling from his earlier possession.

Bonus: by taking the commanding role in making breakfast, he was freeing her to ogle him to her heart's content.

He did look good enough to eat, mouthwateringly tasty in his snug-fitting jeans and the untucked button-down in a shade of blue that accentuated his beautiful eyes. From the top of his glossy black hair to the bottoms of his—she stifled a moan—bare feet, the man looked confident and comfortable and positively lickable.

Forget the waffles. She wanted to devour *him*.

He smiled, an arrogant tilt to his lips that sent bolts of lust through her nether regions. He leaned in close enough for her to get hit with a fresh wave of that warm male scent, inflaming her further and teasing her into a near frenzy.

"Bossy? And here I thought, I was the one making *you* breakfast. I am truly injured, Lacie."

She laughed, realizing just how lucky she was. How many women would give their right arms to have this sexy, caring, intelligent man in their kitchen, doing something so sweet and kind?

Lacie was just about to apologize when Shane

grinned wider and added, "Now, stop badgering me, woman, and tell me where your waffle iron is."

They just ... clicked. Sipping coffee, making breakfast together, sharing little things—it was all done with an ease and comfort that belied their short time together, as if they had spent years learning each other instead of mere days. Being with Shane was so easy.

"Mad waffle skills, huh?" Lacie said doubtfully a short while later as the misshapen item was presented to her with a flourish.

Throughout the process, she'd managed to refrain from questioning his culinary skills, skirting the edge of acceptable teasing, afraid to injure his fragile male pride, but too tempted to resist it entirely. It was playful banter, and he seemed to enjoy it as much as she did.

"It might not look pretty, but it'll be the best damn waffle you've ever tasted," he said confidently.

The only reason it had not been created in geometric perfection, he informed her, was because she had distracted him while he was pouring the batter. That part was true enough, and she refused to apologize for it.

"Hmm." She used her fork to break off a piece, swirled it around in a pool of maple syrup, and slowly brought it to her lips. It was hard to keep her eyes from rolling back in her head—it was that good. The forkful melted in her mouth.

Shane's eyes followed her every movement intently, watching as she chewed and subsequently swallowed.

"Well?" he asked, that smug grin tugging at his lips.

"Jury's still out," she said evasively and cut another bite-sized portion with the side of her fork.

As with the first piece, she took her time, savoring it as long as possible. Shane remained unnaturally still, watching her with such intensity that she could feel her skin warming beneath her loose cotton shirt, waiting for her to pay his skills proper homage.

She continued to work her way through the waffle, one small bite at a time, refusing to be rushed. By the time the last piece was gone, Shane was practically vibrating. She handed the plate back to him, daintily wiping her lips with a decorative paper napkin. Containing her grin was hard as she further ignored him and sipped her coffee. Shane continued to stand before her, arms now crossed, the hint of a smirk across those talented male lips, and one perfect brow arched above eyes that caused her heart to stutter.

"Okay, I concede," she breathed finally. "That was, by far, *the* best waffle I've ever had. I could easily become addicted to these."

"Told you." Shane's smirk widened into a full-fledged grin, and his eyes sparkled like living sapphires.

"Yes, you did." She licked her lips. "Can I have another one?"

His gaze darkened, and his voice lowered until it was purely sensual. "The first one was free. The next one's going to cost you."

Lacie held back the whimper that threatened to

escape and tightened her inner thigh muscles. "Hmm. What's your price?"

He leaned in closer, placing one arm on the counter at either side of her hips, daring her. "A kiss."

"I can do that."

She reached back, dipping her finger in the remains of the syrup and coating his lips. Then, she proceeded to slowly, methodically remove it. By the time she finished, his eyes were glowing, his muscles tight and straining.

"How's that?" she whispered.

"That'll do," he rasped.

Good Lord, the man knew how to kiss! Any further thoughts of breakfast were lost as Lacie wrapped her arms around his neck and pulled him closer, spreading her knees and scooching forward. She needed to feel him against her—against one specific place in particular. His hands went to her waist, stroking back and down with sizzling electricity as he found her bottom and assisted her. A moan sounded deep in his throat; she echoed that sentiment with one of her own as she felt the hard proof of his interest exactly where she needed it. To know that he was feeling it, too, filled her with a sense of feminine power.

Shane's hands lazily explored the curves of her back and waist, stroking along her thighs several times but staying maddeningly away from where she ached. Lacie impatiently tried to work at the buttons of his shirt blindly; she needed to put her hands on the bare flesh of the warm, living marble that so teased her aching breasts. Frustrated with the length of time it was taking and her fingers' inability to correctly unfasten a button, she simply grasped the shirt along the open edges and pulled, sending buttons popping and bouncing along the floor.

∽

SHANE LAUGHED SOFTLY into her mouth, more than a little turned on by her boldness.

His large hands skimmed along her waist, reveling in the contraction of muscles beneath impossibly soft skin with each caress. They moved upward slowly, teasingly, until his thumbs brushed the curve of her breasts. Even through the material of her lightweight bra, the heat of her skin nearly burned him. Lacie moaned audibly, arching into his touch, needing it, wanting it, begging for it.

Shane obliged, cupping her breasts, loving the way they filled his hands. He kneaded them gently, stroking his thumb across her nipples, awed by their pronounced response. Shane's hard length throbbed with the newly discovered knowledge that his sweet-tempered, soft-spoken schoolteacher had been hiding a fierce, fiery passion, one that thrilled him beyond his wildest dreams.

"Shane," she moaned, her eyes closed and her head back.

Hearing Lacie murmur his name with such need was like a hard pull on his cock. He fought for the self-control that was proving so elusive. He'd never had to fight so hard before, but then, his mind rationalized, he'd never been held by his *croie* before either.

The need to mark, to claim, and to possess was almost impossible to ignore. At the rate they were going—and the way she was responding—he would not be able to resist much longer.

A loud knock sounded at the door, breaking into their private world. Shane's hands, filled with Lacie's breasts, paused. Lacie didn't seem to have heard the knock, protesting Shane's sudden lack of movement by pushing into his hands with purpose, tugging at the base of his skull with the pads of her fingers, and kissing the shadow along his jawline. He growled in approval, a low, deep sound in his throat.

The knock was repeated along with a verbal warning. "Open up, Lacie. I know you're in there."

The voice broke through the lusty fog, and she stilled. Shane stiffened at the same time, his protective and possessive instincts roaring into overdrive. His natural impulse was to cover her body with his own and keep her as far away from the other man as possible. Davidson was a threat to Lacie. Shane felt it strongly, and he, like his brothers, had learned never to ignore his instincts.

Her subsequent response only reaffirmed what his gut was telling him. She tensed; her eyes, dazed with desire only seconds earlier, went wide with a mixture of fear and dread before she shielded them.

But why? Was it as Corinne had said? Did Craig have the ability to manipulate Lacie so easily?

Shane had trouble believing it was as simple as that. Lacie might have a gentle demeanor, and she was undoubtedly both kind and compassionate, but he had sensed a strong inner spirit in her as well. It was not something she advertised, but Shane had seen glimpses of it in the way she had managed a week with the pain of a broken hand as well as in the lusty ardor that had burst forth when he kissed her. Lacie was an intelligent woman with a quick wit that would certainly recognize any attempt to control her.

Except Craig Davidson wasn't just anyone. Davidson was practically family, and family was very important to Lacie. He also knew from their conversation in the car Friday night that Lacie made excuses for Davidson, citing his wife's untimely and tragic death, his terrible injuries, and her brother's disappearance as rational excuses for his occasional irrational behavior.

She was too caring of a person not to cut him some slack, but there was a limit. In Shane's opinion, Davidson had passed that mark, and it was time to do something about it. The situation had changed. Shane was in her life, and he would see to it that Lacie would no longer be a dumping ground for Davidson's issues.

∼

"SHALL I KILL HIM?" Shane asked softly against her neck, punctuating the statement with a long, slow lick along her jugular vein. His voice was low, feral, and starkly male, calling to her on a primal level.

She shivered, her nails curling into his shoulders, not knowing if he was kidding, not even knowing if she cared if he could make her feel like this.

"Lacie, if you don't open this door in one minute, I'm coming in." Craig's voice, somewhat muffled through the heavy steel door, was loud and clear enough to be heard.

Shane stilled as the words registered and then pulled away enough to look at her in disbelief, taking all that delicious heat with him. "He has a key to your apartment?"

"For emergencies," she explained for the second time that weekend, her voice thick with the now-receding desire.

Exchanging keys hadn't seemed like such a bad idea when Craig suggested it, but Lacie wasn't so sure anymore. The look on Shane's face at her confession was even worse than the one on Corinne's. Was it possible that they were right and that she wasn't looking at things sensibly?

Shane backed away, his face unreadable as he shielded his emotions. Was he angry? Jealous? Disappointed? She couldn't tell, and that bothered her. She didn't want him to be any of those things. Well, maybe a bit of jealousy was flattering, but Shane had no reason to be jealous of Craig. After the way they'd just been pawing at each other, she thought that would be pretty clear.

"Let me talk to him for a minute. I'm sure he just wants to make sure I'm okay."

Shane's eyes didn't leave her face; his hands did not relinquish their hold.

"Please," she pleaded, imagining Craig readying his key just outside the door, not wanting him to burst in and see her up on the counter or Shane with his shirt hanging open.

Given their brief, heated exchange the day before, Craig would probably hit the roof.

Craig was going to have to accept the fact that Lacie was involved with Shane, but it didn't have to be this morning. She didn't want to deal with his overzealous, overprotective tantrums at that moment. The best thing she could do was reassure Craig that she was fine, send him home, and figure out a way to deal with everything else later when her hand didn't hurt so much and her body wasn't amped up on Shane-induced hormones.

"Just give me a minute, okay?"

Shane nodded, but his expression remained carefully neutral. Without another word, he stepped back. A chill settled over her; Lacie had to resist the urge to pull him right back to her.

"I'll be right here if you need me," he said, kissing her nose before walking away, disappearing into her bedroom to give her some privacy.

Judging by the way his eyes had gone cold and the too-even tone of his voice, he wasn't happy about it, but she appreciated the fact that he trusted her enough to handle the situation.

Bonus points for him.

Craig was inserting his key into the lock by the time Lacie made it to the door and swung it open. Without waiting to be invited in, Craig pushed right past her.

"What the hell is going on, Lacie? Corinne commandeered your phone last night and refused to let me talk to you. You don't answer your door." His eyes landed on her pink cast. "What the hell is that?"

"It's a cast," she said, though she thought it was obvious.

She crossed her arms over her chest, suddenly uncomfortable with the way Craig was looking at her. His eyes narrowed, his mouth set in a scowl, and if she looked really closely, she could see the tiny vein pulsing at his temple.

She licked her lips self-consciously. Did her lips look as swollen and ravished as they felt?

"I know that," he said, irritated. "Why is it on your hand?"

She shrugged, knowing he wouldn't be satisfied until she told him. Best to just get it over with. "I had it X-rayed. As it turns out, I really did break it last week, and the bones weren't fusing properly. They had to re-break it and then cast it." She blew out a breath. "They shot me up with some powerful painkillers, and I went to bed the moment we got home. Corinne was just looking out for me, Craig."

He looked around, his eyes zeroing in on the two coffee mugs sitting on the counter. Then on the waffle iron, the bowl of batter, and the two place settings.

Crap, thought Lacie.

She was a grown woman, but Craig made her feel as though she were a naughty teenager caught in a compromising position. She straightened her shoulders and met his icy glare.

"Where is Corinne now?" he asked.

"She left."

"When?"

"Why the interrogation, Craig?" she huffed. "Does it really matter?"

Lacie turned and started to head back toward the kitchen, already tired of the conversation and wishing she had never agreed to give Craig a key to her place. She looked longingly at the counter where Shane had been so wonderfully attentive only minutes earlier.

"Hell yes, it matters," Craig growled, stalking after her. "Her car wasn't in the lot this morning when I took Shelly back." He accusingly pointed at the mugs, the plates, the forks. "Who made you breakfast, Lacie?"

"I did." Shane stepped out from the back room.

So much for his ability to let me handle things. She tried to be annoyed with him, but the truth was, his presence did make her feel better.

Craig's eyes were murderous as he took in Shane's appearance. Shane's shirt still hung open, and his hair was still tousled from her fingers raking through it, his jaw still shadowed. But his eyes were as bright as Lacie had ever seen them. Bright and yet so very dark. She suddenly knew beyond a shadow of a doubt that the rumors of the Callaghans were true. For all of his gentlemanly charm and easygoing manner, Shane was a lethal man.

"What the fuck is he doing here?" The purplish tinge of rage raced up Craig's neck and into his face; his fists clenched at his sides.

Shane strode through the apartment with the supreme confidence of a man who was exactly where he belonged. His movements were unhurried, almost lazily careless, but there was nothing remotely casual about the look in his eyes. He deliberately placed himself between her and Craig.

Realizing she would have to face this now rather than later, Lacie stood a little straighter, her chin taking a slightly defiant tilt. "Corinne called him when she had to leave."

Craig whipped his gaze back to her. "Why didn't she call me? I could have taken care of you, Lacie. You didn't need to call on a complete stranger." He glanced at Shane as if he were some bum she'd picked up off the street.

Lacie's first instinct was to simply state the truth, but she couldn't exactly tell him Corinne was, in her words, "creeped out" by him.

Instead, she kept to the truth in as nonconfrontational a way as possible. "Shane is not a complete stranger. And you had Shelly. Seeing me like that would have upset her."

"I would have taken her back to her grandparents," Craig said through clenched teeth, his voice strained in barely repressed anger. "They would have understood. Christ, Lacie, I've known you your whole life. You've known him, what, less than a week? And yet you allow yourself to be alone with him in your apartment when you are so vulnerable?"

Craig's eyes roamed around the room, some of the tension in his face vanishing with visible relief when he noticed the pillows and blankets on the couch, but it returned in full force the instant he turned back and saw Shane. Since Shane was standing slightly in front of her, she couldn't see his expression, but Craig could. His entire body went rigid.

"Your daughter needs you more than I do, Craig," Lacie began.

The heated burn of embarrassment and irritation rolled through her, even as her nurturing nature tried to take over. Despite her ire, it was an effort to ignore the stunned and, if she wasn't mistaken, hurt look on Craig's face. Shane's presence gave her the strength and courage to overcome it.

"And one night was enough for me to know that I can trust him," Lacie added defiantly, stepping closer to Shane.

Shane's eyes glittered, the hint of a smirk on his face as he wrapped one arm around her waist.

"Jesus Christ, Lacie, do you even hear what's coming out of your mouth?" Craig said. "You trust a man—and not just any man, a fucking *Callaghan*—

after he flashes you a smile and buys you a cup of coffee?"

"Got a problem with Callaghans, do you?" Shane asked casually, though his voice carried an unmistakable edge.

Lacie felt the slight shift of his body weight.

"You bet your ass I do," Davidson grated, standing taller. "You're a bunch of cocky motherfuckers, thinking you're better than everyone else, thinking you own this town."

Shane's body leaned forward, and Lacie knew they were close to blows.

"Enough!" Lacie bellowed, taking a step forward to place herself between them, arms out, as if to keep them apart. "I won't listen to you speak to Shane that way. I'm a grown woman, Craig, not some helpless child you can bully around. I'm capable of deciding how and with whom I choose to spend my time."

Craig's eyes darkened, and his face paled as her words hung in the heavy silence. The effect was even scarier than when it had been dark with rage. "Thank God Brian's not here to see this"—he said seethingly—"because it would break his fucking heart to see you acting like some crushing teenager. How am I supposed to keep my promise to him to look out for you when you pull shit like this?"

Her sharp intake of breath was loud in the sudden silence. Shane's fingers brushed against hers in silent, unwavering support along with an unspoken question, but he didn't need to ask it out loud for her to hear it.

The same words from a few minutes ago floated, unbidden, into her mind. *"Shall I kill him?"*

Lacie shivered, feeling the quiet, lethal intensity of the man beside her. She knew if she looked up at his face, she would see nothing but an unnerving calmness, but she felt anger rolling off of him in waves. This man would kill on her behalf without question. As horrifying as that thought was, it also made her feel incredibly loved and protected.

Still, she had no wish to see violence, especially not here, not now. Lacie's fingertips met his and gave a quick, gentle squeeze of thanks, but no, thanks.

She turned to Craig. "You need to leave."

Craig's jaw set stubbornly as he crossed his arms over his chest. He was several inches shorter than Shane, but he had the bulk of a man who spent several hours in the gym every day. "We need to talk about this, Lacie." His eyes flicked to Shane. "Alone."

Shane shifted his weight again but only slightly. It was enough to tell Lacie that if she didn't do something to defuse the situation now, she would no longer have any say in what happened. As big and tough as Craig was, Lacie knew with certainty that he would be no match for Shane Callaghan. The stupid idiot was going to get himself hurt.

She took a deep breath and squeezed Shane's hand again in a silent plea for restraint. She would have preferred to discuss things privately, but Craig wasn't giving her a choice. No matter how angry, irritated, or aggravated he got her, he was still like a brother to her, and she did not want to hurt or embarrass him.

"Maybe later, when you've calmed down and I'm not sorely tempted to say something I'll regret," she said, glad that her voice didn't tremble as much as the rest of her. Not out of fear, but out of anxiety.

She hated the fact that Craig was putting her in this position, making her feel like some sort of errant child who needed watching over. After spending the morning feeling gloriously like a desirable woman, being treated like a child was particularly abrasive.

Craig's eyes widened in disbelief. He wasn't used to her standing her ground so boldly. He shot a look of loathing at Shane. Lacie knew he was blaming her sudden show of spine on him, and in a way, he was right. If Shane wasn't there, Lacie would most likely be making a pot of tea and trying to soothe Craig's ruffled feathers instead of showing him the door.

As unpleasant as the current situation was, it was also inevitable and far past due. She'd let Craig get away with too much for too long, good intentions or not.

Craig's lips thinned, but he kept himself in check and did not force the issue. Lacie attributed that to Shane's presence as well and was glad for it. It might make things more difficult later on, but hopefully, by then, they'd both be calmer and be capable of having a rational, adult discussion.

"Fine," he said finally. "You know where to find me."

Craig opened his mouth to say something else, but Shane gave him the barest shake of his head, warning against it. With one final look back at Lacie, Craig let himself out, slamming the door as he did so.

Lacie sagged against the countertop. Any pride she'd felt from standing up for herself was negated by the look in Craig's eyes as he left. They held so much disappointment, so much betrayal, that it physically hurt.

"Hey. You okay?" Shane was there, beside her, once again the charming, soft-spoken man who had stolen her heart.

The pads of his fingers lightly trailed across her cheek, providing the tender contact she needed. He had a way of doing that, of saying and doing exactly what she needed, even when she didn't know herself.

She offered him a weak smile and leaned into him. He felt so good. So strong. So warm. So deliciously *Shane*.

"Yeah. I'm sorry you had to see that."

CHAPTER TEN

Shane kissed the top of her head and tucked her beneath his chin, glad she couldn't see the fire he knew was flashing in his eyes. His mind ran through alternate scenarios of what might have happened if he hadn't been there, and he didn't like any of them. Lacie didn't fully appreciate the depth of Craig Davidson's feelings for her, but Shane did, and they ran far deeper than brotherly concern. After witnessing Davidson's quick temper firsthand, Shane's unease over the man's close relationship with Lacie increased.

Corinne had been dead on. Davidson knew exactly what to say to hit Lacie where it would hurt the most. Shane fought the urge to go across the hall and strangle the bastard right then and there. If he thought for one moment that Lacie wouldn't hate him for it, he would.

"Is he always like that?" Shane asked.

He was already forming a to-do list in his head, starting with getting Lacie's locks changed. Next, he'd ask Ian to set up some extra security cameras that would encompass the main entrance, the fire escapes at the back of the building, and the parking lot as well as install a high-tech security system in Lacie's apartment.

In the meantime, he could take her back to the pub with him, where he knew she'd be safe. He was about to suggest as much and then thought better of it. Things were going well, but she might not be receptive to the idea. After dealing with Davidson's bullshit, she might see it as another attempt to control her or a suggestion that she was incapable of looking out for herself.

Lacie pushed away, a light, tender stroke to his arm silently communicating gratitude for his support. Content with that for now, he crossed his arms over his chest, his posture relaxed, and leaned against the counter, fighting the urge to draw her back to him. He liked the way she was already looking to him for strength and comfort. As his *croie* should. He would give her the space she needed even if doing so made him grind a few molars down in the process.

Shane watched her with thoughtful eyes as she poured them each another cup of coffee. She really was beautiful. Even the worried crease to her brows couldn't take away from the loveliness of her delicate features. Conflict didn't sit well upon them though. Standing up to Davidson, while necessary, had upset her; she was much more comfortable smoothing feathers than ruffling them, he realized.

"No," she finally answered, handing him his coffee and taking a similar position next to him. Her toes were just barely touching his, a slight contact, but one that gave her the anchor she subconsciously needed. "Most of the time, he's helpful and supportive, but he does have his caveman moments, usually when I do something he perceives as foolish or possibly dangerous."

"I would never hurt you, Lacie."

~

"I KNOW." Lacie's voice was soft, her expression contemplative. "I'm not sure how I know that after meeting you less than a week ago, but I do. I feel very safe with you, Shane. It's almost as if ..." She bit her lip before she said anything more. It was on the tip of her tongue to say they were meant for each other, but she decided against it.

Craig's words from the previous morning were still fresh in her mind. Was she, on some level, hoping that she would prove to be Shane's perfect match?

No, she thought, *I can't afford to acknowledge something like that.* If she dared to hope and was wrong, she wouldn't just be hurt; she'd be destroyed. Unmercifully, she shoved, pushed, and jammed those thoughts back into that secret place where she kept her deepest, darkest desires.

If things worked out, awesome. If not, then perhaps she could retain a shred of dignity. That was what she told herself anyway. Yes, Shane did seem really into her, and he obviously cared, or he wouldn't even be there. But did he feel the same soul-deep connection with her that she felt with him? The one that had hit her hard and fast from that first moment she'd opened her eyes in that classroom and found him looking at her with amusement dancing in those beautiful blues?

While Lacie had always been an incurable romantic at heart, she'd had her doubts about the whole love-at-first-sight phenomenon.

Until Shane Callaghan had unknowingly proven otherwise.

From what she'd heard, most men tended to run, screaming for the hills, when a woman started talking about a serious relationship, especially after such a short time. She didn't want to do anything that might scare Shane away. Whether she said it out loud or not, she was quite certain she was falling in love with him, and she was not about to jeopardize that because she couldn't keep her mouth shut. It would be prudent—and preferable—to keep her thoughts to herself until she had a better grasp of his feelings and intentions.

"Almost as if what?" he prompted.

"Nothing." She waved it off, hoping he didn't read the truth in her eyes.

Sometimes, when he looked at her, she suspected he saw a whole lot more than most people did. Given the intensity of her feelings, she didn't have a prayer of hiding them from anyone willing to look. She cared for him, so deeply that it bordered on frightening. It was kind of exciting, too, much like the feeling she got when approaching the crest of a thrilling roller-coaster ride. She had to keep her arms and feet safely planted inside the car for just a little while longer.

Shane reached out and pulled her into his arms. It was exactly what she needed. After only a moment's hesitation, she melted against his chest.

"Thank you," she murmured.

"For what?" A whisper against the top of her head.

"For knowing what I need before I do."

Lacie's muted cell phone vibrated across the countertop. Without completely leaving the comfort of Shane's arms, she reached out and checked the display. Her face flushed a dark pink. "Oh, for heaven's sake," she mumbled, quickly tapping out a reply.

"Problem?" Shane asked, letting his hands drop down to loosely rest on her hips.

"Corinne," Lacie exhaled. That one word carried enough martyred weight to assure Shane that everything was indeed fine. "She wanted to know if we were 'done yet' and whether or not it was safe to come in."

Shane's grin grew. "How very considerate of her to ask."

"Are you kidding? The only reason she hasn't let herself in is because I dead-bolted the back door."

"A voyeur, huh?" He laughed.

Lacie looked him up and down—taking in his slightly mussed hair, shadowed jaw, bare chest, naked feet—and sighed. Corinne was going to have a field day with this.

"You know self-defense, right?" she asked as she forced herself to the door.

Twinkling blue eyes smiled back at her. "I thought you had my six."

An answering mischievous grin. "Right."

It took the better part of five minutes before Corinne could tear her eyes away from Shane and speak coherently with Lacie, and that was only after Shane went into the bedroom to change.

"Oh. My. God. I am *so* slamming my hand in a car door."

Lacie laughed. "Back off, sister. He's mine."

"Yeah, but he has a younger brother, doesn't he?"

Lacie ignored that and inquired about their mom and dad. Corinne assured her that the trip to and from the airport had been uneventful, that their parents had arrived in Florida just fine and in fact set sail on their two-week cruise that morning.

"So ..." Corinne said, flicking a look toward the door behind which Shane had disappeared. "You're going to tell me everything, right?"

Lacie turned her eyes to her sister. "Not a chance."

"But I did good, right? Admit it—calling him was a good idea."

Lacie agreed that it had been. Had she been aware of Corinne's intentions when she crawled into bed yesterday, she probably would have resisted the idea. Their relationship was too new to put to that kind of test. But Shane had passed with flying colors, surpassing every expectation she might have had. He was definitely a keeper.

When Corinne was once again struck dumb, Lacie knew that Shane had emerged. A glance across the room confirmed this. She was at her own loss for words when he flashed a sexy half-grin her way, freshly shaven and changed. She would have to start setting aside money from each paycheck, she decided, to buy him new shirts because the thought of ripping through this one was just as appealing as the last. The desire to see and have access to that stunning chest was shockingly powerful for a woman who, until Shane Callaghan had walked into her life, had neither the time nor desire to get involved with anyone.

And she *was* involved. In the span of a heartbeat, Shane Callaghan had not only captured her interest, but he'd also managed to snag her heart in the process. It was scary, especially for someone like Lacie, who allowed very few people to get close. She loved her kids and those select few within her inner circle, but outside of her immediate family, Lacie guarded her heart fiercely. It was not something she would give easily or freely, but when she did, she would do so completely. Looking at Shane now, she was afraid it had slipped away on its own, and she found she had no desire to call it back.

"Thank you," she said quietly, the sudden realization and intensity of her feelings making her shy. "For ... everything." *For coming. For staying. For watching over me. Making waffles. Kissing me until my insides melted together.* The color rose in her cheeks as she recalled the way it'd felt to have his lips and hands on her, the way his heart had pounded against her chest ...

Desire flared in his eyes, letting her know that he was aware of the direction her thoughts were headed. With Corinne watching them intently, there was nothing either of them could do about it. That smile though suggested he would very much like to.

Soon, his eyes said with a flash of that luminous dark blue that made her think of sapphires lit from within. It was a unique shade that she now associated solely with Shane's desire.

I can't wait, she answered, lowering her lids in the slightest hint of submission.

Their silent, secret conversation thrilled her.

~

SHANE'S GRIN GREW. He was inwardly glad he'd had the foresight to keep his shirt untucked. The woman could make him harder than iron with just a look from those bedroom eyes.

"My pleasure," he answered, his voice a sexual purr that betrayed his illusion of total self-control.

It was just as well her sister had arrived when she did; he would have been less inclined to hit some of those items on his new to-do list otherwise.

"I have some things I need to see to today. Is there anything I can do for you before I leave?"

She flushed and averted her eyes. The little vixen was clearly thinking naughty things, and that knowledge only increased the aching throb in his jeans. Across the room, Corinne sighed.

After ensuring that Corinne would be spending the afternoon with Lacie—he did not want Lacie here alone with Davidson until he had a chance to cool off—Shane forced himself to leave.

There were several other scenarios he would have preferred. One was sending Corinne on her way and spending the rest of the day pleasuring Lacie. Another was to take Lacie with him back to his room at the pub, where he would get Ian started on ramping up security and then spend the rest of the day making love to her. His favorite had him doing both—loving her here and then gathering her and taking her back to his place, safe among his family ... and doing it all over again.

In the end though, he leashed his arousal, caging it for a more opportune time, preferably when Lacie wasn't feeling so vulnerable. But he could not keep himself from claiming her mouth in one final soul-searing kiss that screamed possession, taking satisfaction in the openmouthed shock on Corinne's face and the dazed, entranced look on Lacie's.

◊

Later that evening, when her cell phone chimed, Lacie was prepared. She had it resting beside her as she reread the official, bureaucratic responses to her latest inquiries into what was being done to locate her brother. It bothered her that Craig had been sifting through it. She knew he didn't believe that Brian was still alive, but for her sake, he refrained from saying so very often.

"I'm breaking protocol again by calling so soon, but I wanted your voice to be the last thing I heard before I went to sleep tonight." Shane's deep male voice flowed through the small device and directly into her heart.

Damn if the man didn't make her insides squirm in the most wonderful way.

"I'll allow it," she said. "But only because your voice is pretty fine too."

He answered with a soft hum that made her tingle in the most feminine places. It was exactly the same sound he'd made right before he kissed her earlier. She understood it for what it was—an indication of considerable restraint.

"Is Corinne still there?"

"No, she went back to our parents' house."

"She couldn't stay?" Lacie heard the frown in his voice.

"I'm a big girl, Shane."

"I know you are. I'd be a pervert otherwise, wouldn't I?"

She laughed. "Yes, I suppose you would."

A moment of quiet.

"Has he been by again?"

"No."

There was hesitation, as if Shane wanted to say something but was looking for the right words.

"He seemed very upset earlier, Lacie."

Yes, he had been, but that was just Craig. She was used to his sudden flare-ups. Silently, Lacie vowed to speak to her sister for voicing her overzealous concerns to Shane, obviously thinking she'd found a powerful ally in him, and then immediately recanted that thought. Corinne did what she did out of love, and Shane couldn't be expected to understand that Craig was a lot more about the bark than the bite. Besides, she'd already made up her mind that she was going to talk to Craig and put a stop to this nonsense once and for all.

"He won't hurt me." *Not intentionally*, she added silently, looking down at her casted hand.

Craig just didn't know his own strength sometimes, especially since he'd come back. He'd thrown himself into his physical therapy after Mikaela's death. He would be horrified if he believed he had been a contributing cause to her latest injuries. He'd be constantly underfoot in an attempt to make up for it, just like he had in the past when he realized he'd gone a little too far. She didn't bother telling that to Shane though. Given his fierce reaction to the day's earlier events, he wouldn't be any more receptive to her reasoning than Corinne.

Another heavy pause.

"I worry about you, Lacie. I know I haven't earned that privilege yet, but I certainly hope to."

He considered worrying about her to be a privilege? If he kept saying things like that, she was going to turn into a puddle right then and there.

"I'd say, giving up a Saturday night to watch over me earned you something," she said quietly. Hopefully.

She heard his slight intake of breath.

"That was a privilege in itself," he answered.

Her body felt strangely boneless. And empty. Terribly empty.

"You made me waffles," she whispered.

"I'll make you a thousand more for the chance to kiss you again."

"Deal," she said, breathless.

Just the thought of it had her body flushing with heat, but his soft, almost-silent groan intensified the sensation.

"You don't want me to sleep at all, do you?" he grumbled sexily, making her smile.

She loved the idea that she was having a similar effect on him.

"Of course I do," she said boldly. "But only if you dream of me."

"That's a given," Shane told her. "I can't seem to think of anything but you these days."

"Nice to know I'm not alone then."

"Lacie," Shane breathed her name like a prayer. "What are you doing to me?"

She didn't know, but she wished she did. If it was

anything like what he was doing to her, she could empathize.

~

SHANE EXHALED HEAVILY. Every cell in his body screamed for him to head over to her apartment and finish what they'd started that morning, but he worried about rushing her or scaring her away.

"Promise me you'll call me immediately if anything happens."

"I promise." She sighed. "But I can't run away from this, Shane. Craig needs to understand that I'm a grown woman, capable of making my own decisions with or without his approval. I've let him believe otherwise for far too long."

"I don't think you should do it alone."

"I have to. Craig won't take me seriously if I don't. He'll think I'm acting under someone else's influence."

Shane could see her point, but that didn't mean he had to like it. He didn't give a rat's ass what Craig Davidson believed as long as he was out of the picture.

"Shane?"

"Yes?"

"You've earned the privilege."

Shane smiled into the phone. "Now, say something wicked to give me memorable dreams."

He expected her to laugh softly, maybe give him a gentle chastisement. He imagined her eyes sparkling and her cheeks turning that lovely shade of rose as she did. But she surprised him.

In less than a heartbeat, her sexy purr sounded in his ear. "Syrup tasted better on you than your waffles, but next time, I want to try whipped cream too."

Lacie's sensual laughter was the last thing he heard as she disconnected the call.

CHAPTER ELEVEN

When Lacie walked into her classroom early Monday morning, she found a single perfect rose in the center of her desk. It sat next to a shiny dark-red apple. She picked up the small, tented notecard that completed the set—a heavy, textured cream-colored paper with *Lacie* handwritten in bold male script—and she opened it to read the message within.

Coffee after class tomorrow night?

Then, below it: *Whipped cream optional.*

Warmth flooded her body once again as her lips curled up in a smile. How had he gotten inside her classroom? The windows were closed, the door locked.

Of course, she thought with a flash of pride, *gaining entrance to a kindergarten classroom would be child's play for a SEAL.*

It was official. Shane Callaghan had just managed to completely steal her heart.

With a mischievous grin, she picked up a bright red crayon and block-printed *YES* in the corner. Then, she added a few motivational stickers she put on her kids' papers—*Star Student*, *A+*, and *Super*—and tucked the card into the pocket of her skirt. Rather than call the number he'd given her, she would deliver this personally later.

~

ACROSS TOWN, Shane grinned from behind his laptop as he looked at the clock. Lacie should have found his surprise by now. Wishing he could see her reaction in person, he contented himself with imagining it instead. He checked his phone, turned the volume up a notch, and waited.

~

LACIE WALKED into Jake's Irish Pub later that afternoon. She'd passed it hundreds of times but never actually ventured inside.

It was nothing like she'd expected it to be. Dark wood gleamed, accentuated by polished brass. The room was filled with the aromas of pipe smoke and lemon oil, mixed in with the heady scents of finely aged spirits. The bar took up half of the primary room with comfortable-looking padded stools, inviting patrons to step up and take a load off. Toward the back was another large space, separated from the main area by a half-wall. There appeared to be tables there, old-fashioned high-backed booths, and a small stage. From somewhere farther beyond, out of her immediate line of sight, came the muted sounds of people playing billiards.

Behind the bar, countless shelves held bottles in every possible color, size, and shape, reflecting like stained glass in the mirrors behind them. Soft, muted lighting gave everything a decidedly homey feel, whether from the recessed tracks cleverly hidden above or the antique-looking brass lanterns spaced along the walls. In every corner, a flat screen was suspended, each showing a different sports-based channel.

The place was immaculate and well kept. For someone who had never stepped foot in a bar before and was unsure of what to expect, Lacie was pleasantly surprised.

∼

JAKE WATCHED the young woman taking in every detail of his pub with wide-eyed wonder and unmasked curiosity. Even without the telltale pink cast, he would have known who she was. With the conservative skirt and blouse, the soft blonde waves held in check at the back of her neck, and a presence that exuded a patient gentleness, he would recognize Shane's *croie* anywhere. She was perfect for his soft-spoken, organized younger brother.

The pub wasn't crowded at this hour, just a couple of locals. More would be stopping in as it got closer to evening. Those who were already there regarded the newcomer with interest. A woman like Lacie would have stood out even if she hadn't been standing in the middle of the bar, looking around as she was. Jake chuckled.

"Looking for someone, sweetheart?" one of the patrons asked, rising from his stool.

Jake allowed it. Stan Campbell was well into his seventies and a real old-fashioned gentleman.

"Yes, actually," she said, smiling at Stan. "Shane Callaghan?"

Stan chuckled. "Well, you've come to the right place. Can't shake a stick without hitting a Callaghan boy." He winked. "No guarantee it'll be the right one though."

She laughed easily, her eyes sparkling, even as a hint of color rose in her cheeks. Jake instantly liked her and decided to take pity on her.

"You must be Lacie," he said, emerging from behind the bar. "I'm Jake."

"It's nice to meet you, Jake. This is a beautiful place."

He acknowledged the compliment with a nod and a smile. "First time?"

"That obvious, huh?" She grinned. "I'm afraid my sister and I grew up with the *nice girls don't go to bars* lesson drilled into us from our father."

"Smart man." Stan nodded approvingly.

"I don't think this is the kind of place he was talking about though." Lacie's eyes met Jake's head-on for a long moment before taking in the room again. "This is really nice."

The fact that she was able to look him in the eye without turning away was an encouraging sign; Callaghan women had to be made of strong stuff regardless of how docile they appeared on the outside.

"Thanks," Jake replied. "Shane's not here, but I'm expecting him shortly. You're welcome to wait for him."

She looked around uncertainly. "Well, I really just wanted to give him something ..."

She pulled out a small notecard and handed it to Jake. He looked down at it, saw it was sealed with stickers, and grinned.

"Sure. But before you leave, my wife would love to meet you. Do you mind?"

∽

Caught by surprise, she fumbled for words and came up empty. Why would Jake Callaghan's wife want to meet *her*?

"Shane mentioned that you were a kindergarten teacher, and our daughter, Riley, will be starting next year," he explained. "My wife, Taryn, is a little anxious about the whole thing. Maybe meeting you will help alleviate some of her fears."

Lacie relaxed instantly. "Of course. I would love to. Your first, I take it?"

Jake nodded.

"It's always harder on the parents than on the kids," she told him truthfully.

"Come on," he encouraged, leading her to the private kitchen in the back and doing a few quick introductions. "Lacie, my wife, Taryn. Taryn, baby, this is Lacie McCain," he said, his eyes twinkling. "I told her you were a little anxious about Riley starting school in the fall."

A beautiful woman looked up from the counter, where she was slicing up carrot sticks. Not much older than Lacie, she had a mane of riotous hair, streaked black to platinum, and the most unusual violet eyes. She was wearing faded jeans and a black maternity tank, and Lacie's eyes were immediately drawn to the brightly colored eyes of the dragon peeking over her shoulder. The tattoo was hypnotizing.

Two small children looked up from a table covered in Lincoln Logs and Legos. One was a lovely little girl who had the trademark Callaghan hair but her mother's violet eyes; the other was a little boy who couldn't be mistaken for anything but a Callaghan. They eyed her warily.

Two baby swings moved in the background, each holding a sleeping infant.

"Hi," Taryn said, her smile friendly and welcoming. She turned to Jake accusingly. "You told her *I* was nervous?"

Jake grinned, unrepentant, and returned to the bar.

Taryn snorted and then looked at Lacie. "Coffee?"

When Lacie nodded, Taryn continued, "I don't suppose he told you that *he's* already done background checks on everyone associated with the elementary school and their immediate families."

Lacie's eyes widened. "No, he didn't mention that."

Taryn shook her head and poured a cup for Lacie. "Don't sweat it, sweetie. Comes with the territory."

"The territory?"

"Yep. Callaghan men. Irresistible but overprotective as hell. You get used to it after a while."

Was there a warning in there somewhere? Lacie wondered. "So, I suppose the fact that I'm sitting here with you now means I passed inspection?"

Taryn grinned. "And then some."

∽

Fifteen minutes later, Shane walked into the bar. He was in an ill temper. Checking his phone once more, he frowned. Surely, Lacie was home by now. Why hadn't she called to confirm their coffee date tomorrow night? He'd thought the rose and apple were a nice touch, but maybe he'd freaked her out by leaving them on her desk.

No, he argued internally, *Lacie isn't the type to get spooked so easily*. She knew he'd been a SEAL, and her brother was in the Army.

There must be some other reason she hadn't gotten back to him. His scowl deepened. Maybe Davidson was giving her a hard time again. Maybe the bastard had been lying in wait for her when she returned to her apartment, itching for a chance to warn her away from Shane again.

That thought had him quickening his stride. He was going to run upstairs, change, and then head right over to Lacie's and make sure she was okay.

The huge grins on Jake's and Ian's faces didn't improve his mood any.

"What are you dickheads grinning about?" he asked sourly.

"This." Ian tossed Shane the folded note, embellished with stickers.

His heart leaped as he snatched it up and unsealed it. His bad temper instantly vanished until he started to wonder how it had come to be in Ian's hands. His head snapped up, and he scanned the bar. "Lacie was here?"

"Still is. She's in the kitchen with Taryn," Jake told him, pointing his thumb over his shoulder.

Shane's heart stuttered when he walked into the private kitchen. Lacie and Taryn were sitting at the table, sipping coffee as if they had been friends forever. Jake's daughter, Riley, was in Taryn's lap, and Ian's son, Patrick, was on Lacie's. It was such a perfect image that he stopped for a moment to savor the beauty of it.

It was Taryn who spotted him first. Lacie's attention was on the small Lincoln Logs dwelling she and Patrick were constructing together. Taryn winked and gave Shane a discreet thumbs-up.

"Is this a private party, or can anyone play?" Shane asked, stepping into the room.

Lacie looked up, and the smile she gave him felt like a hundred supernovas firing in his chest.

She turned to Patrick. "What do you think? Should we let your uncle play too?"

At Patrick's enthusiastic nod, Shane sat down next to them.

"Miss Lacie's gonna be my teacher next year," Patrick said proudly.

Shane shot a questioning look at Taryn. It was a well-known fact that Patrick was very much opposed to the idea of starting school.

"Changed your mind, have you?" Shane asked.

"Uh-huh."

"How come?"

Taryn coughed back a laugh when Patrick gave Shane what could only be described as a *duh* look. " 'Cause Miss Lacie says I'm really good at stuff and I can help her out with the other kids who aren't so good as me."

"I see. Well, Miss Lacie's pretty smart. I'd listen to her if I were you."

"Is that why you like her, Uncle Shane? 'Cause she's so smart?"

Lacie's face turned pink. Taryn had to look away to hide her laughter. Shane took it all in stride.

"One of many reasons," he said honestly. "She is also very kind, and she laughs at my jokes."

"She's pretty too."

"That she is."

"Okay, runt," Taryn said affectionately. "Your mom's

going to be here any minute. Let's get you cleaned up, huh?"

Taryn shepherded both children over to the sink, where step stools awaited.

"He's a great kid," Lacie said to Shane, scooping the Lincoln Logs back into their container. "I'm going to enjoy having him next year."

Shane didn't respond. When she looked up, she caught him staring at her, a questioning expression on her face. She couldn't possibly know that in watching her with Patrick, he'd had visions of her with their own children. Crystal-clear visions that had been so real that it felt as though he could reach out and touch them.

"You're wonderful with kids," he said, his voice unusually thick, simply because she was still looking at him and he had to say something.

"Thanks," she said, her lips twitching. "It helps with the job, you know."

"Do you want kids of your own?" he asked bluntly.

"Yes," she admitted shyly. "Do you?"

"With the right woman, yes." He pinned her with his gaze, silently communicating just who that woman was.

"Yeah?"

"Yeah," he whispered, pushing a strand of hair away from her face, leaning toward her until his lips hovered over hers.

Catching him by surprise, Lacie took the initiative and pressed her lips to his.

Shane's hand slipped beneath her hair, cupping the back of her neck, and he deepened the kiss. He thought he had accurately remembered the impossible sweetness of her mouth. He'd been wrong. His tongue danced with hers, playfully, sensually, taking everything that she would give him, binding her to him that much more.

Lacie McCain was his, and he would never have enough.

"Ugh, they're kissing!" complained Patrick before Taryn could grab his hand and snatch him back to the sink.

"Busted." Shane grinned as Lacie began to laugh. Her cheeks turned the prettiest shade of pink. Holding up the stickered notecard, he asked, "So ... does this mean you'll have coffee with me tomorrow night?"

"Yes," she said. "The rose was beautiful, by the way, and the apple was delicious. Thank you. You made my whole day brighter."

Shane grinned, pleased. He would spend a lifetime doing little things to make her smile, especially if it got her to kiss him like that.

"Well, I guess I'd better be going," Lacie said, rising. "I promised Rinn I'd hang out with her tonight. She doesn't like staying in the house all by herself."

"Big plans?"

"Huge. Takeout and some serious binge-watching."

That sounded safe enough.

"Make sure you lock the doors."

Lacie gave him a patient smile. "Always."

"I'll see you tomorrow then."

"Tomorrow," she confirmed.

The knot of worry eased a little, as he knew that Lacie would be with Corinne. He'd spent a good portion of the day with Ian, investigating Craig Davidson. The more he'd learned, the more anxious he was to put as much space between Lacie and Davidson as possible.

∼

"A SINGLE ROSE, YOU SAY?" Corinne said later when Lacie told her about the presents awaiting her when she arrived at the school that morning. "What color?"

"Why? What difference does that make?"

Corinne rolled her eyes. "You might be the older sister, but you are woefully naive." At Lacie's blank look, she explained with exaggerated patience, "*Because*, my dear sister, roses are like a secret code, a very specific language. Everything matters; number, color—it all says something."

Lacie shook her head. "I doubt he put that much thought into it."

Corinne arched a brow. "We are talking about Shane Callaghan, aren't we? Lace, I would bet that man has a reason for everything he does." She pulled out her phone and started tapping away.

"What are you doing?"

"Decoding your secret love message," Corinne said, waggling her eyebrows.

Corinne opened a browser window and typed in *meaning of roses*. Lacie looked on curiously even though she continued to mumble her skepticism.

"Okay, just one rose, right? That means ... ah, here it is. *The gift of a single rose of any color depicts utmost devotion.* See? That means he's really into you."

Lacie tried not to put too much faith in that. It was a romantic interpretation. It might just as well have meant *I like you, but I'm not that into you* or *I'm only getting you one, so you don't get ahead of yourself*. After all, it wasn't as if they'd post *that* as a possible meaning.

Then, she thought about the way Shane had kissed her and felt bad for doubting him. It was just so hard not to when everything about him screamed *perfect*. She might be a hopeless romantic at heart, but she'd seen enough to know that ninety-nine-point-nine percent of the time, something that seemed too good to be true, was.

"And, hmm, that is a really interesting color," Corinne said, studying the rose more closely.

Lacie had placed it in a delicate bud vase the minute she'd gotten inside. During the school day, it had sat regally in the small, reusable water bottle Lacie brought with her every day and had stood proudly in the cupholder on the ride home.

"I'm going to say that it's ... peach. Okay, here it is."

"What does it say?" Lacie asked despite herself.

"Oh, a believer now, are we?" Corinne chuckled. "It says that peach means *let's get together*. Well, that makes sense, doesn't it? His note was asking you out for coffee."

"It says it could also mean sincerity, gratitude, and appreciation," Lacie pointed out, tapping the screen with her finger.

"Yeah, okay. So ... he's sincere about wanting to go out with you, he's grateful for the chance to ask you out, and he appreciates the fact that you like to spend time with him." She tapped a perfectly manicured nail against her teeth. "But really, he already took you out to a fantastic dinner and came over to stay with you when you were so out of it. Maybe *you* should get *him* a peach rose."

Corinne paged down, skimming the screens of information. "Hey, does that rose have any thorns on it?"

Lacie imagined holding the delicate flower in her hand, how smooth it had been. "No. Why?"

"Because it says here," Corinne said with a devilish grin, "that thorn-free roses mean *love at first sight*."

ON TUESDAY MORNING, Lacie found another perfect rose on her desk. This one was a beautiful shade of lavender. It was balanced upon a small house, constructed entirely of Lincoln Logs, artfully done with windows and even a small porch. She laughed out loud into the silent classroom.

She fished her mobile out of her pocket and tapped out a query on the tiny keyboard. It was still too early to call—Corinne had been up way past midnight, studying—but a text message would do the trick.

What does a lavender rose mean? she asked, hitting Send before she could change her mind.

Lacie could barely hold the shiver of excitement when her phone vibrated in her pocket two hours later. She slipped it out and looked at the display, her heart doing that odd fluttering thing again.

Love at first sight. Enchantment. Told you. ;-)

CHAPTER TWELVE

Never has ninety minutes lasted quite so long, Lacie thought as she willed the clock to move faster.

Normally, she enjoyed Professor Stevens's lecture, but tonight, she simply couldn't concentrate. Had it only been a week ago that she sat in this very spot, sound asleep, while one of the most compelling men she had ever met spoke in that rich, sensual voice? Dear Lord, what was wrong with her?

"Everything happens for a reason." Lacie's mother's words floated across her mind, atop the sea of white noise that had become Professor Stevens's monologue.

If Lacie hadn't uncharacteristically drifted off, Shane wouldn't have given her a second glance. They would never have met. Never gone for coffee. Who would have thought such an embarrassing event could result in something so ... wonderful?

Finally—*finally*—the lecture was over. Lacie gathered up her book and notes—she'd managed to capture a couple of key points at least—in record time and was the first one out of the classroom. Perhaps such overeagerness wasn't proper, but she didn't care. All she could think about was seeing Shane again.

"Lacie." If the familiar voice hadn't caught her attention, the strong hand gripping her upper arm certainly would have.

Her forward progress was stopped so suddenly that her backpack slipped from her shoulders and landed on the floor with a thud. She winced as her shoulder wrenched painfully.

"Craig! What are you doing here?"

Oblivious to her discomfort, he tugged her out of the way as the classroom continued to empty out behind her. "I thought maybe we could grab a coffee and talk. You haven't been around much."

"I've been really busy, Craig," she said, bending over to pick up her bag the same time he did. The result was a solid thump to the head that sent her reeling backward and onto her behind. Her casted hand reached out reflexively to catch herself, further rewarding her with a shooting pain that reminded her it had recently been broken. Twice.

"Ah Christ, Lace, I'm sorry," he said apologetically. "Are you okay?"

"Yeah," she managed through gritted teeth as Craig hauled her to her feet. "I'm fine. You can let go now." Lacie felt herself turning red as the others shot curious looks their way.

Craig did not release her immediately, prompting Lacie to shrug out of his grasp.

"I can't have coffee with you tonight, Craig."

"Why not?"

"I made other plans."

His eyes narrowed. "Don't tell me you're meeting Callaghan again. I'm warning you—"

"And I'm warning *you*," she interrupted, her eyes blazing. "*Back off*."

She turned and started walking away, but Craig reached out for her once more.

"*Lacie*."

"Let me go," she hissed.

"Not until you hear what I have to say." Craig held her in place along the wall, using his bigger body like a blockade.

Lacie tried to wrench free of his grasp without drawing attention to herself; there were already a few uncomfortable glances being thrown their way. The last thing she needed was for someone to call campus security or for Shane to show up before she had a chance to handle this.

"I suggest you let her go now." Shane's voice was cold, lethal.

They both turned to see him behind them, his eyes like blue ice.

"Or what?" Craig sneered.

In answer, Shane's lips curled upward in a smile that didn't reach his eyes, promising both pain and humiliation. Craig saw it, too, his own presence intensifying at the silent challenge, unconsciously squeezing Lacie's arm until she yelped. Lacie saw Shane's entire body tense, saw the ice in his eyes morph into flames, and knew she had to do something to defuse the situation before someone really got hurt.

She lifted her foot and stomped on Craig's. *Hard*.

"Ow! What the fuck was that for?" he grouched, but the move had done the trick. Craig released her.

"For being an idiot," she told him.

As much as she appreciated Shane's willingness to stand up for her, he had to know that she was capable of fighting her own battles, and so did Craig.

Lacie stood tall and faced Craig first. "You and I are going to talk about this, but not here and not now."

The two men glared at each other. Craig's expression was one of unmitigated loathing. Shane's promised retribution for daring to touch Lacie. So much for her standing up for herself. She didn't think either one of them had even noticed.

She lightly touched her hand to Shane's arm. "I think I'd like that coffee now, if you're still up for it."

Without taking his eyes from the other man, Shane put his arm at Lacie's back and gently nudged her toward the exit. "You and I are going to have a little talk too, Davidson," he promised quietly.

"I look forward to it," Craig growled.

Lacie felt the heat of his glare all the way to the exit.

She and Shane walked in silence along the pathway until they were out of sight of the building.

Shane guided her to a bench beneath a standing carriage light to examine her more closely. "You're hurt."

"I'm fine," she exhaled, relieved that the confrontation was over—at least for now.

It was only a temporary respite, she knew. She was dreading having *the talk* with Craig, but it had to be done sooner rather than later. For now, however, she just wanted to forget about him and concentrate on the beautiful man looking at her with genuine concern. Even with his brow creased in worry and that serious expression on his face, he took her breath away.

"The tears in your eyes say differently," he chastised gently. "Is it your hand?"

She nodded, sniffling, hating that once again she was appearing as the helpless female. "Yeah, but it's okay. My head hurts more right now."

Shane pushed away a few tendrils of hair, spotting the emerging bump on her forehead. In a tender gesture, he pressed his lips to it. "We can get some ice for that when we get your hand X-rayed."

"Not again," she murmured.

"Yes, again," he said, his voice kind but firm.

His hand massaged her upper arm, where Craig had had such a bruising grip on her. She was glad she was wearing three-quarter-length sleeves, knowing that her flesh was probably already starting to darken. As it was, she could sense Shane's rage simmering just below the surface despite how gentle he was being with her.

"Does anything else hurt?" he asked.

Lacie's face flamed at the question. With her injured hand all but useless in stopping her fall, she'd landed hard on her rear end. She couldn't bring herself to tell Shane that though.

As if he'd read her mind, his eyes glistened, and the corners of his mouth quirked. "I'd prefer to take care of that particular injury privately," he said in a husky whisper, and Lacie forgot all about the pain in her hand, her arm, and her head as a new ache began to take over, one that had nothing to do with her latest fall from grace.

"Come on," he said, holding out his hand to her. "Let's get that hand checked out. I'll drive."

Shane guided Lacie into the passenger seat. When he leaned over to fasten her seat belt for her, it placed the base of his neck right by her lips. Unable to help herself, she leaned forward and kissed him there, connecting with the hollow of his throat, where his shoulders met his neck.

Shane froze, closing his eyes. "Do that again," he commanded softly.

She did, feeling the ache re-blossom when he gave an involuntary shudder of pleasure.

Shane turned, his eyes that lovely glowing sapphire, and placed his lips over hers. "You know how to give a man incentive, don't you?"

Lacie squeezed her thighs together at the husky quality of his voice just as he dipped his head lower and kissed her.

By the time he released her, she was barely lucid. She thought she heard him speaking to someone briefly. The next thing she knew, he was sliding into the driver's seat, giving her his sexy male grin.

It just made the evening's events more suckish.

"Spending this night in the ER is not what I had in mind," she grumbled.

"Don't worry, sweetheart; we won't." He winked. "My brother Michael is at the hospital tonight. We're getting express service."

Michael Callaghan was every bit as kind, soft-spoken, and gorgeous as his younger brother. He had a gentle touch and easy manner about him that Lacie liked immediately. Lacie asked about Maggie, and they spent a few minutes chatting about the farm and how much Lacie's kids enjoyed it every year.

"Well, everything's where it should be," Michael said a short while later while he examined the images. "Just continue to be careful, and you'll be fine."

∽

Lacie thanked him. While she visited the ladies' room, Michael pulled Shane aside.

"I like her," he said with approval.

Shane nodded. It was hard not to like Lacie. But he knew his brother well enough to know that Michael hadn't pulled him aside to tell him that.

"Spit it out, Mick."

"Is she ... accident-prone?" Michael asked carefully.

Shane thought back to the first time they'd met. She'd been a bit clumsy at first. When she stood up and discovered him so close, she tried backing away, tripping on the desk in the process. And when they walked outside, she ran into the doorframe, whipping around the moment she felt his hand on her lower back. Both times had been a reaction to some small gesture he'd made, almost defensive in nature.

Now that he thought about it, Lacie hadn't stumbled, tripped, or bumped into anything in their subsequent times together. At the restaurant. In her apartment. At the pub. On the contrary, her movements had been smooth and graceful. Until tonight. Until she tried to step away from Craig Davidson. Something unpleasant wriggled in his gut.

"Why?"

Outwardly, Michael's expression didn't change, but Shane was adept at reading people and was damn near psychic when it came to his own family.

"It looks like that hand has been broken several times," Michael said quietly, keeping his tone neutral. "Bones heal over time, but old injuries often show up on high-resolution images."

Shane said nothing. Michael glanced down the hallway to where Lacie was emerging from the ladies' room.

"If this were Maggie we were discussing, I'd keep her as close as possible."

Shane nodded, understanding Michael's message. Michael had already figured out that Lacie was Shane's *croie*, and the need to protect family was a strong one.

After thanking Michael again, they left.

"Your brother is really nice," she said. "I'm glad Maggie married him."

Shane glanced at her and offered her a smile. "Mick and Maggie were made for each other. I can't even imagine one without the other anymore."

Lacie was quiet for a moment and then asked, "Do you believe in soul mates, Shane?"

He didn't hesitate. "Absolutely."

"You sound awfully certain."

"That's because I am," he told her. "I've seen it happen five times in as many years."

"Your brothers," she guessed.

Shane nodded. "They knew right away when they met the women who eventually became their wives. My father says a Callaghan man will always recognize his *croie*, and when he does, there is no other woman for him."

"*Croie*?" she repeated, entranced.

"A variation of the Irish word for heart," Shane translated. "It is how we refer to our soul mate, the one and only woman capable of capturing and holding our heart."

"How incredibly romantic," she whispered.

"It's a lot more than romance, Lacie. Our *croie* really is our heart. She becomes the center of our whole universe, our very reason for being. We would do anything for her."

"Your brothers told you this?"

"They tried to explain it to me," Shane said slowly, forcing his eyes to stay on the road in front of them instead of the beautiful woman at his side, "but it's not something that can be adequately expressed in words. It has to happen to you to gauge the depth of it."

"Oh." The silence was broken only by the subtle hum of the car for several heartbeats while Lacie thought about what he'd said.

"It was not something I fully understood until I met you."

He heard her small but definite gasp. Shane glanced sideways at Lacie. She was staring straight ahead, her expression unreadable in the muted lights of the dash. For several moments, Shane thought he might have made a grave error. Everything he'd said was true, but perhaps Lacie hadn't been quite ready to hear it yet. Not so long ago, he would have scoffed at the idea himself, but thanks to his brothers, he'd accepted the possibility that perfect mates did exist.

If their roles were reversed and Lacie had said something like that to him this early in their relationship, he wasn't sure he would have taken it well, no matter how strongly he felt about her. Acceptance was a huge but critical step. In retrospect, he probably should have asked if she believed in soul mates, too, before blurting out the depth of his feelings for her, but it was too late for that now.

By the time he pulled the sedan next to Lacie's Passat back at the college parking lot, he was a nervous wreck. Lacie still hadn't said a word. Hadn't moved really. He thought he might have seen her blink once or twice, but even that was questionable.

Ten years of military training and covert ops had done nothing to prepare him for dealing with anything like this. For a man so adept at reading people, he was suddenly at a complete loss. He couldn't even venture a guess at what she was thinking.

He cut the engine and took a deep breath. There was nothing else for it. He was an idiot. Things had been going so well. He should have stuck to the traditional stuff—flowers, little gifts, midnight phone calls, and stolen kisses. He should have been patient, allowing her time to grow accustomed to the idea of having him around before he dropped a bombshell like that on her.

Shane Callaghan—the soft-spoken, lethal special ops man—stared unseeingly at the steering wheel, wondering how the hell he was going to fix this when he felt the gentlest of touches on his arm. He turned, and his heart went from thumping wildly to nearly stopping completely. Lacie was looking at him, silvery moonlight and soft carriage lights playing across her beautiful face, her eyes impossibly large and blue and filled with ... *love*.

"Did you mean that?" she said, her voice barely more than a whisper but easily heard in the silence.

"Yes," he said, his voice thick. "Every word."

He watched her intently as a slow smile spread across her face.

And right there, in the parking lot of the university, Shane Callaghan kissed his *croie* with all of the passion of a man who had just found his heart.

CHAPTER THIRTEEN

"Do you still want coffee?" he asked sometime later, his head swimming dizzily as he finally broke their kiss.

"No," she said, sounding every bit as dazed and breathless as he did. "I've got a better idea. Follow me."

"Anywhere," he murmured.

Lacie grinned and got out of the Lexus. The cool night air was a welcome shock to his senses; kissing Lacie was enough to make a man lose himself.

Shane followed her back to her place. It was a short distance, but it seemed interminable with her in another vehicle. He kept telling himself not to get his hopes up, that it was still too early to consider the kinds of things running through his mind.

His body didn't listen. Every cell was alive and vibrating with hopeful anticipation. He was going to be ready for her, no matter *what* his mind said.

He was pretty proud of himself. He made it all the

way to Lacie's apartment without wrecking the car. He managed to get out of the car and walk—fairly normally, too, despite the ache between his legs—over to hers and open the door for her. The smile she gave him made him weak in the knees, and when she entwined her fingers with his and started leading him to her apartment, his mouth went dry.

"Maybe I should say good night," he said when she opened the door. If he went inside, he wasn't sure he would be able to control himself. Everything about her called to him on a very base, primal level.

"Do you want to say good night?" She rose to her toes and kissed beneath his jaw, down his throat, and along his collarbone. Her lips were so soft, so warm, and when they touched him *right there*, the sensation rocketed throughout the rest of his body.

"No," he answered truthfully, his voice a strained whisper.

"Then, don't."

A single tug on his hand, and he was over the threshold.

Shane stood as still as a statue—at least until Lacie stepped up and began to wrap her arms around his neck. Shane kissed her then. He couldn't have stopped himself if he wanted to. He lifted her in his arms until her feet dangled above the floor, pulling her to him, tasting her sweetness, growing drunk with pleasure on it. His desire flared to dangerous levels again, threatening to engulf them both.

It was only with great effort that he eased their

passionate kiss, gently setting her down on the ground again, though he did continue to hold her close.

"Lacie ..." Her name was a tattered prayer on his lips. It was all he could do not to lay her down right then and there and spend the rest of the night loving her, as he longed to do.

"Shane, please don't stop," she whispered.

"I have to," he replied, his breathing ragged as he carefully tugged her shirt back down, more to give his trembling fingers something to do than anything.

"Why?" Her face was so guileless, her eyes so innocent and yet filled with such desire.

It was a true test of his will to resist when she clearly wanted him with the same clawing hunger that had claimed him.

"Because, Lacie, once I start, I'm not going to want to stop. And when I take you, it will be all of you. You will become mine, totally, completely, and irrevocably. Know this, Lacie, and be absolutely certain it is what you want."

∽

"Oh." Had he not been holding her, she was sure she would have swooned. Then, his words really sank in, the implications clear. "It works both ways, you know," she said, gaining strength from the bond she could already feel between them, growing stronger with every passing minute. "You will belong to me as well."

His eyes blazed. "Yes."

"Then, there's no reason not to."

"You're sure?"

Lacie had never been more certain of anything. She didn't just want this man; she needed him. "Yes."

Shane kissed her again, wildly, passionately, sweeping her up into his arms and carrying her to the bedroom. Lacie's arms held on tight, her hands finding purchase on his muscled shoulders, taut with the tension of holding her.

He laid her down on the bed, sliding next to her when she refused to release him. His hands eased over her curves, as if he was memorizing them. Her body bowed and stretched, begging shamelessly for more of his touch. Her soft, feminine flesh yielded to his every tactile command, burning beneath him.

Lacie arched hard, desperate to feel more of his body against hers, wanting, needing those hard planes pressing against hers, knowing he was the only one who could soothe the unbearable ache deep within her. Shane nipped her bottom lip in warning.

"Easy, baby," he said, his voice roughened with the effort of keeping his hunger leashed. His tongue caressed over the bite, soothing it.

If he thought to stem her desperation with the punitive act, he was sorely mistaken. Lacie's hands clutched at him tighter, her nails curling into his upper back like a tigress flexing her claws. Haze filled her mind, incited by that bit of subtle pain, even as one leg curled over his hip and pulled him closer.

Could it be that his mild-mannered schoolteacher burned with a darker passion than he'd realized?

His mind flashed back a few days to when Lacie had perched on the kitchen counter with him between her thighs and she had grabbed the edges of his shirt and pulled hard. At the way she had wrapped her legs around his waist and willed him closer with her heart, mind, and body.

Deciding to put his theory to the test, Shane exerted enough force to pin her beneath him, taking both of her arms in one of his much larger hands, being extra careful not to exacerbate her injury. He moved them above her head and held them there while he used his other hand to trace small circles across her chest, pausing to pinch her diamond-hard tips through her cotton blouse. Straddling her hips, Shane let his hand alternate between sensual caresses along the column of her neck and encircling her throat —not enough to hurt, but enough to clearly assert his dominance. Her blue eyes darkened, and her lids fluttered closed, as if in ecstasy.

"Look at me," he commanded, and her eyes snapped open in immediate obedience. Though he wouldn't have believed it possible, his cock swelled even more as an ever-increasing throb built within.

With a wicked grin, he let his fingers stroke down to the neckline of her blouse. Then, in a swift tug, he ripped it right down the center. Lacie writhed beneath him, her keening whimpers threatening his control.

"You like that," he breathed in awe, his fingers tracing the outline of her silky bra, a pretty pink that he knew would be a lighter shade of her nipples.

He leaned down, retaining eye contact, and took one breast in his mouth. An impassioned moan echoed from deep within her as he tongued her hardened peak through the material, her hips desperately trying to move against him.

"Shane," she said, his name a ragged plea from her lips. "Please ..."

"Please what, baby?" he purred, lightly biting her, delighting in the hiss that escaped her lips.

"Please ... take your shirt off ... want to feel you ..."

"You do it," he commanded, releasing her hands and moving back enough to allow her to sit up.

Her hands grasped at his shirt; her small growls of frustration were like music to his fevered ears when her fingers couldn't undo the buttons fast enough. Finally, she gave up and gave one wrenching pull, solving the problem. Shane laughed at her enthusiasm, a sexy, answering growl that gave way to a hiss when she pushed the sides away and found his bare chest. Nails raked over his skin, sharp enough to send ribbons of pleasure streaking through his nerves but not enough to draw blood.

Then, her mouth was suddenly around his nipple, biting and sucking, mimicking the things he had done to her. Shane's head flew back as he fisted his hands in her hair, pulling just enough to earn a few more feminine snarls.

While her mouth worked hungrily at his chest—licking, biting, and teasing—her hands moved down, stroking his sides, his abs, and his back, desperate to touch every exposed inch of his flesh. His muscles contracted and rippled beneath the contact, responding to her with a will of their own. He lost himself in the bliss of it, only to realize moments later that she had managed to unfasten his pants and her hand was reaching in ...

Shane nearly shouted when her hand closed around him. He had expected her touch to be tentative and gentle. It wasn't. It was firm and fiercely possessive, branding him down to his soul. He had warned her that she would belong to him, totally, completely, and irrevocably. She had answered him in kind. And she hadn't been kidding.

Unable to withhold himself any longer, Shane pushed her onto her back, looming over her like a predator. Her eyes widened, and she licked her lips in anticipation. One by one, he discarded pieces of her clothing until she lay naked beneath him.

He allowed himself one scorching look. He would spend hours, days, years learning her body. Worshipping it. Pleasuring it. Discovering all of its hidden secrets. But at that moment, neither her desire nor his would allow it.

The need to claim his *croie* surged inside of him. To mark her. Claim her. Brand her soul so that there was no question what she was to him or what he would do for her.

He pulled away only long enough to get rid of the rest of his clothes, and then he settled his weight on top of her. Her legs opened in invitation, her body forming a perfect cradle. He paused above her, cupping her face with his hands.

"*Mo chroie beloved*," he whispered, his breath mixing with hers.

"*Mo chroie beloved*," she repeated, and his heart sang with joy.

He tenderly kissed her on the lips ... and then slid himself into her warm, welcoming depths.

Lacie rolled her hips to provide a better angle as Shane eased forward. As desperate and hungry as they were, he would not hurt her. Her sheath was so incredibly tight, hot, wet, and perfect. Even with her desire, it was difficult. He cursed himself for not having the patience and self-control to prepare her better as she stretched around him.

A low moan filled his senses as she lifted to take him deeper; he'd never heard a sweeter sound. He worked himself inside, his penetration absolute until he filled her to capacity, swollen and pressed against her slick folds.

He paused, allowing her to become accustomed to him, kissing her face, her neck, and her jaw until he felt her start to move beneath him. Then, he began slow, easy thrusts.

"Shane," she moaned again, drawing out his name

so it sounded like a song upon her lips. "Oh, how I've dreamed of this ... of you ..."

Her admission broke his last thread of control. He began to move harder, faster. She opened further to him, begging him to crawl inside her, to possess her. Her legs wrapped around his waist, her feet rode his ass and the backs of his thighs, and he pumped into her over and over again while she clutched feverishly at his arms.

He felt her inner muscles begin to tighten and her body coil around his. She called out his name in one last desperate plea, and he obliged, driving hard and deep. Lacie shattered around him, her body seizing in ripples of pleasure, her sex squeezing like a tight fist around his cock.

His own release was imminent. He continued to thrust, prolonging her climax until he joined her in ecstasy. He exploded within her, filling her, marking her, over and over again until she wrung every last drop from him.

Exhausted, Shane dropped to the side, afraid of hurting her. Instantly, Lacie rolled into him, burying her face in his neck and wrapping one leg around his hip to keep them joined.

Shane's heart pounded against the walls of his chest. He had never before experienced anything like it. No victory had ever been sweeter; no adrenaline rush could have compared to the high he felt in this woman's arms.

He'd thought he understood the intensity of a

man's feelings for his *croie*, but he realized now that he hadn't even scratched the surface. This was far beyond anything he could have imagined; he could no more have comprehended this than a blind man could witness a spectacular sunset or a deaf man, a symphony. It was as if a whole new sense had come into being, one open only to those who had found their other halves.

Lacie was his. Forever. His heart. His soul. His universe.

She snuggled in closer, murmuring against his skin while he held her to him. It awed him.

As he lay there, sated, basking in absolute peace and a sense of completeness, he realized that he should have known all along. His perfect mate was everything he needed even if he hadn't known exactly what that was.

"Baby," he purred against her neck. "Time to get up for school."

Lacie, he'd learned, was a full-body-contact sleeper, wrapping herself around him like a blanket. He loved it.

She murmured something into his neck, making him chuckle.

"No," he answered, stroking her back, "I don't think we have time to do it again."

The entire night had been an alternating series of mind-blowing sex and brief, restorative catnaps. While he was used to operating on little or no sleep, it was apparent that Lacie was not.

She grumbled, but with a few imaginative, motivational words and some well-placed caresses, Shane got her up, showered, and dressed with several minutes to spare—minutes he made the most of. While she slipped on her casual sandals, he sipped his coffee, trying to reconcile the sweet, wholesome image now standing before him with the woman who had mounted him in the middle of the night. The thought made him smile.

"And just what are you grinning about?" she teased, coming over and rising on her toes to place a chaste kiss on his jaw.

"Same thing you are, I imagine," he said, grabbing her for a more substantial kiss.

She melted against him. "Mmm. It's going to be a very long day, isn't it?"

Shane laughed. "That it is. When can I see you tonight?" There was no longer a question of *if*.

His body, heart, and soul were already protesting the realization that he would have to spend the day apart from her. That would take some getting used to.

Lacie frowned. "Not until late, I'm afraid. There's a staff meeting after work to plan for the year-end carnival." She sighed. "It always runs late. Bill Schaeffer and Carole Simms will have their usual pissing contest and make the rest of us suffer."

She gave him a martyred look. "I don't suppose you can think of a way to get me out of it, can you?" she asked, petting his chest with tender strokes. She couldn't seem to keep her hands off of him, and he loved it. "I'll make it worth your while."

Shane groaned. Even a simple caress had him hard and heavy. After the night they'd just had, he should not be as eager as he was. "That I don't doubt. But it's just as well. I have a couple of things I've been putting off that I should take care of." At the top of that list was gathering more intel on Craig Davidson. He kissed her nose. "Call me when you're done?"

"I will," she promised and then cursed. "Damn. Rinn's staying over tonight. She's got early morning classes tomorrow."

She looked so adorably put out at the thought of spending an evening away from him that his heart swelled.

"Call me anyway," he said. "We can talk dirty to each other."

Lacie laughed, the sound pure music to his soul. "You're on."

CHAPTER FOURTEEN

There were no flowers awaiting Lacie when she walked into her classroom that morning, but then she hadn't expected any since Shane had been with her up until the time he closed her car door and watched her drive away. As thoughtful and romantic as his gifts were, spending time with him was infinitely preferable.

She was thrilled, however, when half a dozen roses arrived at lunchtime. Since it was between classes, she wasted no time in pulling out her phone. According to the internet site Corinne had been consulting, the single dark red rose meant *I love you*, and the brilliant orange that made up the remainder of the bouquet signified enthusiasm, desire, and fascination.

She sighed, resolving to spend time during the long, boring planning meeting thinking of all the ways she would thank him later.

. . .

It was getting dark by the time Lacie finally emerged from the school. The meeting had lasted even longer than expected. Joan Engle had decided to dig her heels in against both Bill and Carole, and it had been an all-out free-for-all after that. Lacie shook her head. Her kindergarten kids handled themselves with more maturity.

She offered a parting wave to the others as she slid into the front seat of her VW and finally exhaled. Several hours of bickering on top of a full day and a lack of sleep—along with some very intense, exhausting physical activity throughout the night—was catching up with her. Not to mention, she felt like she was starting to come down with something. A nasty bout of flu had been running rampant through the school these past two weeks; she certainly hoped she'd avoided it, but the dull ache in her muscles and joints was suggesting otherwise. Perhaps if she took something the moment she got home, she could nip it in the bud before it took a solid hold.

All she wanted to do was take a hot bath and crawl into bed. Ideally, she would do so in Shane's warm, strong arms, but that would have to wait because Corinne was expecting her. Maybe it was just as well. If this was the beginning of the flu, then she didn't want to get him sick too, and Corinne had already had it.

At least she'd get to talk to him later. Just the thought of hearing his voice sent delicious ribbons of warmth through her. *Had he been serious when he suggested they talk dirty to each other?* Her lips curved upward at the thought. She'd never done that before; it just seemed so ... naughty. Then again, Shane Callaghan and naughty seemed to go hand in hand.

Naughty, but oh-so good, she thought with a smile.

Lacie let her head fall back and closed her eyes, pondering the possibilities ...

A LOUD CRACK of thunder boomed and rumbled, jolting Lacie awake. It took her a moment to recall where she was. There was an unpleasant cramp in her neck from where it had lolled to the side.

Blinking furiously, she realized it was pitch-dark. The streetlamp she'd parked under was out. A quick perusal of the surroundings confirmed that not a single light shone in the parking lot; nor were there any silvery shafts of moonlight to illuminate the area around her. She knew that the school turned off the lot lights after a certain time—an effort to save a few taxpayer dollars on energy costs. *Could it possibly be that late?*

She tried checking her inexpensive but practical watch, but it was too dark to see. A shiver slid down her spine; she'd never realized just how spooky an unlit parking lot could be.

Muttering a few soft, G-rated curses, she felt around blindly for her keys. They must have fallen from her lap while she napped. It took several minutes, but she finally managed to locate them between the seat and the center console. Fighting another shiver, she jammed her key into the ignition, turned, and ... nothing happened.

The slight click that came from the rotation was the only sound in the silence; there was no attempted start, no whir of a weak battery, nothing. Lacie tried several more times but to no avail.

Achy and beyond weary, she was more than ready to call it a day. With a long-suffering sigh, she fumbled around in her purse for her cell phone, somewhat surprised that Corinne hadn't been calling every five minutes. Despite the fact that she was several years younger than Lacie, Corinne often acted like a mother hen, especially these last few months. Lacie wasn't sure how long she'd napped, but surely, it was well past the time Corinne had expected her back at the apartment.

Maybe Corinne was already asleep. She had been cramming for exams and staying up till all hours of the night lately. It might be better just to call Callaghan Auto. They had a twenty-four-hour towing service, and since it was right around the block from her place, they probably wouldn't mind dropping her off.

Lacie emptied the contents of her bag in mounting frustration. She sifted through them one by one in the dark, identifying each item by feel, finally coming to the unwelcome conclusion that her phone was not among them. She closed her eyes and tried to think back. The last time she'd used it was to order out for pizza when the meeting ran into dinnertime; it was probably still sitting on the conference table, where she'd left it.

Lacie took a deep breath in, a deep breath out. It wasn't the end of the world. Her warm bath and soft bed would be delayed a bit longer, was all. The doors to the school were probably locked, but the second-shift custodian, Daryl, would still be there.

Gathering her courage, Lacie opened the door and stepped out into the darkness. The air was still, heavy with the moisture and silence that preceded a storm. The tread of her soft-soled sandals was barely audible as she carefully made her way across the empty lot. Each step required effort.

A few inside lights were still on, visible through the windows. Lacie knocked on the door several times, but there was no indication that anyone had heard her. Once, she spotted Daryl through the floor-to-ceiling panes of glass outside the main office, but his head was down, his earbuds in, and he passed without a single glance her way. After a while, she had to face the fact that she was not going to get back into the building to retrieve her phone.

Lacie looked heavenward into the inky blackness of the night sky. The way she saw it, she had two options. She could stay here, where the tiny bit of light that spilled out through the school windows gave her some small measure of comfort. Or she could go back to the empty parking lot and sit in her car until someone came looking for her. Between Corinne and Shane and their similar penchant for worrying about her, it shouldn't be long at all.

That was a comforting thought.

A sudden flash of lightning and subsequent crack of thunder made her jump, even as the first few fat drops of rain splattered in front of her.

Decision made. Back to the car it was.

A vicious wind whipped up, lifting the maple leaf seeds into miniature tornadoes made visible with each subsequent streak of lightning. The storm was approaching hard and fast, which wasn't unusual for the late spring when the daytime temps rose in stark contrast to the cool nights. Within seconds, the sky opened up, and Lacie forced her legs to move quicker until she was running toward the safety of her car.

She rounded the corner, already drenched to the bone from the icy downpour. Huge puddles formed along the sidewalk; the rain came down in torrents, faster than it could drain away. Another booming crack of thunder hit so close that she could feel the charge lifting the fine hairs on her soaked arms, and behind her, the school went dark.

It was impossible to see where she was going; she knew only that she was headed in the right direction. She stepped off the sidewalk and right into a patch of mud. She'd been running so fast that it was impossible to stop her forward momentum, and she skidded. There was a sharp stabbing pain in her ankle as her foot caught on something. The next thing she knew, she was weightless and looking up at the stormy sky.

She hit the ground hard. All of the air was knocked out of her lungs with a huge *whoosh* upon impact. Instinctively, she opened her mouth to gulp in air, only to choke on the deluge of water pouring down onto her from the flooding gutters above. Forcing herself onto her side, she expelled the water in a series of racking coughs until she was finally able to take a breath.

She almost wished she hadn't. A new rush of pain seared along her back, making it hard to expand her rib cage as she gasped for air. It joined with the burning flame shooting up from her ankle, the ache from her broken hand—which now extended to her wrist as well, and the sensation of a metal spike being driven into the back of her shoulder.

Lacie would have cried if she had been able to find enough air to do so. Instead, she clenched her teeth together and tried to push herself up, only to flop down in the mud several more times when her ankle refused to hold her weight. Resigned to crawling on her knees and one hand, she began moving forward. If there was any consolation, doing so kept the rain out of her face while she sought shelter.

"Lacie!"

Strong hands were suddenly lifting her upward. She screamed at the pain the movement brought and heard a series of muttered curses in response. Then, she was scooped up into powerful arms and held against a body covered from head to knee in a dark, hooded rain slicker.

"Craig?" she croaked, recognizing the familiar scent of his aftershave. Her mind was so fuzzy; the sound of the rain mixed with a loud buzzing in her ears, making it difficult to hear a response.

"I've got you. Jesus. Don't talk. Hang on."

Craig shifted her against his body while he opened the door to his SUV and lifted her inside.

"Your truck ..." she protested, knowing that she was covered in mud, dripping wet, and—if the warm, sticky stuff on her upper back was any indication—bleeding all over his new vehicle. The Durango was Craig's pride and joy.

"Fuck the truck," he growled.

Her next feeble objection was lost as the passenger door slammed, reducing the noise of the storm to the muffled deluge against the metallic exterior.

He joined her a minute later. The cab was so warm, and she was shivering uncontrollably. She felt a blanket being draped over her and heard Craig asking her questions, but it was hard to concentrate when her head hurt so badly. She didn't think she'd hit it—her shoulder had taken the brunt of the impact—but she must have jarred it enough to give her a nasty headache. And why was she so dizzy all of a sudden?

"My car wouldn't work," she mumbled as she fought to keep her eyes open. She should stay awake—she knew that—but it was a losing battle. "I lost my phone. Couldn't call for help. I fell. Hurts." Forming a coherent sentence was becoming increasingly difficult; single words were so much easier.

"No one knows where you are? What happened?" Craig sounded rushed. He was reaching for the seat belt, tugging to get it to extend around her, blanket and all. Lacie let out a cry as he pulled tight to secure it. "It's okay, baby."

The SUV roared to life.

"It hurts, Craig," she told him, shifting in an attempt to alleviate some of the pressure. "And I'm so tired. What's wrong with me?"

"Close your eyes, Lacie." Craig pulled out of the parking lot, and the powerful heater continued to fill the inside with such lovely warmth. "Everything is going to be okay now."

∽

SHANE RUBBED at his chest again, the persistent ache growing stronger with each passing minute. He looked at the wall clock. Nine p.m. Lacie should have called by now.

He pulled out his phone and called her cell. It rang a few times and went to voice mail. *Again*.

Shane paced the length of his room and told himself he was overreacting. Lacie had warned him that the planning meeting would probably go late and that her sister was going to stay over at her place. There must be a good reason Lacie hadn't called yet. The meeting had probably run late, just like she'd said, and then she and Corinne had gone out for a bite to eat.

No big deal. She'd call any minute now, and he'd realize how paranoid he was being. It was only natural. He wanted to be with Lacie, craved her so much that it made him overly agitated when something kept them from being together. His brothers were the same way with their wives. The desire to be with his other half was part of the experience. It would take some getting used to—that was all.

He glanced at the now-closed file folder on his desk. That was the real source of his unease—a two-inch-thick dossier that Ian had managed to compile on Craig Davidson. With each page he'd read, the more disquieted Shane had become. While the official profile painted a decent enough picture, anyone with experience deciphering official government documents could read between the lines.

On the surface, Craig Davidson had served his country, had sustained grievous injuries on his final tour, and had been honorably discharged on medical grounds.

What the official documents had hinted at but had not come right out and said was that Craig Davidson was a borderline psychopath. At least, that was the opinion Shane had formed.

Ian had obtained enough "unofficial" evidence to support that theory. A history of insubordination. Disorderly conduct. Use of excessive force. Allusions to problems in the civilian sector, such as brief mentions of fights and "coerced sexual relations." There were even a few psych evaluations Ian had managed to get his hands on. Terms and phrases like *obsessive*, *skewed perception*, and *predilection toward violence* leaped off the page and into Shane's photographic memory.

The items that interested Shane the most were the so-called investigations into the events that had resulted in Davidson's injuries and the loss of the rest of his unit. The cause of the incident was officially ruled as an accident, the result of "weapons malfunctions," but so many of the pages had been black-lined in the interest of national security that it was difficult to get a complete picture of exactly what the mission had entailed and what had gone wrong.

Ian was working on getting the full reports, but even the little bit Shane had seen was enough for him to know that the information in Lacie's apartment did not match up with Ian's results, not even at the official level.

It was also enough to convince Shane that something was off. The pieces just didn't fit.

Davidson's activities after his discharge didn't foster any warm and fuzzy feelings either. He had been in bad shape when he came home—that much was true. He'd spent much of the first year in and out of hospitals and then rehabs as they sought to rebuild the parts of him that had been so badly damaged. The local news had done a series of interviews with him over that first year. Shane had read every one of them. Each one had given him the same instinctual feeling that Craig Davidson was not a man who could be trusted.

Then, Davidson's young wife had died tragically in a car accident, leaving him with a three-year-old daughter. The maternal grandparents got custody of the little girl, but Davidson had visiting rights. Why?

Was it that Davidson was still in bad enough shape that they felt it would be in the girl's best interests to be with the mother's parents instead? Or was it something else?

What Shane had found particularly interesting were the handwritten sticky notes Ian had placed on various documents, reminders to speak with the lawyer in town who had drawn up the custody arrangement. Ian must have been thinking along the same lines. Shane would have to ask him about that later; Ian had already left for the night with Lexi and the kids.

Shane sighed, looking at the clock again. Nine thirty. Maybe he should try calling Corinne's phone. Lacie did have a tendency to be a bit forgetful with hers. It was probably sitting in the pocket of her skirt at the bottom of her hamper. The thought made him smile.

Then again, maybe he shouldn't call again so soon. It might come across as too possessive. Lacie might think that he was checking up on her. She certainly didn't seem to appreciate it when Davidson acted over-protective. The situations were totally different, he knew, but he was averse to anything that might put him in the same light as Davidson until Lacie fully accepted their *croie* bond and could understand.

He pushed his phone further back on the desk. He could wait a little longer. He would force himself to.

Flipping up the screen on his laptop, he decided to check out a few things. Ian had managed to get a lot of information over the past couple of days, but he had his hands full too. In his typical orderly fashion, Shane created a list of items on which to follow up on as he perused the data Ian had already provided. Ian was the uncontested digital genius, to be sure—he could bypass any security system, given enough time—but Shane was no slouch either. Research was a big part of what he did too.

He interlaced his fingers and gave them a stretch. Ian had concentrated on Davidson at Shane's request, but the more he'd read about Lacie's self-appointed big brother, the more agitated he became. Shane decided to switch gears. His fingers glided over the slick black keys, using Ian's custom search engine to find out more about the woman he would soon be calling his wife.

Several hits came up right away. All generic things from public sources, and all good. Pictures of Lacie with her "kids" at Maggie's farm. A graduation announcement placed in the paper by her proud parents on achieving her bachelor's in elementary education. A wedding portrait, where Lacie stood as maid of honor to Mikaela (Daniels) Davidson.

Shane froze at that last image. At first glance, Lacie and Mikaela looked identical. They had similar features and were of similar build, but Lacie was a bit shorter and curvier. It was the hair that really did it—both the same shade of golden sunlight at dusk, cut into waves layered and angled around their faces.

He revised his search to include Mikaela. He brought up the obituary announcement and placed that picture side by side with the wedding photo. Though, chronologically, only a little more than three years had passed between the wedding and her death, Mikaela looked much older. There were small lines around her face, a soulful, haunting look in her eyes despite the smile. Her hair was back to what Shane suspected was her natural color—a light brown, much shorter than it had been in the wedding photo.

One of his brothers had mentioned that Mikaela bore a resemblance to Lacie, but he'd had no idea just how striking it had been. The ache in his chest intensified, and a cold shiver slithered down his spine.

No longer worried about appearing overly protective, Shane grabbed his phone and called Corinne. She answered on the first ring.

"Corinne? This is Shane Callaghan. Can I speak with Lacie, please? She's not answering her phone."

The brief moment of silence on the other end of the line sent waves of foreboding through him.

"Corinne?"

"She's not with you?"

It was Shane's turn to pause in surprise. "No. She told me she was spending the evening with you."

"That's what I thought, too, but she's not here. When she didn't answer her cell, I figured she was with you ..."

"When was the last time you spoke with her?"

"This afternoon. She texted me about the roses you sent."

"Before the planning meeting or after?"

"Before. It was right before her afternoon class."

Shane used his years of training and experience to tamp down the sudden rush of panic he felt. His psychic sensors were screaming. "Corinne, stay there in case she calls. I'm going to drive over to the school. Maybe she had car trouble or something."

He hoped.

CHAPTER FIFTEEN

Lacie's VW was the only vehicle in the lot, but the asphalt was covered in wet leaves and an assortment of twigs and branches from the storm. None of the lot lights were on. Shane angled his vehicle so that the Passat was bathed in the glow of his headlights, but he knew it was empty before he got out.

He checked it out anyway. The rain had slowed to a constant, gentle shower. The lightning and thunder that had racked the valley earlier had moved toward the northeast. Occasional glimpses of eerie white-gold strikes backlit the clouds, but they were too far away now to be heard.

Shane opened the driver's door—it was unlocked—and Lacie's scent hit him head-on. So fresh, so feminine. Sunshine and flowers. It made his stomach clench in worry. When the inner dome light did not come on, Shane used a flashlight to do a quick check of the interior. The keys were still in the ignition. Lacie's purse and the contents of it were strewn across the passenger seat. Her wallet was among the items he saw there, leading him to conclude that robbery was not a motive. What he didn't see was her phone.

With a few quick taps, he dialed her number and listened. There was no telltale ring in the VW, no muted vibration. This time, however, his call was answered.

"Hello?" a male voice said through the small device.

"Who is this?" Shane asked, fighting down the sharp twist in his gut.

"Daryl, night custodian. Who's this?"

"Shane Callaghan. I'm trying to reach Lacie McCain."

"Ah," the man said with a slight chuckle. "I should have known this was Lacie's phone. I found it lying in the conference room. Didn't know who it belonged to."

"Is Lacie in there?"

"Nope. They left hours ago."

"Lacie's car is still in the lot. I think she might have had some trouble with it. May I come in and look around?" The polite request was a courtesy. Shane was going in whether he received permission or not. There might be some clue in there.

"I'm not supposed to do that," the man mused. "Your name is Callaghan, you say?"

Shane confirmed that it was.

"Guess it'd be all right then. Come around to the southern entrance."

As Shane made his way toward the building, the powerful beam of his flashlight searched the ground and surrounding areas for clues to Lacie's whereabouts, but he didn't have much hope. The storm would have wiped out anything useful.

The night custodian was waiting for him at the door. Shane immediately pegged him as a veteran; he had the haunted look of a man who had seen enough horror in the world and was trying to live out the rest of his life in peace.

Daryl took one look at Shane and nodded. "Yep, you're a Callaghan all right. Your brother Kane saved my ass in Iraq. He is one scary son of a bitch but a hell of a good man."

Shane nodded. His eldest sibling was roughly the size of a small mountain and had the personality of a deadly tsunami. He was quiet; no one ever heard him coming, but once he got there, everything around him was decimated. There were hundreds of men like Daryl who owed their lives to Kane.

Unfortunately, Shane didn't learn much from his look around. Daryl told him he'd had his earphones in most of the night and that he hadn't heard or seen anything out of the ordinary until the storm knocked the power out briefly. It was after it had come back on that he found the phone in the conference room. He walked Shane around the building, but again, no luck.

Daryl flipped the switches to turn on the lot light and the floodlights around the grounds, bathing the outside in light. Shane had already called Sean and Kieran; they were on their way to assist in a search of the grounds. Daryl said he wanted to help too.

"Lacie's a good woman. Nice to everyone, you know?"

Yeah, Shane knew. Her gentle, compassionate nature was one of the first things that had drawn him in.

"She got me these Bluetooth earbuds for Christmas," Daryl continued as if he needed to impart the knowledge. "Said the music would keep me from getting lonely when I was here at night by myself. Sometimes, she leaves Yodels on her desk for me. She knows they're my favorite."

Shane nodded. That sounded exactly like something Lacie would do.

Sean pulled up in the family Hummer H2, and Shane was grateful that Nicki had come along too. His twin's *croie* was a former agent of an elite, unsanctioned group known only as the Chameleons. As the only woman to ever be actively included in the Callaghans' off-the-books team, she had proven herself invaluable time and time again. Kieran jumped out of the backseat with his usual enthusiasm, all business and raring to go.

Together, they methodically covered the grounds. It was Sean who found an area near the far back end of the building, where it looked as though some of the landscaping had been crushed. Closer inspection revealed shallow grooves in the seeping mud, consistent with someone crawling—or being dragged. They ended where the walkway picked up again.

"Sean." Nicki's voice was barely more than a whisper, but Shane's head whipped up.

His heart sank into the bottom of his shoes when he saw Sean crouch down next to Nicki, touch his fingers to the foot-high stone retaining wall, and then draw them up to his nose.

Shane didn't need his special connection with Sean to know that he'd found blood.

"How bad is it?" he asked.

"Not bad," Sean answered evenly. "We have to call this in, Shane."

Shane heard the words Sean hadn't said aloud. *This might be a crime scene.*

"I know." *Lacie is fine. She has to be.*

"Kieran's calling in the others." *We'll find her, Shane. Fuck yes, we will.*

"Maybe there's something helpful on her cell," Nicki said, standing. "Sean said you found it inside?"

Shane cursed. He'd been so intent on finding Lacie that he'd forgotten about the mobile. He pulled it up and glanced at the display. Twelve missed calls. He pressed a couple of buttons and started scrolling through the list. Four were from him. Six from Corinne. He skipped over those for now. One was from someone named Cindy Sheridan, a brief message concerning a booth they were working on together for the upcoming carnival. And one from Craig Davidson.

That was the one he listened to first.

"Hey, Lacie. It's Craig. Are you screening or something? Listen, I'm sorry, babe. I know you're angry with me, but believe me when I tell you, I'm only trying to look out for you. You might be all grown up, but in my eyes, you'll always be that skinny little thing with big blue eyes, who used to follow me and Bri around all the time."

There was a small chuckle, a brief pause.

"I have to head out of town. Gotta help an old friend. But I'm only a phone call away if you need me, you hear me? And if that bastard so much as causes you a single tear, I'll take care of him, just like I did that bully in first grade who pushed you on the playground and tried to steal your lunch money. Love ya, babe."

Shane exhaled heavily. It was going to be a long night.

~

LACIE MOANED as both pain and consciousness returned with a vengeance.

"Lacie, baby, shh. It's okay. I'm right here."

Her mouth felt as though someone had stuffed it full of cotton. Every part of her ached, and there was an awful pounding in her head that made her stomach roil. With substantial effort, she forced her eyelids open. Thank God it was relatively dark; even the soft, muted light from the single lamp felt like a blade driving into her eyes. Her surroundings were fuzzy and out of focus, but she knew that voice.

"Craig?" she rasped.

Strong hands pushed her back when she tried to sit up. Yes, she knew those hands too. Hands that didn't know their own strength.

"Take it easy, babe. Here, sip this."

Craig held a straw to her lips, and she did as he'd commanded. Cool, delicious water eased down her parched throat.

"What happened? Where are we?" *Is that my voice?* That didn't sound like her, and it seemed to be coming from far away.

The side of the bed lifted slightly as Craig rose to ease another pillow beneath her head, so she could swallow easier. Even that small movement made her wince.

"What do you remember?"

Lacie closed her eyes and tried to think. It was like trying to swim through mud. Visions of lightning and thunder burned the insides of her lids, and her body shivered, recalling the icy-cold rain. "There was a storm ..."

"Yes, there was a bad storm," he confirmed, his tone low and soothing.

Disjointed images popped briefly into her mind, fading almost as quickly as they'd appeared. It took a while to piece together enough to make sense of it. *Why can't I think straight?*

She recalled sitting in her car, relieved that the teachers meeting was finally over. And that she was tired. She was just going to close her eyes for a moment ...

"I fell asleep, I think," she mumbled. "In my car. And then it wouldn't start."

"Why didn't you call for help?"

Yes, why hadn't I? The images jumbled together again. Lacie tried to take a breath, but a sharp stabbing sensation kept her from inhaling too deeply, effectively disrupting her train of thought, and she had to start all over again from the beginning.

"I couldn't find it. It wasn't in my purse."

Craig lifted the straw to her lips again, encouraging her to take another sip when her voice cracked.

"I ... I went to the school, but Daryl didn't see me. I fell ... and then ..." Her brows furrowed together as she struggled to recall what had happened next. She looked into his face and blinked. "Then, you came." She frowned. "Why were you at the school?"

Craig gently placed his hand on her arm. "Thank God I found you when I did, Lacie. How do you feel?"

Well, that one was easy enough to answer. "Awful," she groaned truthfully. If only the terrible throb in her head would let up, she might be able to think ...

"Tell me where it hurts, Lacie."

"Everywhere ..." She tried to do an inventory—she really did.

She'd heard once that when the body experienced more than one painful stimulus at a time, the brain's pain control system perceived some as less painful than others. She now knew that was total bull. So many different parts of her were screaming out simultaneously in agony, her mind incapable of sorting them out. Craig's outline was blurring again.

"Corinne ... I need to call Corinne ..."

"Shh, relax," Craig said quietly. "It's okay, babe. I'm here, and I'm going to take good care of you."

She mumbled something. It was getting harder to form words again; she could feel the darkness creeping up on her, surrounding her.

"Here, drink this. It'll help." Craig exchanged the water for a small glass of juice.

She didn't have the strength to fight him. She was tired, and she just wanted the pain to stop. Craig was here, and he would watch over her until she could think straight again, just like when they had been kids and that bully had pushed her into the slide and she'd hit her head ...

"Can't ... stay ... awake," she murmured.

"I know. Sleep now, babe. Everything's going to be all right."

Craig sat next to her, holding her hand. She could feel it, but she lacked the ability to move. A glorious dullness began to spread through her. She still had so many questions, but it was hard to think past the fog and the lovely numbness, and her mouth didn't seem to be working properly.

"Sleep, Lacie. Let the medicine help you."

He didn't say what it was that he'd given her, but it was some powerful stuff, dragging her under. Her eyes grew heavy, and the pain faded until she was floating on the most wonderful cloud. It felt good to relax into it, to let her body settle into the warmth and comfort of the bed and the pillows.

"That's my girl," she heard him whisper as his lips touched her forehead. "Pleasant dreams, baby."

∾

ONCE HE WAS sure she was asleep, Craig put the rest of the potent meds back in his locked cabinet. It would not do to have her get her hands on them by accident. They'd been dosed for his height and weight, which was substantially more than hers, designed to help him with the terrible pain he suffered at times. Tonight, they would help Lacie. She'd gone out a lot quicker than he'd expected; perhaps even half a dose was too much for her smaller frame. Or maybe he should have waited until the other stuff wore off.

"Sweet Lacie," he murmured, pulling back the blankets he'd so hastily wrapped around her in an attempt to stem her shivering.

His first priority had been getting her warm. Now that she no longer felt like a bag of ice, he could look toward other things.

Her clothes clung to her, still damp and splattered with mud and blood. He checked again, lifting her eyelids, talking to her, squeezing her hand, ensuring that she was completely out. Lacie would not be pleased with what he was about to do next, but he had no choice. She needed care, and he would be the one to provide it.

As he should be.

Craig removed her clothing, piece by piece. He'd known Lacie all her life, yet now, his hands were trembling. How many times had he touched her, held her over the years? But never like this. Never with so much intimacy, so much reverence.

He sucked in a breath when she finally lay in nothing but her pretty underclothes before him, her normally sun-kissed skin looking pale. It was so soft, so beautiful, except for the bruises. Not all of them had been caused by her recent fall, he knew.

Craig scowled at the discolorations around her hips, echoes of fingers that had gripped her too roughly in the throes of passion. He gritted his teeth at the telltale red marks in the tender flesh between her neck and her shoulders, where that animal had sunk his teeth into her like the rabid beast he was.

He couldn't dwell on that now though; Lacie needed him. Craig forced himself to put all that aside and evaluate her injuries. Her ankle was swollen and turning an ugly shade of purple, most likely sprained. He'd have to tape that up. The pale pink cast about her hand had been reduced to a soft, pulpy mass that he carefully cut away, section by section. Underneath, her hand was a mottled mess of purple and black, extending down through a wrist that was now swelling quickly as well. Turning her ever so carefully, he saw the blossoming bruise and an ugly gash along her back and winced. That was going to need stitches.

He continued to run his hands over her, eventually concluding that nothing was broken, but she was going to hurt like hell for a while. Overall, he was pleased to see that it wasn't as bad as he had feared.

Now that he had assessed her needs, he felt better. There was nothing he couldn't deal with. He had the supplies he needed and enough basic first aid training to care for her, though he would have to monitor her closely. For now, there was no reason to seek help elsewhere, and for that, he was glad. It was just another among a series of signs and events, all of which he now believed were nothing less than destiny leading them to this moment.

Lacie was meant to be his. Craig had always known that, but *she* hadn't, and life had certainly thrown a few curveballs in the way. Her brother, Brian, for one. Brian shouldn't have warned him off Lacie. They'd been like brothers from the moment Brian had stood up for him on the first day of school when all the other kids were making fun of him because his clothes were old and dirty and not the right size. They could have been real brothers if Brian had just accepted the truth.

Craig hadn't wanted to leak their location overseas. He still felt bad about that. But he couldn't take the chance that Brian would continue to try to keep them apart. And he'd paid his debt, hadn't he? The explosions he'd rigged as distractions had backfired and nearly taken him out too.

It was fate's way of intervening. And now, fate was giving him the opportunity to show Lacie the truth, to finally get her to see what had been right there in front of her the whole time. She'd made a grave mistake in trusting Shane Callaghan and in giving herself to him, but Craig would forgive her. He would show her the error of her ways, and she would know who truly loved her.

He ran a warm bath as he pondered the events of the last twenty-four hours. Fate was a funny thing. He had been so out of his mind with jealous rage when he viewed that video recording of her and ... *him*. Thank God she'd been at work when he saw it, or who knows what he would have done?

God, she made him crazy in a hundred different ways! But he loved her. Loved her so much. And after he'd had a chance to calm down and think through things, he knew that if he was to have her, he would have to be smart about it. The brute-force method had only pushed her further into Callaghan's arms.

He shouldn't have yelled at her in front of Callaghan. That had been a mistake. But he'd been so angry! If only he'd waited until he calmed down and then talked to Lacie, surely, she would have seen reason. She would never have done what she did.

It was defiance—he saw that now. A need to prove that she was her own person. He of all people should understand that about her. As kind and compassionate as she was, she needed to feel that she had some control over her life. For as long as he could remember, someone was always telling her what to do—her parents, her overprotective brother, her interfering little sister. And if he was honest, even him sometimes. But only because he loved her.

Unlike other teenagers and young adults though, Lacie had never rebelled. As the oldest and only boy, Brian had been wild. Corinne got away with everything because she was the baby. But Lacie? She was the good girl, the responsible one. These last few weeks had been nothing more than Lacie finally asserting her independence, of flipping everyone the proverbial bird. It had been a bit delayed perhaps but inherently overdue.

Once he'd realized that, everything had fallen into place. He had known then what he had to do. Oh, he wanted to spend a week making Shane Callaghan suffer for what he had done, the fucking dog, but he couldn't blame Lacie. Callaghan was a pro after all, and Lacie … well, she wasn't exactly schooled in seduction. It was a well-known fact that good girls were attracted to bad boys, and there was no one better than his sweet, naive Lacie.

How could she not be taken in by Callaghan's smooth lines, slick car, and extravagant dates?

Craig blamed himself. He should have been more aware of what was going on and found a way to show Lacie the truth before things went too far. He sighed.

What was done was done. Now, it was up to him to make everything right.

Craig tested the bath water, making sure it wasn't too hot, mentally chastising himself for not thinking of something bubbly and flowery-smelling to add in. Lacie always smelled so good—her hair, her skin, her clothes. Maybe next time he drove into town for supplies, he'd pick up something nice for her to use. Something soft and feminine, just like her. Yeah, she'd like that.

He shut off the water and set towels within reach of the tub, and then he returned to thoughts of his good fortune. He couldn't have planned it better. Everything had come together so nicely.

Lacie's meeting had run late. Then, Lacie had fallen asleep in her car, and how perfect was that? Originally, he'd tampered with the engine so that she'd need a ride home. Lacie was always the last one out of the building; he'd counted on the fact that few, if any, would be around to offer assistance. He'd conveniently be driving by, stop to help, and—*bam*—she'd have no other choice but to talk to him. And if she'd balked and tried to blow him off again, well, he'd had that preloaded syringe in his pocket. Craig believed in being prepared, and he'd had it all worked out.

Lacie getting herself hurt hadn't been part of the plan, but again, he saw it as a sign.

Really, this was so much better. He was not just the guy who had given her a ride; he'd actually *rescued* her. God, the way she'd clung to him like he was some kind of hero! He would remember that feeling forever. And when she had spoken his name, had practically melted in relief to discover it was him who held her, who carried her into the warmth and safety of his truck —*fuck!* It was better than anything he could have hoped for.

He probably hadn't even needed the sedative, but why take the chance?

Her sister thought she was with Callaghan. Callaghan thought she was with Corinne. Lacie had lost her phone, so neither of them could confirm or deny their theories before it was too late.

Now, he had her all to himself, far away from those who would try to keep them apart. No one would ever think to look for them here; no one else knew about this place. Roger used to talk about it all the time when they were in-country and had some downtime, how he used to come here to get away from it all.

Lacie needed him. She was injured and sick, and he would take care of her. What better way was there to make her see the truth? They belonged together. He knew her. Understood her. Loved her. No one could care for her better than he could.

After some consideration on the best course of action, Craig stripped down to his skivvies and carried her into the tub with him, hissing at the feel of her bare flesh against his. Lacie never even flinched, remaining limp and pliant in his arms. He hadn't intended to get this intimate so quickly, but it was the best way to care for her while she was unconscious.

He stepped carefully into the tub and rested her across his legs and torso. The setup allowed him to wash her and keep a tender hold on her at the same time, ensuring she didn't slip into the water or exacerbate the injuries she already had.

He washed her with reverence, taking his time, his attentions thorough. She was soft in all the right places, just like he had known she would be. Not skinny, not hard-bodied, but feminine and yielding with just enough to squeeze.

Afterward, when every inch of her was cleaned and warmed, he dried her with soft, fluffy towels. Taped her ankle and wrist. Gently rubbed mineral oil into her bruises. Stitched the gash behind her shoulder and bandaged her cuts and scrapes. Dressed her in his soft flannels. When he was finished, he sat back and admired her.

Beautiful. She was so damn beautiful. She was a precious gift to be treasured. He would never hurt Lacie, not ever. Not like that bastard Callaghan.

Cold fury began to flow through his veins when he thought about what Callaghan had done to his Lacie. If he hadn't seen it for himself, he wouldn't have believed it. The bastard had been so rough with her, almost brutal, taking her over and over again. The tiny security camera Craig had installed in her bedroom all those months ago had shown him the horrific truth. Callaghan was nothing less than an animal, completely undeserving of someone as pure as Lacie. Once things settled, he was going to put Callaghan down like the rabid dog he was.

Craig threw on some pajama bottoms and crawled into bed beside Lacie. He would make himself get up and out of the bed long before she awoke, but for now, he would hold her to him, protect her, and keep her safe and warm as only he could.

CHAPTER SIXTEEN

Shane slammed his fist through the drywall with a strangled curse. His brothers exchanged glances, but no one said a word. It was shocking to see the unfettered rage coming from the quiet, soft-spoken Callaghan, yet they understood what had driven him to this point. Each of them had faced similar crises. The love they felt for their mates and the fear they felt when they were in danger greatly surpassed any physical pain and stretched all limits of control.

And when they had needed him, Shane had been there for them without question, without fail. With a sense of profound empathy, they would do the same for him. They would rectify the situation and bring his woman back to him. As Shane had claimed her, so Lacie had become part of their family. In this, they were united.

The search in and around the school had been

extensive. The Pine Ridge police were called in out of necessity. They combed every inch of the building and grounds and even brought in the canine unit. It'd all added up to the same thing—Lacie had been on the grounds, and then she wasn't.

She was injured—they knew that much. Michael had confirmed that the blood discovered at the scene matched Lacie's, using skin and hair samples. The only thing keeping Shane relatively sane was that all signs pointed to it being an accident and, judging by the amount of blood, not a life-threatening one at that. But if someone *had* intentionally hurt her ...

He punched the wall again, needing an outlet for the crushing emotions overwhelming him.

Her car didn't have much to offer in terms of additional information. It had been towed back to the garage, and Sean had meticulously gone through it. It had taken less than five minutes for him to find where the lines had been disconnected, effectively disabling the vehicle, but whether or not this had been done deliberately or something had just worked its way loose was unclear.

Lacie was out there somewhere, hurt, and no one knew where.

Questions pounded in his brain, tormenting him. *Was she alone? Was she scared? How badly was she hurt? Why hadn't she called?*

Someone must have found her. It was the only explanation that made sense. But that brought even more questions. *Who had found her? Why hadn't they taken her to a hospital? Called the police? Brought her home?*

He didn't like the answers he kept coming back to —someone had Lacie, and she was unable to contact him or anybody else for help.

"*Goddamn it*," Shane cursed, smashing through the wall a third time.

Why were they standing here instead of finding her and bringing her back home? They'd gone all over the world, doing just that for people they'd never met, people they didn't love. Yet here they were, in their own fucking backyard, and they couldn't find his *croie*.

"Finished yet?" Ian asked somberly.

Shane shot him a withering glare. "Davidson has her." His gut screamed with the knowledge.

"We don't know that, Shane," Michael said quietly.

"*I* know it." Shane seethed, pacing back and forth like a caged tiger while blood dripped from his hand, unchecked. "That call was bullshit, placed after the fact. He's obsessed with her; he can't stand to see her with anyone else. I saw the look in his eyes. I should have foreseen he'd do something desperate like this. When the fuck is Nicki going to call anyway?"

Nicki was in Craig Davidson's apartment with Sean, using her particular CSI-type expertise to look for something, anything that might give them a clue to what had happened. Despite what anyone said, it was just too coincidental that Davidson had happened to choose that particular time to go "help an old friend."

The words had just left his mouth when Jake's cell

went off. The fact that it was Jake's phone and not Shane's was telling.

"Yeah," Jake barked into it.

Outwardly, his expression didn't change, but the temperature in the room dropped as he listened, his body hardening into stone. "Got it."

When Jake shoved the phone back into his pocket and his eyes met Shane's, Shane's heart nearly stopped. He'd only seen that look on Jake once before when his wife, Taryn, was in danger.

Shane couldn't bring himself to ask what it was that they'd found. He already knew it was bad.

"Davidson apparently had surveillance cameras hidden in Lacie's apartment," Jake said, his voice like ice. "They found a series of recordings." He blinked but didn't look away. "Including one of you and Lacie."

Davidson had been spying on Lacie?

For a few moments, it was hard to breathe as random images of his *croie* filled his mind.

Lacie, soft and sleepy, snuggled in her bed.

Lacie, emerging from the shower, scrubbed and pink.

Lacie, sweet and beautiful, just being herself.

Lacie, flushed with desire, screaming his name as she came.

Those were *his* images, for him and him alone.

Red haze obscured Shane's vision as his heated blood turned to ice in his veins. He was so enraged that everything went silent, into a perfect, deadly calm. It was a state he'd never experienced before; it was ... chilling.

And just like that, the picture came together with startling clarity.

"He wanted her. Seeing her with me pushed him over the edge and drove him to do something desperate." It was Shane's voice but not. This was his alternate persona, the quintessential black ops man who was now entirely focused on only two things—find Lacie and bring her home, and kill Craig Davidson.

He'd been right all along. Davidson was a psychopath. And right now, he was holding Shane's heart.

∽

DAYLIGHT STREAMED THROUGH THE WINDOWS, causing Lacie to blink against the light as she rose to wakefulness. Her body was stiff and heavy, as if she hadn't moved in a long time. Everything was sore. Her head. Her back. Her arms and legs.

Where am I? She squinted at the unfamiliar surroundings. It appeared to be a man's bedroom. The colors were dark, natural shades of brown, green, and blue. Basic, practical furnishings. The bed took up a good part of the space. A Shaker-style matching dresser and night table were the only other pieces; they were simple, sturdy, wood-grained—pine maybe. Even as disoriented as she was, she knew it wasn't a room she'd ever been in before.

What am I wearing? Like the room, her clothing clearly belonged to a man—a soft, heavy flannel shirt and lightweight sweats that were way too big for her. Her ankle, wrist, and hand were securely taped. A few twists of her torso confirmed what the dull throb had already suggested—that she had sustained an injury below her right shoulder blade.

Craig entered the room, his face breaking into a smile when he saw she was awake. "Morning, sunshine," he said with cheer, carrying a small tray with toast and juice. "How are you feeling?"

"Craig," she croaked. The memories started to come back to her along with the uncertainty, the fear, and the feeling that something wasn't right.

He grinned wider and sat beside her, slipping a thermometer under her tongue while pressing his other hand to her forehead. "Got it in one. I guess that rules out a serious concussion." He winked.

"Where are we?" she asked, removing the thermometer.

Craig put it right back in. "My uncle's cabin. Now, keep that in there, or I'll find somewhere else to stick it."

She scowled at him, making him laugh. He was in unusually high spirits.

"Brat. Show some gratitude, will you?"

She remained quiet until he removed the thermometer and looked at it, frowning.

"One hundred point seven. Could be worse, I guess, given the shape you were in last night. Let's see if we can get some more fluids in you and keep that fever from going up any higher."

He stood, stacking pillows behind her and helping her to sit up. She winced at the pain in her back.

Last night. The storm. She'd been cold and wet, covered in mud and hurting. Now, she was warm and dry, wrapped in soft flannel, and the excruciating pain was reduced to a series of dull background aches.

Realization dawned.

"You undressed me," she said, her eyes widening while heat flooded her face.

He rolled his eyes. "Trust me. You don't have anything I haven't already seen, sweetheart," he assured her. "What was I supposed to do? Leave you in your wet, muddy clothes all night? It's not like you were in any shape to do it yourself."

Lacie bit her lip. He wasn't wrong. Still, the thought of Craig seeing her naked felt like a violation. He smiled, but thankfully, he refrained from commenting further. It was awkward.

Time to move on to question number two. "Why are we at your uncle's cabin? Why didn't you take me home?"

Craig's eyes darkened. He stilled momentarily, and then he wiped the thermometer and placed it back into its plastic sheath. "I can care for you better here."

His carefully modulated tone sent a chill through her.

"Craig, what's going on?"

"You tell me, Lace."

Lacie blinked slowly; she hadn't expected him to throw the question right back at her. "Since I'm just waking up and you're the one who brought us here, I'm not sure I can."

Craig's lips thinned as he checked the wraps, made her wiggle her fingers and toes, and had her follow his finger with her eyes as he moved it from side to side. She humored him, knowing it was the only way he would answer her questions. Repeating the query would be useless; Craig would answer in his own time. Defiance at this point would only get his hackles up, and she needed information, not attitude.

Apparently satisfied that everything was as it should be, Craig exhaled heavily. "Lacie, I've known you a long time. You haven't been acting like yourself lately. I'm worried about you."

She blinked. "There's no reason to be."

Craig shifted, averting his eyes. "See, that's where we disagree. You've been especially moody lately and doing irrational things."

"Moody? Irrational?"

He nodded, his eyes bright. "Yes. You missed pizza and movie night, Lacie. You never miss pizza and movie night. Shelly was devastated."

Lacie frowned. She thought Shelly had seemed just fine but refrained from saying so. Craig was acting very strangely, even more protective than usual, and he was speaking to her as if she were a child prone to temper tantrums. Normally, if Craig had something to say, he just came right out and said it, subtlety be damned.

This cautiousness was out of character, and something told her that whatever he was referring to was about more than one missed pizza and movie night.

"And you yelled at me, Lacie. *Twice*. You'd been angry with me before, but you never yelled at me. Scowled at me, told me I was wrong, walked away, sure, but never yelled." He gave her a look of such suffering that she felt a slight twinge of guilt. "I was only trying to look out for you."

If she didn't know better, she might think Craig was actually *pouting*. Whatever medication he had given her last night must have hallucinogenic side effects. Had she not felt like Alice in Wonderland, falling down the rabbit hole, she might have laughed, but her instincts told her this was no laughing matter. She decided to go with her instincts on this one.

"I'm sorry I yelled at you, Craig," she said slowly, gauging his response. "I shouldn't have done that."

"Damn right you shouldn't have," he agreed, slightly mollified, and she knew she'd made the right choice.

She would have to tread lightly until she understood more about what was happening because at that moment, she was well and truly lost.

"I know you get stressed out sometimes, Lacie. And that's okay. You can always vent to me, babe." He stroked her hair. "But I knew something was really wrong when you brought a man back to your apartment. The Lacie I know would never have jumped into bed with a man she'd just met."

Lacie stiffened, ignoring her body's protests, her cheeks flaming. "How did you know about that?"

"I saw him leaving your apartment at six a.m., babe, and he was smiling and whistling. There's only one thing that makes a man smile like that at six a.m." He sighed. "*My* Lacie wouldn't have given herself away so easily."

She was speechless, torn between embarrassment that Craig knew what she'd done and rage that it bothered her. She was a grown woman. A responsible adult capable of making her own decisions. What had happened between her and Shane was a beautiful, wondrous thing. It was hard to feel shame for what she and Shane had shared, not when it'd felt so right, so perfect. The feelings she had for Shane—even after only a week—was the stuff of fairy tales. Never before had she felt a connection with another quite so strongly, and she would not apologize for it.

That didn't mean she wanted everyone to know that he'd spent the night. No matter how right it was, there were still those who wouldn't understand. Craig's reaction was a prime example of that.

"That's really none of your business," she said, ignoring the red flags her common sense was waving, her voice noticeably cooler.

"The hell it isn't," he retorted. His voice was louder than it had been. This was more like the Craig she knew. He might be mad, but at least this was a familiar field they were playing on now. "*Everything* you do is my business, Lacie."

"How do you figure that?" Lacie was getting angrier with each passing tick of the clock, ignoring the warnings firing left and right in her addled brain. The red flags were multiplying and waving frantically now.

"Goddamn it, Lacie!" He stood up and paced away from her, attempting to get himself under control. "How can you even ask me that? Christ, I've been looking out for you since you could barely walk."

Lacie flinched, as if he had slapped her. "I'm not a kid anymore, Craig."

"No," he agreed, his voice oddly strangled. "You sure as hell aren't." He paused near the window and exhaled heavily, dragging his hand down over his face. "You are a beautiful, sweet, grown woman, Lacie. And I ... care for you. I always have."

Whoa. Lacie was stunned by his blatant admission. She'd been expecting him to argue with her or to give her yet another lecture on her poor choices, but this? Nothing could have prepared her for this.

Feeling off-balance, she took a minute to regroup. Had she, on some level, suspected he had feelings for her? Maybe. But deep down, she'd refused to accept them as anything more than brotherly affection. It would have complicated things too much. She didn't want things to be weird between them. But now, he was giving her no choice. He was forcing her to address the issue head-on.

She steeled herself for the words she'd hoped she'd never have to say. The last thing she wanted to do was come across as ungrateful or to hurt his feelings. Yes, he could be arrogant and overprotective, but she had known him forever. And despite him being loud and overbearing, she did love him as if he really were her brother. That was how family was. You loved them regardless of their faults.

Still, she owed him the truth. "I care for you, too, Craig, but not ... not like that. Not like I do for Shane."

Shane ...

As she thought of him, a feeling of warmth enveloped her. Warmth and comfort and love.

Where is he now? Is he looking for me? Is he worried?

She thought about how concerned Shane had been over her hand and the murderous look in his eyes when Craig had been waiting for her in the hallway outside of class that day.

At the mention of Shane's name, Craig's entire body tensed, and she reflexively pulled the blankets tighter around her, as if to form some sort of protective shield between them.

"He's only using you, Lacie," he spat out. "Can't you see that? You are nothing more to him than a quick fuck. Another notch on his goddamn bedpost."

Lacie gasped, immediately sorry she had when her ribs protested. "That's not true!"

"Don't be so naive, Lacie." Exasperated, he ran his hands through his hair and paced away from her. The condescension was back in his tone. "A man doesn't jump into bed with a woman he really loves, a woman he wants to marry. He courts her, loves her, and builds up a relationship with her over time."

Craig ran his hand over his face again, as if searching for the right words to make her understand. He took a deep breath and softened his voice. "When a man really loves a woman, Lacie, he cares for her. He's always there when she needs him, no matter what, looking out for her. Keeping her safe."

She shook her head. What was Craig saying? That *he* loved her? That all this time, he hadn't been acting out the role of the big brother, but a potential husband?

Deep down inside her, things started clicking into place, filling her with a sense of dread. Her mind refused to accept it. It was unthinkable. This was *Craig*.

"No ... you're confused," she said, grasping at the most logical explanation.

Because Craig Davidson couldn't possibly love her that way. He just couldn't.

"Confused?" Amusement quirked around his mouth, but his expression was as weary as she'd ever seen it. "Lacie, I've never been more lucid in my life."

The dull throb at the back of her skull grew stronger. Shaking her head didn't help. Craig wasn't himself. Despite what he said, hee wasn't thinking clearly. He didn't love her, not like that. He'd married another woman and had a child with her ...

That's it! He was lonely, missing Mikaela, and he was projecting those feelings onto her. *That* made sense. She grabbed on to that theory with a two-handed death grip.

"It must be so hard for you since Mikaela is gone,"

she said, infusing as much empathy and understanding into her voice as she could.

How could she have been so blind? Craig was hurting. He'd had a terrible experience overseas, returned home in awful shape, and just when things had started to look hopeful again, his young wife had died in a horrific car crash, leaving him alone with a small daughter. It must have been devastating. Of course he would look to her. She was one of the few constants he could cling to.

Craig's head snapped back toward her, all traces of weariness evaporating. "What?"

"Mikaela. You must miss her terribly."

He looked at her as if she'd lost her mind, and then he did the most unexpected thing of all. He laughed. "You're kidding, right?"

Lacie's uncertainty gnawed at her from the inside. It didn't sit well with the ever-increasing ache in her head. "No, of course not. You loved her. It's perfectly understandable that you would—"

"I never loved Mikaela."

"What? But ..."

"Mikaela Daniels was a simpering, pathetic fool of a girl. I'd be lying if I said I missed waking up to that hell every day."

Lacie felt like she was in some kind of bizarre dream. "Then, why did you ..."

"Marry her? Because I'd knocked her up, Lacie. Her father threatened to ruin everything if I didn't. Interfering bastard," he muttered. "He should have been in that car with her. That would have been fucking perfect. Let *him* spend eternity listening to her whine and mewl." He laughed again, a choking bark. "That's probably why he was so anxious to marry her off. He couldn't stand being around her any longer either."

Lacie felt the air leave her lungs in a whoosh. Reality was caving in around her, melting in a surrealist rush like a Salvador Dalí painting. The sky was blue. The sun rose every morning. Mikaela Daniels had been her friend. And Craig Davidson had married Mikaela because they belonged together.

"You loved her." Without air in her lungs, her voice came out as a barely audible whisper.

"No, Lacie. I love *you*. I always have." He blew out a breath. "Stupid cunt that she was, Mikaela knew that, at least. She came to me one night in yet another attempt to get you out of my mind—if only for a little while." He smiled sadly. "She was wearing that pink sundress. The one that you always wore. The one that drove me fucking crazy."

Pink dress? Lacie remembered that dress. It was one of her favorites—a soft checked pink-and-white gingham of light, airy cotton. It had a long flowing skirt, cinched waist, and a halter top with a low-cut sweetheart neckline. Wearing that dress had made her feel like a princess.

Mikaela had asked to borrow it the night she had a date with Craig because she wanted to impress him.

Craig dropped down into a chair, putting his head in his hands. "I thought she was you."

What?

"I was ... ah hell, there's no other word for it. I was drunk, Lacie. Way past my limit. It was the night you were going out with that tool, Gary something or other."

Gary? It took her a few beats to place the name. Given that she didn't go on that many dates, it shouldn't have been as hard to remember him as it was. *Oh yeah. Gary.* Not exactly a tool, though he was a bit on the intellectual side. They'd had a nice, pleasant dinner and seen a movie. Apparently, he hadn't felt any sparks either. He never called again. She hadn't been disappointed.

"God, you looked so beautiful. You wore black jeans and strappy little silver sandals that put you up to chin height with me and that navy silk top that made your eyes sparkle like sapphires. I thought he was the luckiest son of a bitch in the world."

How could Craig remember what she had worn so clearly? She couldn't even recall what she had worn yesterday.

He paused for a moment, shaking his head. "I made the mistake of telling Brian what I thought about you dating that idiot, and he got all weird. We got into a huge fight, and it came to blows." He smiled ruefully. "He kicked my ass. Told me to stay away from you. As if I could. Christ, I wish it were that easy."

Now, *that* was news. Yes, Brian had been acting strangely the last time he'd been home on leave, but she'd assumed it had something to do with his first tour overseas. She would never have guessed he and Craig had had a falling-out. And over her, no less.

The ache in her head increased; it was a lot to take in, especially feeling as lousy as she did. She blinked several times and tried to stay focused while Craig continued.

"So, I took my beaten ass home to lick my wounds and grabbed a case of my closest friends to keep me company. And then ... there you were ... at my door! At least, I thought it was you in my fucked-uppedness. A vision in that pink dress, your blonde hair clipped up on your head, looking like a fucking angel and smelling like sunshine and flowers. You came to me, took care of me. Cleaned me up and held me. I thought I'd died and gone to heaven."

Oh my God. Mikaela!

Lacie had been so flattered when Mikaela said she wanted her hair cut and dyed to look like hers. She'd said it would be a blast when they took their annual trip down to the shore; they could tell everyone they were twins.

He exhaled heavily. "But it wasn't you. It was Mikaela. And the next morning, when I woke up hungover and saw her in the cold light of day, that's when I realized what she'd done. God, I was so pissed. She'd tricked me, Lacie. Made herself up to look like you, knowing I wouldn't be able to resist."

Mikaela had known? Brian had known? How was that possible?

"He's starting to give me the creeps. Have you seen the

way he looks at you sometimes? There's nothing brotherly about it." Corinne's words from only a few days ago came rushing back into her mind.

Was there anyone besides her who didn't know? Her subconscious laughed at her. Of course she had known. She'd just chosen to hide her head in the sand and ignore it.

It had been so easy to deny that unease in the back of her mind, especially once Mikaela and Craig had hooked up. There it was—definite proof that Craig was nothing more than an affectionate big brother. She could lay all of her fears—the ones she'd refused to recognize—to rest.

But this ... this made a mockery of what she now knew had been nothing more than self-effacing rationalizations on her part.

Not all of it had been a farce though. Mikaela had had very real feelings for Craig—Lacie was sure of that. She had forever talked about him, trying to find some way of gaining his attention.

"She loved you."

"Yes," he admitted heavily. "At first anyway. I think after a while, she began to accept I could never feel the same way about her. That realization was probably what drove her to do something so monumentally stupid."

Icy dread trickled down the back of her neck, momentarily overpowering the horrible ache. In her mind, she was running around, closing all the doors and windows, as if a storm was coming, not wanting to hear what came next. The communication link between her brain and her mouth lagged behind though, and the words came out before she could stop them.

"What did she do?"

"She threatened me." His body tensed in remembered anger, his eyes hardening right along with it.

"Threatened you? How?"

He shook his head, returning from some faraway memory. "Doesn't matter. None of it does. The only thing that matters now, Lacie, is that you are here with me, where you belong. I'm going to take care of you. I'm going to show you once and for all that I am the right man for you."

Her swift and sudden intake of breath was loud in the silence of the cabin as she fought the panic rising within her. She needed to be calm and rational. She needed to keep *Craig* calm and rational. He had been through so much. He was just confused. No one could be expected to go through as much as he had and emerge unscathed.

He might *think* he loved her, but he was probably just projecting his feelings to someone familiar, someone he felt comfortable with. When they returned to Pine Ridge, she would see to it that he got the help he needed to work through it.

"Craig, we need to go home. Now."

He stared at her for a long time, so long that she was forced to release the breath she hadn't realized she was holding.

Finally, he shook his head, looking disappointed. "No, I'm sorry. I can't do that."

She decided to play upon his sympathy and appeal to his protective nature. "But I need medical attention. I need to go to a hospital. You're the only one who can get me there, Craig. Please."

"You are right about that, Lacie," he said quietly. "I am all you need."

He turned his back to her, rearranging some items on the tray he'd carried in earlier.

"You can't keep me here," she said bravely.

Craig's shoulders slumped before he set them with renewed determination. He stirred her glass of juice and turned slowly. "Yes, actually, I can."

The grim reality of the situation hit her. She didn't know their location, but she could guess that they weren't in close proximity to any neighbors. Even hale and hearty, she'd think twice about trying to strike out on her own. She was not a rugged survivalist by any means, but in her current state, striking out solo would be tantamount to suicide. She wasn't even sure she was capable of getting out of bed unaided.

How was she going to find her way home from a cabin in the wilderness? Were they even still in Pennsylvania? Vague recollections of Craig mentioning fishing trips up in New York came back to her.

"Why are you doing this?"

"Because," he said, returning to sit down beside her, handing her the juice, "you need me, baby." He pushed a stray lock of hair away from her face. "And I'm going to take care of you, just like I always have."

Lacie raised the glass to her lips, sipping the juice. It was hard to swallow with the incredible lump currently sitting in her throat.

"Corinne is going to be worried sick," she said, trying for reason. "You have to let me call her and let her know I'm okay."

He smiled enigmatically, interlacing her fingers with his. "I've taken care of it."

"How?"

He shook his head, and then he brought her hand up to his mouth and kissed it. "I'll take care of everything, babe. You just need to rest and get better. Then, you'll see."

CHAPTER SEVENTEEN

"It said what?" Shane asked carefully, certain that he had heard incorrectly.

Corinne bit her lip. "It said she was okay, not to worry. That ... that things were happening too fast and she just needed some time to think."

"Time to think about what?" he snapped, making her flinch.

Ian shot Shane a warning glance and moved out from behind the bar to sit next to Corinne. "What time did the text come through?" he asked gently.

"Um ..." She thumbed a few keys on her cell. "Four a.m."

"That was eight hours ago," Shane said, his voice growing even quieter.

Corinne's eyes filled with tears as she looked from Shane to Ian and back again. "I know. I'm sorry. I didn't hear it. I had it charging ... I must have slept through it ..."

"It's okay, Corinne," Ian said, shooting Shane another withering glance.

Shane understood why. Lacie's sister looked like she hadn't slept in days. She shouldn't be made to feel guilty for succumbing to the exhaustion and strain.

Shane knew this, but he wasn't thinking clearly. The only thing on his mind was getting Lacie back safe and sound. If anyone should be able to relate to that, it was Ian; he'd been through his own personal hell.

"May I?" Ian held out his hand, and Corinne placed her cell phone into it. Ian's fingers moved faster than Shane could follow. After mere seconds, he blew out a breath. "The call source was blocked. My guess is, it was sent from a throwaway. But I might be able to trace it back through the towers based on the time frame. Probably not to a specific location, but enough to narrow down the area."

Corinne's eyes widened in desperate hope.

"Do it," Shane commanded, but Ian was already on his way to their private quarters.

Shane ran his hand through his hair—a signature gesture he'd seen each of his brothers make time and time again whenever one of their women had them so riled up that they couldn't think straight.

"I'm sorry, Corinne," he apologized. "I shouldn't have snapped at you like that."

∽

"It's okay," she said, rubbing her eyes. "You can't make me feel any worse than I already do."

She'd been beating herself up seven ways to Sunday. Why hadn't she called Shane earlier? Why hadn't she driven out to the school herself? She was Lacie's sister. She should have known something was wrong when Lacie didn't show up when she was supposed to.

Lacie had fallen fast and hard for Shane—that was true—but she had retained her wits about her. She would have known Corinne would worry when she didn't show up, and she would never have let her do so without calling to tell her where she was and why she hadn't come home when she'd said she would. Lacie was nothing if not considerate of others, often at her own expense.

Instincts, instincts, instincts. She should have listened to them then. She should be listening to them now. That text message wasn't right. Lacie would have called, not texted, knowing Corinne would need to hear her voice to be satisfied. And if Lacie really did need to sort a few things out—which Corinne didn't believe for a moment—she would have done so in the traditional, tried-and-true method of the McCain sisters—with Chinese takeout and a half-gallon of Turkey Hill's finest Rocky Road.

"You don't think Lacie sent that message," Shane said, as if reading her mind.

Corinne let out a breath. Why was it so hard to admit it? Maybe because if she did, then she would also have to accept that if Lacie hadn't sent that message, someone else had. And if she acknowledged *that*, then Corinne might lose the fragile hold she had on her sanity. "I don't know. Maybe."

"But you don't think so, do you?" he pressed. "It doesn't feel right, does it?"

His ability to read her so easily bordered on eerie. She opted for honesty. If anyone could help Lacie, Shane and his brothers could.

"No," she confessed. "It just doesn't make sense. I've never seen Lacie more certain of anything than she was of you. What would she have to think about?" Corinne shook her head, her conviction growing with each word she spoke aloud. "And even if she was confused about her feelings, she wouldn't walk away from her kids like that. *Never*. She might shut out everyone else while she tried to work through things but not her kids."

~

Corinne's thoughts confirmed what Shane had already suspected. Lacie wouldn't do this. There was only one person he could think of who would.

"Have you heard anything from Davidson?"

Corinne looked at him, her face somber. Her lack of surprise proved she had been thinking along the same lines. "No. His truck's not in the lot. I tried texting him again this morning but no response. My calls are going right to voice mail too." Corinne's blue eyes, so like Lacie's, met his. "He's got her, doesn't he?"

Shane nodded. "I believe so."

"Oh God. I knew he was obsessed with her, but I never thought he'd go this far." Tears started rolling down her cheeks. "Brian was right."

Beside her, Shane stilled. "What did you say?"

"Brian, our brother. He was right. He said Craig had some issues."

"I thought he and Davidson were best friends." Shane thought back to what Ian had alluded to earlier, that there had been a falling-out between Brian McCain and Davidson over Davidson's feelings for Lacie, but that was just speculation. He wanted to hear what Corinne had to say, guessing that her perception would be pretty accurate.

"They were, at one time," Corinne said, wiping hastily at her eyes. "But something happened the last time they were in on leave. He wouldn't tell me what it was about, but I think it had something to do with Lacie. All I remember is, Brian wouldn't let Lacie out of his sight."

"When was this?"

"About five years ago," Corinne told him. "I was still in high school; Lacie was attending the university. They were here for three months between tours. Craig ended up getting Mikaela pregnant. They were married right before he and Brian had to ship off again."

Shane felt the hairs on the back of his neck prickling. "Tell me about Mikaela."

Corinne took a deep breath and accepted the drink Shane had placed in front of her. "She transferred into Pine Ridge High when her dad retired from the Army and decided to get into local politics. She kept to herself mostly. Well, you know Lacie. She couldn't stand to see someone moping around the sidelines. Lacie kind of adopted her. She brought her into the fold and made sure she was included in everything. Pretty soon, Mikaela was around all the time. I think she had a thing for Craig, but he didn't seem to notice her much. It was a huge surprise when word got out about the baby."

"How'd that go over?"

"Oh, Mikaela couldn't have been happier. Craig, not so much. He didn't want to get married. Mikaela's daddy didn't give him much of a choice though. I don't think Craig was going to re-up until that happened."

Ian reentered the bar. "I've kicked off a couple of things. We should have the results in a few hours."

Corinne nodded, rising. "I'd better get home. Mom and Dad are due to arrive anytime now. Lacie is so going to kick my ass for calling them home early." She blew out a breath. "And she'll kill me if I tank finals on her account. She'll probably make me take a full course load over the summer or something." She attempted a smile. "You'll text me if you hear anything?"

"Of course. You too. You've got my private number, yeah?"

She nodded and turned toward the door.

"Corinne?"

"Yes?"

"We'll find her. We'll bring her home."

She nodded. "I know you will. I'm really glad she has you, Shane."

∽

CRAIG RAN THE WARM, damp cloth over her gently, reverently. He felt bad about upping the amount of pain meds he was giving her, but it was for her own good.

It had been a battle to get her to drink more juice. He smiled as he remembered how she'd tried to defy him. He liked her spirit, but in the end, she'd listened to him and done what he'd said. It would always be like that. She would challenge him, get his blood pumping, make him feel alive, and then she would give him what he needed. She was perfect that way.

His words had been a revelation to her. His naive, innocent Lacie. Of course she would believe that he'd loved Mikaela. Love, marriage, children—they went hand in hand in her world. Maybe that was why she had refused to see what was between them. Mikaela had been her friend. It was entirely possible that Lacie felt that acknowledging what was meant to be would be betraying Mikaela's memory somehow.

Mikaela. That stupid bitch had ruined everything! If she hadn't made herself up to look like Lacie and seduced him when he was three sheets to the wind ...

She'd planned it down to the very last detail, leaving nothing to chance. It was Mikaela who set Lacie up with Gary, ensuring that Craig would be there when Gary came to pick her up. It was Mikaela who worked him into a jealous fury with a few carefully orchestrated insinuations. It was her suggestion that he say something to Brian about Lacie's clear lack of judgment in choosing a date. And she was the one to play dress-up, to come to him when she was fertile and make sure they didn't use protection. She *wanted* to get pregnant.

Oh, she denied it at first. Told him it was meant to be, that she would make him happy. That Lacie didn't love him and never would.

Hateful, spiteful bitch.

As time progressed and she realized that he could barely stand the sight of her conniving ass, she grew nasty, threatening to tell Lacie everything. How she'd found his secret stash, he'd never know, but she said she was going to take all those photos of Lacie and show her, her brother, her parents, the police. He'd had to do something; she'd left him no choice. A few well-placed nicks here and there beneath her car, and ... problem solved.

Poor Lacie. She'd been so distraught over her friend's death. But Mikaela had never been her friend, not really. He'd done Lacie a favor. She'd never know how Mikaela had betrayed her.

In the end, it had worked out for the best. Mikaela was no match for fate. She was out of their lives forever. Lacie was especially nice to him and lavished attention on Shelly. Shelly adored Lacie. And Lacie would be a better mother than Mikaela had ever been. Soon, she would realize that they were meant to be together, and they would finally be a real family.

Lacie would be a better wife than Mikaela too. She would never have to stoop to tricks to have him in her bed. Already, she was pleasing him beyond his wildest dreams, providing him the haven he so desperately needed. And soon, she would willingly welcome him into her body and scream his name in orgasmic pleasure.

He just needed to be patient for a little while longer, capturing these stolen, intimate moments when he could until they could enjoy them together.

~

"THE ENDLESS MOUNTAINS," Ian told Shane, Jake, Sean, and Kieran. They'd been working around the clock in shifts, looking for any information that would lead them to Lacie. Michael and Nicki had gone home to get some much-needed rest.

Ian cast a map onto the mounted flat screen and zeroed in on an area near the Pennsylvania-New York border. "Sullivan County, to be more specific." It had taken longer than expected to narrow down the source of the text sent to Corinne's number, but Ian had come through.

"Shit. Are you sure?" Sean asked.

"Positive. Can't get an exact location, but that's where the signal originated from."

"That's right in Kane's backyard," noted Kieran.

Unlike the others, Kane and his wife, Rebecca, chose to spend most of their time at the family compound high up in the mountains and only ventured down into the valley of Pine Ridge for special occasions and brief family visits.

"Yeah, he's on it," Ian assured them. "He's got the whole area mapped out; he knows every hunting cabin within a hundred square miles. He's going to do some checking, see if there's been any unusual activity."

Shane nodded. They were closing in—he could feel it. The familiar hum resounded through his gut, preparing him for action. Soon, he would have Lacie back where she belonged, and Craig Davidson would learn what it meant to beg for death.

"Something else came up too," Jake said, his face looking especially somber. "I got a call back on the bat phone today from Commissioner Gordon."

Shane raised his eyebrows at the reference to the direct, secure line used only for official—or "unofficial" —business.

"The commissioner was very careful about what he said, but he hinted at a couple of things."

"What kind of things?" Kieran asked, curious.

Their youngest brother was always up for a mission, anytime, anyplace.

"Things that might be well suited to our particular area of expertise," Jake said slowly.

"Extraction? Recovery?" asked Sean.

Jake nodded. "A very specific recovery as a matter of fact. One that involves a local boy who went missing about three years back."

"Brian McCain?" guessed Shane.

Jake's eyes glistened.

"Jesus. Lacie was right, wasn't she?" Sean murmured, respect clear in his tone. Shane felt a sense of pride swelling within him. His woman was fierce, determined, and unwaveringly loyal.

"Maybe," Jake said carefully. "Apparently, there've been some new developments—thanks to what Ian was able to find—but not enough to sanction official action."

"What's your gut telling you, Jake?" Kieran asked.

They often deferred to Jake's instincts when considering which missions to accept. They all had them, but Jake's were flawless. He hadn't been wrong yet.

Jake paused for a moment and then blew out a breath. "It's legit. God knows what we're going to find though. Three years is a fuck of a long time to be in hostile territory." He looked pointedly at Shane. "Your call, man. How do you want to play this?"

Shane considered carefully before answering. Until he had Lacie safely back in his arms, he wouldn't be worth a shit, and he needed his brothers in on this. But if he could give Lacie her brother back, he'd do it in a heartbeat.

"Lacie's my first priority," he said. "Once I know she's safe, I'm going for her brother."

Jake nodded knowingly. "Thought you'd say that. Go on then. Take Kier and get your ass up to Kane's tonight. Pick up Mick on the way. The rest of us will handle the prep on this end and have everything ready to go when you get back."

"Something you're not telling me, Jake?" Shane asked quietly.

Jake had slipped in the suggestion to pick up Michael casually enough, but Shane sensed it hadn't been an offhanded thought. Jake met his younger brother's eyes. Kane might have been the alpha among them, but Jake was a close second. It was an effort to hold his gaze, but this was Shane's woman they were talking about.

Jake reached out, placing one hand on Shane's shoulder. "Just a precaution, little brother. We don't know exactly what we're dealing with here, but we do know she sustained some injuries the night of the storm. I'd feel better, knowing Mick was there with you."

Shane nodded, appreciating Jake's candor, even if he did sense there was more to it than that. This couldn't be easy for Jake. The situation was too reminiscent of one Jake's wife had been in a few years earlier. Shane remembered what it had been like when they went after Taryn, and the shape she was in by the time they got to her. She'd lost the son she'd been carrying, but if Michael hadn't been there, they would have lost her too.

Everything in Shane stilled at that moment as he felt the blood drain away in a rush, leaving him weak. What if Lacie was pregnant? They hadn't used protection. He'd released in her several times. It was possible. Hell, it was more than possible. Jake had gotten Taryn pregnant in one night. Ian, Mick, and Kane had gotten their wives with child right off the bat as well, in no more than a week. The only reason Sean and Nicki hadn't had a kid right away was because Nicki had been on birth control when they first hooked up.

His eyes met Jake's head-on. He didn't need his psychic sensors to tell him Jake was thinking the same thing.

Fuck.

CHAPTER EIGHTEEN

"You need to eat, Lacie." Craig held the spoon up to her lips and tried to coax a bit of soup into her.

It had been days since she'd had anything solid, surviving on little more than juice and broth. Even that had been an effort. In those few hours when she was awake, she said she felt weak and dizzy, and her appetite was nonexistent.

"I can't."

Maybe he would need to start cutting back on the meds. Every time he did, she started talking about wanting to go home. She wasn't ready yet. She was still recovering. And he wasn't willing to let her go.

"You want to get better, don't you?"

"I'm trying," she whispered. "I want to go home."

Damn it. He hated seeing her like this.

Each day, she seemed weaker than the day before. She was supposed to be getting better under his care, not worse. How else was she going to see how good he was for her?

"Come on, babe. Just a few more."

Dutifully, she opened her mouth and allowed him to feed her. She barely had any fight left in her. The fever, while low-grade, was still tenaciously hanging on, sapping her strength. Combined with her injuries and the potent painkillers he was pumping into her and her inability to eat, it was taking everything out of her.

He wanted her compliant but not like this.

"No more," she murmured after he got a few more spoonfuls in. "Please."

She pushed feebly at his arm, and he was alarmed at how weak she was.

"You did good," he lied encouragingly, wiping gently around her mouth. "Want to go out on the porch for a bit?"

Her eyes brightened a little. "Yes, please. Maybe the fresh air will help."

"I'm sure it will," he said. "It's raining lightly though. Is that okay with you?"

She nodded, her eyes half-closed. She liked the rain. She said she liked the way it made everything smell fresh and clean.

"All right, babe. Wait there till I take this stuff out to the kitchen, and then we'll go outside."

When she didn't answer, he turned to look at her and saw that her eyes were closed. He exhaled heavily. This was turning out to be much more difficult than he'd thought. He wasn't giving up though. He'd waited too long for this chance to prove his love.

∼

Lacie relaxed into the pillows while she waited for Craig to return, trying to keep from going under again but she was just so damn tired. She hated this feeling of helplessness. Surely, she should be showing some signs of improvement by now.

How long had she been here? Three days? Five? Longer? Days and nights ran into one another; she spent so much time sleeping that time passed in a blur.

Her aches and pains had lessened considerably, but she suspected that had a lot to do with the painkillers Craig was giving her. That, in addition to whatever bug she'd happened to pick up, was keeping her down and out. She was as weak as a newborn kitten and just as shaky with frequent bouts of dizziness and general muddle-headedness. It was hard to focus on anything. The days, dreams, nightmares, and reality were melding together, overlapping and interweaving, and it was becoming harder and harder to distinguish what was real and what was not.

She liked the dreams the best. In them, she was with Shane, making love for hours on end in some remote location, just the two of them. He would hold her in his arms, whisper words of love and endearment against her skin, and tell her how they were meant for each other and that they would always be together.

Then, the dreams would morph into something darker. It wasn't Shane's voice whispering to her anymore; it was someone else's. Shane's gentle lover's touch became harder and rougher, almost punishing. She would try to scream, but no sound came out. Her arms and legs were useless; no matter how much she struggled, she could not move, held down by a heavy weight draped over her, battering her already-broken body over and over again as she fought for breath.

Just when she thought she couldn't bear any more, the pain would lift, the heavy weight would ease, and she could breathe again. Then, the darkness would return—the blessed, lovely darkness—and shush quietly in her ear, stroke her hair, and tell her that everything would be all right. She was safe, she was loved, and all she had to do was let go ...

Eventually, she'd swim up through the darkness into the light again, and her world was recognizable once more.

In her brief periods of lucidity, Craig was kind, caring, and attentive. He massaged her arms and legs. Made her tea and soup. Read to her when she couldn't focus on the words herself. Carried her out to the porch for fresh air and to watch the sunset each evening.

But the darkness was always there, lurking just out of sight, hiding in the shadows, waiting for her to succumb and start the vicious cycle once again. It was exhausting.

Craig was taking good care of her, but all she really

wanted was to go home. Craig would hear nothing of it. She was safer here, he insisted, away from the "negative influences." It was clear by now that Craig knew Corinne didn't like him hanging around Lacie so much, and he had alluded to that fact more than once. And they both knew what he thought about Shane's influence. She'd learned not to mention Shane's name; doing so only agitated Craig and made things more difficult.

No, her best option was to bide her time and get better. The only way she would be leaving this place was by her own power or on a stretcher. Unfortunately, with each passing day, the stretcher was looking like the likelier of the two. Something inside Craig had snapped, and she needed to get him some help. He refused to listen to reason and believed that he was protecting her by keeping her here.

"Craig?" she called out feebly, wondering what was taking so long.

He was probably making her tea. He often did after a meal, saying that it would help settle her stomach and relax her. It did. But at that moment, the last thing she wanted to do was fall asleep again. She still had chills from her last series of dark dreams. She was unable to recall them clearly, but the soul-deep sense of horror lingered. It was as if her mind was shielding her, knowing it was beyond her ability to cope. She dreaded the idea of falling prey to them again.

A cold shiver ran up and down her spine, punctuating that last thought. She couldn't dwell on that. It was best to focus on the here and now. If she could manage to stay awake and strengthen her hold on reality, she'd be better equipped to fight her unseen demons.

She took a slow, cleansing breath, as deep as her healing ribs would allow. Lacie attempted to shed the residual fear of her dreams and concentrate on her body and how her recovery was progressing. Her head still ached, but it had been reduced to a dull, background throb. Her hand, wrist, and ankle were sore if flexed but otherwise not bad. Unfortunately, flexion was all she could manage; her limbs didn't seem inclined to do more. Sometimes, it took several minutes of concentration before she could get them to move the way she wanted them to.

With much effort, Lacie struggled to sit up. A wave of light-headedness conspired with her protesting and underused muscles, but she clenched her teeth and breathed through it.

There, she thought proudly when she remained upright. *That wasn't so bad.*

Once she silently celebrated her small triumph, gravity and her new position provided her with her next challenge—the increasingly urgent need to use the bathroom.

She called out to Craig again.

Ah hell, she thought when he still didn't answer.

She could do this. It wasn't that big of a room. Surely, she was capable of making it those few steps to the bathroom by herself. Craig had been helping her whenever she needed to get from point A to point B, but as long as she took it slow and kept one hand on something for support, it was totally doable.

Feeling encouraged by the fact that she'd eaten twice today and managed to hold everything down—even if it was only a couple of spoonfuls of broth—she forced her legs over the side of the bed, giving herself a moment to let the blood flow back into her feet. She winced at the pain in her ankle but was glad for it. She'd been numb for so long; any sensation, even the pins and needles firing up and down her calves, was welcome.

Her brief sense of accomplishment shattered quickly when she attempted to stand. Sitting up and standing up were vastly different. The room spun around her; her stomach lurched sickeningly as she felt herself falling.

"Lacie!" Craig shouted, lunging forward to catch her before she crumpled to the floor. "What the hell were you thinking?!"

"I just wanted to go to the bathroom," she whined, encaged by Craig's strong arms as he pulled her to him.

Temporary panic overwhelmed her, dark shadows lurching up from her subconscious at the close contact. Suddenly, she was violently thrown back into her nightmares—only this time, she could move. She writhed and scratched with everything she had, struggling against the evil attempting to restrain her.

The bindings tightened and squeezed even harder, encompassing her arms and her chest, and then another heavy weight wrapped around her legs, subduing them, too, until she could do little more than gasp for breath.

"Fucking hell, Lacie, it's me! It's Craig!" a voice repeated over and over again until her screams died down into choking sobs.

Entirely spent, her body went limp in his arms, nothing but dead weight against him.

"Craig?" She sniffled, her voice hoarse and thick.

"Oh, thank God," he mumbled. "Yes, baby. Yes, it's me. Shh. It's okay; it's okay," he repeated, rocking her back and forth. "Jesus, Lacie, what the fuck was that about?"

He loosened his grip, shifting her into a cradle hold.

"A nightmare, I think," she finally answered.

"Must have been pretty bad."

"It was ... awful."

"Do you want to tell me about it?"

She shook her head, squeezing her eyes tight, but nothing could dispel the overwhelming sense of horror that had gripped her.

"Well, it's all over now, sweetheart. I've got you, babe. Everything is going to be all right."

The words, spoken quietly against her ear, were so familiar. As was the scent, the feel of those muscular arms, and the solidity of the chest. No ... no ... no ... it wasn't possible. Those were just dreams, bad dreams brought on by fever and pain meds. They weren't real.

They couldn't be. This was Craig. The man she'd known her entire life.

She stilled in his arms as the cold, hard truth tried to force its way into her conscious mind. Were the nightmares actually her subconscious trying to warn her? Or was it already too late?

"Lacie, what is it?" he asked, a frown forming on his brow.

"Bathroom," she rasped past the terror constricting her throat. "I still have to ..."

"Ah, right," he said, relaxing his grip.

Oh God, oh God, oh God. The words repeated themselves over and over again in her mind.

Lacie tried to swallow down the worst of the fear. Panicking wouldn't do her any good, and it sure as hell wasn't going to get her out of here. She tried to take a few deep breaths, wincing when her ribs protested the expansion.

"Easy, babe," he crooned again. "Slow breaths now. Easy. That's my girl." Craig's arms were like steel bands around her, but his embrace was as gentle as she'd ever felt it.

On some level, he really did care for her. He wouldn't hurt her, not intentionally.

She gave herself a mental shake. He couldn't have done any of those horrible things. They were just nightmares—that was all. Hallucinations from her fever, the meds, and her overactive imagination.

Weren't they?

Lacie looked into eyes that had been watching out for her as long as she could remember. The boy who had teased her beyond mercy but beaten up every single boy who had ever made her cry—from the playground bully in first grade to the prom date who dumped her the day after he got her drunk and took her virginity. It was always there, but her mind would never allow her to see it.

She swallowed the scream that wanted to erupt from her throat and forced herself to speak. "Will you help me to the bathroom, please?"

Craig's face broke into a worried grin. "Of course, Lacie. Always. Anything."

He carried her to the bathroom, getting her situated while catering to her modesty. He offered to stay, but she convinced him that she was awake and capable of managing on her own for this small but necessary task. With a doubtful look, he agreed to remain outside the door, just in case.

At least he was affording her some privacy. Lacie said a silent prayer of thanks for that. It was impossible to look into his eyes and believe he was capable of any of those awful things.

But he's not the Craig you know anymore, whispered a tiny voice in the back of her mind.

The Craig she knew might openly and loudly disagree with her choices, but he wouldn't whisk her away and keep her from her family and friends.

She just managed to grab the trash can before the soup made a quick and sudden reappearance.

∽

CRAIG WAITED OUTSIDE THE DOOR. What the hell had just happened? One minute, Lacie had appeared to be dozing peacefully after finally managing to eat something. The next, she had been biting and scratching at him like she was fighting for her very life. It was scary as hell.

Things were going to have to change. He was going to have to start weaning her off the pills. She simply wasn't strong enough to handle them. He was getting fluids into her, but without solid food, she had to have dropped at least five pounds in the past week, and he didn't want her skinny. He loved her soft, feminine curves. He was looking forward to having her awake and actively participating in their lovemaking.

It wouldn't be long now; she was coming around, just as he had known she would. These last few days, she had been noticeably more compliant. Today, she had actually eaten something and even asked him outright to help her! That was definite progress.

This latest episode was worrisome, however. The way she had looked at him! For several moments, it had been as if she was terrified of him. But she had no reason to feel that way. He loved her. He would do anything for her. Surely, she had to realize that by now.

He heard her retching and cursed, bursting through the door without bothering to knock. He cursed again as he held her hair and stroked her back. His poor Lacie. He hated seeing her suffer.

When nothing remained in her but dry heaves, Craig took off his shirt, socks, and shoes but left his jeans on. He stripped her and then carried her into the shower. He kept it quick and efficient; this was no time for play. He expected an argument, but when none was forthcoming, he counted that as yet another positive sign. He refused to consider that she had simply become too ill to protest.

Craig dried her carefully, dressed her in clean, fresh clothes, and then scooped her up and carried her back to bed. After changing out of his own wet jeans, he joined her and brushed her hair.

By the time he was finished, she still hadn't said a word, nor had she resisted him in any way. He might have been dressing a rag doll.

"There," he said, sitting beside her. "I bet that's better, huh?"

Lacie didn't answer. She continued to stare at her hands resting in her lap.

"Lacie, baby?" He tucked her hair behind her ear. The pallor of her skin was alarming. "How do you feel?"

∽

"Lousy," she mumbled. "Dizzy. Weak." *Confused. Afraid.*

"Worse than before?" he asked, frowning.

Worse? Yeah, it's worse. Infinitely.

She nodded, avoiding his eyes. She couldn't look at

him. Couldn't look into those brown eyes and see the truth. She couldn't face it. She couldn't. Because that would mean everyone had been right and she had been wrong.

And she had allowed this to happen.

"Do you still want to go outside? I know how you like the rain. I'll make you some fresh chamomile tea, okay?" Without waiting for an answer, Craig kissed the top of her head and left her alone.

Lacie laid her head back on the pillows and closed her eyes. The tea. Was that how he was drugging her? It certainly couldn't be what she was eating. Her stomach cramped, reminding her of just how true that was.

What am I going to do? She needed to remain lucid and find a way to get help.

What would he do if she refused the tea? Would he just put the drugs in something else? What if she asked him to stop the pain meds again? Would he?

The waves of nausea began to rise once more as she tried to wrap her mind around it all. Shame, disbelief, confusion, hurt, betrayal—they all warred for the most powerful emotion at the same time.

It was simply beyond her comprehension. How could the man she'd known her entire life—her self-appointed big brother, her protector, the same man who had been taking care of her with nothing but tenderness during her waking hours—do something like this?

Her mind grasped desperately for another explanation. Maybe he hadn't. Maybe those images really weren't warnings but nothing more than bad dreams, made to seem real because of the drugs on her battered system. That could happen, couldn't it? After all, there were other side effects, weren't there? Nausea, vomiting, blurred vision, slurred speech, dizziness, cramps. She didn't know what day it was or how long they had been there. How could she trust anything her mind concocted?

The bottom line was that she couldn't be sure of anything. Could she vilify him based on nightmarish images recorded in a dream state when every waking moment, he had been sweet, kind, and caring? *No, I can't*, she decided, *not without proof.*

Craig might be misguided, but his intentions were good. The sick feeling in her stomach eased a little. *Where is your faith, Lacie?*

But she wasn't a complete fool either. As much as she didn't want to accept the possibility that those horrific visions could be real, she had to face the fact that she didn't *know*. It was now more imperative than ever that she keep her wits about her until she could get out of here on her own—or at least find his cell phone. There had to be some way to communicate with the outside world.

Which brought up another problem. Assuming she could find a way to contact Corinne or Shane, what would she tell them? She had no idea where they were. From the little bit she had seen of the surrounding area, it was very remote; there hadn't been any sign of other people—no cabins, no roads, no steeples in the distance or tendrils of wood smoke curling up into the sky.

What had Craig told her? Something about an uncle's cabin? It wasn't much, but maybe it would be enough for them to go on. Craig never talked much about his family, but Lacie knew his home situation hadn't been very good. It was one of the reasons why he had always hung around their house when they were kids.

She was kept from musing further when Craig reappeared.

"Ready, babe?"

Feeling a bit braver and a whole lot more determined, Lacie looked up into his face and saw the genuine concern etched there. She did her best to give him a weak smile. It was enough. He beamed back at her, and Lacie knew that she had just bought herself a little more time.

One way or another, she was going to find out the truth.

CHAPTER NINETEEN

Kane spread the detailed map out on the large wooden tabletop while Rebecca made a fresh pot of coffee and their infant daughter napped quietly in the back room.

"He's here," he said, his deep voice rolling like thunder as he pointed to what was clearly a cabin in the photo-quality satellite map. "The place is owned by a Roger Crawford."

"Why does that name sound familiar?" Kieran asked.

"Roger Crawford is one of the missing men from Davidson's unit," Shane said, shifting his weight. It was the only indication of his impatience. He pinned his eyes on Kane hopefully. "You've seen her?"

Kane straightened slowly and regarded his younger brother. Shane was big, but Kane dwarfed him. "Yes."

Shane shifted his weight back to his left leg. "And?"

Rebecca appeared between them, her hand resting

lightly on Kane's lower back. It was her way of calming him. Kane exhaled. He would not reveal everything he'd seen during his earlier recon; the last thing he needed was Shane going batshit and rushing in, fueled purely by blind rage, which was exactly what was going to happen if Kane told him what he had seen. That Lacie didn't seem capable of moving around on her own. That the few times he'd observed her yesterday, Davidson had been carrying her. Exactly why Davidson had been carrying her, Kane couldn't say, but two scenarios seemed the likeliest. Either Lacie was sick and injured or she was being drugged and held against her will. Shane wouldn't take either possibility well.

Kane's preference would have been to say nothing now and spare Shane the grief. There would be enough time for the truth once they had Lacie safely in their hands. However, Rebecca's gentle touch reminded him that it was Shane's *croie* they were talking about and therefore one of their own.

Shane needed something to hold on to. But what could Kane tell him that wouldn't rip out his heart? Even Kane had had to stop himself from rushing down into the cabin and retrieving her himself when he saw how visibly weak she was. As much as he'd wanted to, he had known that it was better to wait until his brothers arrived. Davidson was an unknown, and he was staying very close to Lacie. In her current state, she wouldn't be able to help at all. Since she didn't appear to be in any immediate danger, the safest option was to sit tight. Given the guy's mental instability, it was highly likely that Davidson might decide that if he couldn't have her, then no one would.

"She was on the porch last night, watching the sunset," he finally said, choosing his words carefully. "Davidson doesn't leave her side for a minute."

"Is she ... did she look ... okay?" Shane pressed, the need to know etched in his features. His jaw was clenched, his eyes dark and intense. His muscles were bunched so tightly that the veins were clearly visible in his forearms.

Fuck, Kane thought. He wasn't good at this kind of shit. His natural tendency was to speak the truth, however brutal it might be, but finding his own *croie* had tempered him somewhat. He tried to put himself in Shane's place, imagining that Rebecca was the one being held in that cabin, but that was too painful.

Sensing his distress, Rebecca lightly stroked his back with the pads of her fingers. God, he loved her.

Kane was going to make damn sure his younger brother got to experience the love of *his croie*.

He said the most positive thing he could. "She's holding her own."

He felt Rebecca's approval when she discreetly slid her hand down his back and patted him on the backside. She was the only one he would allow to get away with that, and she knew it.

Shane opened his mouth to ask more, but a glance from Kane warned him not to. Instead, he pressed his lips together and nodded.

"Right," Kane said, anxious to move on. "We'll move in right before dawn when Davidson is most vulnerable. Set up positions here, here, and here." He touched a series of marked areas on the map as he spoke. "Kieran, you go in first and take care of Davidson."

Kieran nodded; Kane ignored Shane's bold, pointed stare.

"Mick, when Davidson's secure, you go in next. Based on what I could gather, he seems to be keeping Lacie in this room here." Kane circled the rightmost back corner of the building. "We'll have the Hummer here for immediate transport back to this location, where Rebecca will have a room set up for Lacie. Understood?"

"Aren't you forgetting something?" Shane asked through a tightly clenched jaw.

Kane pinned him with another look. "No. You hang back until I tell you otherwise."

"That's bullshit, Kane! Lacie's my—" Shane didn't get to say another word as Kane's large hand shot out, making contact with Shane's chest and effectively pinning him against the wall.

"I know exactly what she is to you," he growled. "Which is why we are not going to take any chances of her getting hurt. Feel me?" He let up on the pressure, releasing Shane. "You're too close. You're not thinking clearly."

Rubbing his chest and looking as if he wanted to kill something, Shane stalked outside.

"You can't keep him away from her, Kane," Michael said quietly. He knew, as did all of his mated brethren, that Shane would stop at nothing to get Lacie back safely.

"I know," Kane exhaled. "But he's going to lose his shit when he sees her."

"That bad?"

Kane didn't answer. Instead, he said, "I'm counting on you two to keep your heads. Kieran, you've got to take Davidson out of commission double-time. He's fucked in the head, but he's a hell of a soldier. There's no telling what the crazy bastard might do if he knows he's cornered. Treat him with extreme prejudice."

Kieran nodded confidently. He was nearly as large as Kane and just as deadly. Davidson didn't stand a chance. "No problem."

"And Mick ..." Kane shook his head. He couldn't think of a single piece of useful advice. Michael was the best. No matter what they found, he would handle it. There was no better medic in the field, no one Kane would rather have taking care of his family and Lacie now fell into that category.

But at least he could give him a heads-up.

Kane rubbed the back of his neck, where a large knot was forming. "From what I saw, Lacie's not going to be in any kind of shape to be helpful."

Michael met Kane's eyes and understood what Kane wasn't saying. He took a deep breath and nodded.

"Get her back here as soon as possible. Rebecca's

already prepared the spare room with everything you might need. She can assist you."

Rebecca, looking as serene as ever, acknowledged Kane's words with a slight inclination of her head.

Kane had shared what he'd found with her. And if what he suspected was true, Rebecca would be invaluable. She had spent a decade working in impoverished Third World nations. She had seen more than her share of the world's horrors and yet somehow retained her gentle soul. Her capacity for caring for others knew no bounds, and Kane had a bad feeling Lacie was going to need that.

∼

Finally! Lacie was asleep. She'd fought it for as long as she could, but eventually, her exhausted, weakened body had just taken over.

Craig sighed.

She hadn't wanted to drink her tea and begged him not to give her any more of the pain meds. At first, he agreed, since he'd already made the decision to start weaning her from them. As the day progressed, however, she began to shake from the sudden withdrawal, and he went back to his original plan of cutting down her doses instead.

It hadn't been easy. Lacie had eyed every beverage with suspicion, and he'd had to drink from each glass before she would take some. He could have forced the meds into her, he supposed—she barely had the strength to hold her own cup—but he didn't want to do that unless she gave him no other choice.

Thankfully, he'd managed to empty a capsule into a small jar of applesauce, and for whatever reason, she hadn't challenged him on that.

They were running out of time. He could feel it. Lacie had been looking at him strangely all afternoon, as if she didn't quite know who he was. She'd asked lots of questions about the cabin, about his "uncle." Maybe it was the meds, maybe not. But he didn't like it. She was supposed to be growing closer to him, not moving further away.

Crawling into bed beside her, he pulled her close against his body and buried his face in her hair. He loved holding her like this, with her spooned against him, safe and warm in his arms. He'd become addicted to it in fact, and he never wanted to spend another night without her. He just wanted to love her. Lacie had the power to renew his faith in everything good, and he so desperately needed that.

∼

LACIE SHIVERED. She was so cold. Not the kind that came from the frosty mountain air—that would have been most welcome. No, this cold came from somewhere deep inside of her, more chilling than anything nature would create. It was in her very bones, the center of her soul. So very cold.

It was dark too. Still. Silent. As if everything were

waiting. A familiar sense of dread began to creep over her. It was skimming her arms, the outside of her thighs, her breasts. Something hard pressed against her from behind as puffs of moist, warm air pulsed against her neck and shoulders like some panting beast.

Tonight, the nightmare was different. There were no comforting dreams to ease her into it. Shane's presence wasn't there to give her the strength she needed to make it through this one. Tonight, there was only incomprehensible grief.

She screamed silently in her mind, knowing that her body would ignore the commands she desperately tried to give it. Her arms hung uselessly at her sides, unable to push and scratch and fight. Her legs remained immobile, incapable of kicking out. Her body was utterly powerless to twist away or curl into a protective ball.

But it was even worse than usual. Tonight, her mind registered everything.

She could do nothing. She was frozen in a drug-induced paralysis, her body unmoving, but her mind was unbearably alert and aware.

Something inside of her snapped. The last thread of hope, reduced to a fragile gossamer-like strand, was gone. The walls that had shielded her mind, the ones that had kept her safe and blissfully ignorant, shattered like paper-thin crystal. No more illusions.

She couldn't hold them at bay any longer. She was helpless, unable to save herself.

No one was coming.

There was no way out.

An eerie serenity came with acceptance—she knew this now. With a silent prayer asking for forgiveness, Lacie relinquished the last of her consciousness, giving in to the fatigue and weariness of her body and mind.

As the dark clouds built around the edges of her mind's eye, finally offering the peace she so craved, she hoped she never, ever woke again.

And then ... it was the strangest thing. Lacie felt completely weightless, as if she were rising, buoyed by a cloud. There was no pain, only peace. All of the discomfort, the aches, the soreness was mercifully gone. Lacie tentatively flexed her hands, her arms, her legs. Everything seemed to be working perfectly.

She opened her eyes and gasped, but there was no sound from the action. She was no longer in bed; she was floating above it, looking down.

Lacie felt no fear, only the mild interest of an impartial observer. Dawn was just breaking over the horizon, the first rays of the sun slanting in through the cabin window, illuminating everything in a soft, washed-out glow. Beneath her, Craig was lying facedown, just beginning to stir from sleep. His large body was wrapped around something, holding it tightly to him as a child might hold a treasured stuffed animal. He nuzzled it and drew it closer before stilling.

Then, she saw that it wasn't a stuffed animal he held at all. It was *her*.

Lacie drifted serenely above the surreal scene,

watching Craig as he began to realize that something was terribly wrong.

Her hair was splayed across the pillow. When had it gotten that long? Her skin was deathly pale, her lashes looking exceptionally dark against it. She looked so peaceful, lying there, unnaturally still. She felt at peace too.

Free.

Craig was shouting—at least, she thought he was. Her ears didn't seem to be working properly; she could hear nothing but silence. It was like watching a movie with the television muted and cotton in her ears. She could see his mouth moving, a look of panic on his face as he shook her body and slapped her cheeks, but she remained limp and unresponsive. He bent his head and pressed it against her chest, listening for a heart that had gone still.

Then, he was turning away, looking toward the door. Someone else was here. Ooh, he was big, dark, and muscular. He hauled Craig away from the bed like he was a small child. He looked so familiar.

Another man came in behind the first. He looked like the first guy but leaner. He had a black bag with him. Lacie watched as he quickly checked for a pulse at the side of her neck, lifted her eyelids, put his face near her nose.

She recognized him ... Michael! Shane's brother, the doctor. So, the other one must have been a brother too. That was why she thought she had seen him before. The family resemblance was strong, just like in the two who had been at the pub that day.

Uh-oh.

Michael looked upset. He was talking into something, and then he was straddling her body, pressing rhythmically against her chest, calling out to someone else, someone she couldn't see.

Then, Shane was there, and she felt a pang of sorrow. He was so beautiful, and he looked so lost. Michael was talking to him, telling him to do something.

Michael moved back, and Shane bent over her, kissing her. Ah, Shane was the most wonderful kisser! No, no, he wasn't kissing her; he had his mouth over hers, and he was breathing air into it, pinching her nose to keep it closed as her chest rose and fell.

It was mesmerizing.

Where had Craig gone? Oh, there he was. He was crying, trying to get back to the bed but the big guy wouldn't let him.

A fourth guy entered. He was even bigger than the first guy. One huge fist shot out of nowhere, and suddenly, Craig was laid out on the floor, quiet.

Michael looked like he was yelling again, and the big, bear-like guy was rummaging around in Michael's bag, pulling out a syringe. Michael stopped compressions long enough to jab the long needle into her chest. When the plunger was fully depressed, he removed it, carelessly tossing it aside. Then, he hit her chest so hard that the entire bed shook.

Lacie felt a strange tingle somewhere deep behind her rib cage. What was that? It grew stronger, joined by an irresistible tug right behind her navel. Her vision was getting cloudy, too, as if she were being encompassed by a fine silvery mist. It felt surprisingly cool and pleasant.

Was it time to go already?

She hadn't had enough time. There was so much more she'd wanted to do. She'd wanted to bring Brian home safe and sound. To tell her parents how much she loved and appreciated them. To stand proudly beside Corinne when she graduated with honors.

And Shane. She had dreamed of a whole lifetime with him and a houseful of children. He would make such lovely babies ...

Inwardly, she sighed and gave herself over to whatever force was leading her now. The power of it was immense; there was no hope of fighting it. She'd never been overly religious, but she'd tried to live a good life and be a good daughter, sister, friend, and teacher. Hopefully, it had been enough.

CHAPTER TWENTY

Shane gathered Lacie up into his arms, pulling her close against him, warming her with his body heat as Michael wrapped a blanket around both of them. Her heart was beating again, but it was too slow, laboring harder than it should have. The shot Michael had given her was keeping her going —but just barely—until they could get her to an ER.

She hung limply, like a lifeless rag doll, as Shane held her, murmuring into her ear, words of love and apology. Michael sat beside them in the backseat, constantly monitoring her pulse and breathing, while Kane drove like a bat out of hell down the mountain to the nearest medical facility, using the Hummer to create his own shortcuts and bring their ETA as close as he could. They should have had the foresight to have Sean standing by with the chopper. Kane radioed ahead, repeating Michael's commands to the waiting staff verbatim.

Shane held on tight, cushioning Lacie against the rugged terrain, but the situation was dire enough that a few more bumps and bruises were the least of their worries.

Kane executed a perfect horizontal slide into the emergency entrance. Michael was out before it stopped moving, barking orders.

"Shane." Kane's voice was sharp and cold, but it needed to be to get through to his brother.

Shane glanced at him, holding Lacie against him, his eyes wild. He'd gotten out of the vehicle, but he made no move to place Lacie on the waiting stretcher.

"She needs help, Shane. Let Michael do his thing."

Shane blinked as if he didn't understand.

"*Shane*. You have to let her go. *Now*."

"*Never*." Shane's eyes narrowed in warning as Kane took a step forward, but Kane refused to back down.

"*Shane*. She's dying, man."

The words were harsh but true and probably the only ones that could have gotten Shane to release his death grip on Lacie. Reluctantly, Shane loosened his hold and put her into Michael's arms. He swallowed hard and looked to Michael with a silent, desperate plea.

"I've got her, Shane," Michael assured him.

Then, without wasting another second, they were moving her inside.

Shane watched, frozen, praying for one of Michael's medical miracles.

Kane laid his large hand on Shane's shoulder.

"Mick's got this, Shane," he said quietly. "He won't lose her."

SHANE SAT BY HER SIDE, holding her hand as the fluid dripped into her body. For all that she'd been through, she'd never looked more beautiful. Like a fairy-tale princess. Silken blonde waves framed her face, her expression one of supreme peace as she drifted in the throes of some ancient magic spell.

His heart.

He was vaguely aware of the others standing in the background, talking in muted tones. He knew it was out of respect for him that they didn't speak of it, but he knew. He had seen the evidence of what Davidson had done to her. He had drugged her and taken what she would not freely give him, and it had nearly killed her. Had, in fact. It was only through the grace of God and his brother's medical skill that she was still with them.

Silent tears dropped onto her hand, each one a prayer that she hadn't known. That she'd been unconscious for it all.

"Come back to me, *mo chroie beloved*," he whispered. "I need you."

From somewhere very far away, Lacie heard the words, floating to her as if in a dream, spoken in a voice she longed to hear.

∼

"How is she?" Jake asked quietly.

The bizarre irony of the situation was not lost on him. Nearly five years earlier, it had been Shane asking Jake the same question as Taryn lay still and unmoving after the psychotic stalker who had murdered her entire family caught up to her ten years later.

And just as Jake hadn't been able to answer then, so Shane couldn't now.

Everyone else had gone home with the exception of Michael, who had left only to grab a shower and a sandwich. The day had been a constant parade of support. Jake knew from personal experience that on some deep level, Shane was registering their silent presence, but on the surface, he was thinking only of Lacie. Of how much he loved her. Of how she had to come out of this all right because anything else was simply unacceptable.

Jake also knew that Shane was blaming himself, berating himself for all the things he could have or should have done differently. How he should have known, should have sensed Davidson's level of psychosis. How he shouldn't have waited so long to speak with Corinne. How he should have found her sooner.

Jake knew, because he had been there.

Unfortunately, Shane would have to fight those demons on his own. There was nothing anyone could say or do to ease the clawing grief in his heart and mind. The only one who had any hope of helping him heal and get past it was Lacie.

Jake stepped up to the bedside and looked down at the woman who had captured his brother's heart. The last time he had seen her, she'd been beaming, radiant with happiness over some small gift Shane had left for her. With her shy smile and contagious ebullience, she was a perfect mate for Shane, and Jake had liked her instantly.

It was hard to reconcile that woman with the pale, fragile form before him. Her hair, carefully braided for practicality of care, was tucked along the pillow. A mask covered her nose and mouth, providing the oxygen her lungs needed to hasten the effects of the drugs on her tortured body, as did the fluids that flowed through her veins, attempting to flush out the narcotics.

At least the padded restraints had been removed; they'd been an unfortunate necessity when they first brought her in. Her body had been racked with seizures—symptoms of withdrawal from the powerful narcotics Davidson had been giving her. Michael had said that her body chemistry was way off-kilter, but chemical genius that he was, he'd devised the right combination to stabilize her fairly quickly.

It brought back such painful memories. Memories Jake had thought he'd reconciled.

He exhaled heavily and then returned to resume his place against the window. He would share this vigil with Shane, lending his own quiet support, as Shane had for him.

An hour passed, maybe two. Nurses came in and checked her vitals, disappearing again without a word spoken. Monitors and machines blipped and hissed in the private room; the only light came from neon lines on the screens and the automatic night-light just inside the door.

∼

It felt as if only minutes had passed since the silvery mist had enveloped her. Gone was the ethereal sensation of being comprised entirely of light; in its place was an aching heaviness, as if someone had poured concrete into her limbs. This was different from before though. Instead of the painful, muddled disorientation she'd experienced at the cabin, this felt cathartic.

Something was strapped lightly over her nose and mouth—a soft, rubbery plastic. Each breath filled her lungs with the most wonderful cool, clean air. Gentle whirs and hums filled the quiet space around her, and there was the unmistakable scent of rubbing alcohol, noticeable, even through the mask.

With some effort, Lacie opened her eyes. The room

was dark, but there was no mistaking it for anything but a hospital room. And at her side ... *Shane!*

Relief and joy flooded through her at the sight of him along with a pang of sorrow. He looked so sad, so weary, but still, he was the most beautiful man she had ever seen, and her heart lifted.

Hypnotic blue eyes blinked once and then widened. "Lacie ..." he whispered her name like a prayer. "I've missed you."

"I'll get Mick," Jake said quietly, disappearing from the back of the room.

Lacie's heart pounded in her chest; tears formed in her eyes. All of the emotion of the last week flooded into her, overwhelming her. It was okay to let go now. Shane was here, and nothing bad could happen to her when Shane was with her.

"Don't cry, Lacie," Shane whispered, yet she clearly saw wetness on his own sinfully long lashes.

She reached up, attempting to remove the mask over her face, but Shane caught her hand in his and pulled it to his lips.

"No," he said, his voice hoarse. "Don't say anything, sweetheart. Just listen."

Lacie blinked to clear her vision.

Shane kissed each of her knuckles and then held her hand to his cheek. "I thought I'd lost you, Lacie. I don't ever want to feel like that again. I wouldn't survive it."

Lacie tried to stroke his jaw, but her fingers weren't working properly. She could feel the growth of a day or more against her palm, however. It was surprisingly soft.

How much did he know? Would he feel the same way if he knew what Craig had done?

Michael came through the door, hair still damp, smelling of soap and shaving cream. Jake followed closely behind.

"Welcome back, Lacie," Michael said with a smile.

Lacie thought he looked tired, too, and realized that she was the source of his weariness as well as Shane's.

He lifted her lids—he had such a gentle touch—and peered into her eyes. "I'm Michael Callaghan. Do you remember me?"

She answered with a brief flutter of her eyelids and a slight movement of her head. Her fingers tried to grip the hand that held hers, filling her with warmth, but it was little more than a twitch.

"Good girl," Michael praised. He felt her pulse, nodding. "Lacie, listen to me, sweetheart. Don't try to talk; I want you to keep that mask on. Answer me with your eyes. One blink for yes, two for no. Do you understand what I'm saying?"

Another flutter.

"Excellent. You gave us quite a scare, but thankfully, you're a lot stronger than you look." He winked. His expression grew somber, but he kept his tone very soothing. "You had a hell of a lot of narcotics in your system, Lacie. In your weakened state, your body started shutting down. We're flushing everything out, and you are doing beautifully. We're going to have you hang out here for a while, make sure it's all good."

Michael proceeded to listen to her heart and then checked her reflexes with expert skill. "Okay, so here's how it works. You rest. Period. We'll take care of everything else. If you feel any discomfort at all, you let us know. No heroics, no brave fronts. Got it?"

She blinked and nodded ever so slightly.

Michael turned to Shane and grinned. "I wish all of my patients were as accommodating as she is. I take it, you're staying?"

Shane nodded.

"Yeah, I thought so," Michael said, but he didn't seem annoyed. On the contrary, he seemed quite pleased. "We'll bring in something more comfortable for you."

"Mick ..." Shane couldn't find the words.

Michael saved him the trouble. "Do me a favor though. Eat something. And for God's sake, take a shower, will you?"

Lacie's eyes widened, but a quick glance showed Shane's mouth twitching and Michael's eyes dancing with amusement. She knew then that everything was going to be okay.

THE NEXT DAY, Lacie was quietly discharged under Michael's care. Officially, she had been treated for dehydration, exhaustion, and a few minor bumps and bruises incurred while on a hiking trip with friends.

There was no reference to Craig or anything that had happened while she was kept at the cabin. Lacie wondered vaguely what kind of influence Michael had to be able to do that.

She was still weak but remarkably improved. Michael had said it would take a few weeks to start feeling normal again—at least physically. Never in her wildest dreams had she imagined she would be a recovering addict, but essentially, that was what she was now.

The other stuff, well, that was harder to deal with. No organic mix of detoxifying ingredients was going to help with that.

Rather than make the long ride back to Pine Ridge, they took Lacie to Kane's cabin to give her a chance to rest and prepare before facing her family and the police back home. Lacie was grateful for that. She needed to try to wrap her own mind around everything that had happened before she could discuss it with anyone else.

Rebecca sat by her side, adjusting her pillows and blankets, speaking in that quiet, gentle way she had. Michael had suggested that Lacie might feel more comfortable speaking to her about the events that had occurred, but Lacie wasn't ready to talk to anyone. She'd spoken very little other than to answer direct, medically relevant questions, content to simply hold Shane's hand. When her eyes were open, they were on him and nothing else, afraid he might leave if she looked away.

SHANE STEPPED out to give them some privacy but promised Lacie he would be just outside in the next room. Only then did he lean against the wall and close his eyes. It was impossible to see it for anything but what it was—a gut-wrenching pain that went so deep that he wasn't sure he would survive it. He ached for her, for what she had endured, and for what was yet to come, vowing that he would do anything and everything in his power to make it easier for her.

He heard the murmurs of Rebecca's soft, comforting voice through the door and knew she was addressing some of the more horrific events Lacie had been subjected to. Things he couldn't bear to ask himself. While Rebecca wasn't a doctor, she'd spent more than a decade in relief and aid organizations all over the world. She had seen more than her share of cruelty and violence, and the unmistakable air of kindness and serenity that surrounded her invited others to confide in her. There was no one Shane would rather have for his *croie* to talk to.

Shane gave Michael a grateful nod, taking some small comfort in the knowledge that his brother was doing everything he could to make it easier, for all of them. He was overseeing Lacie's care, ensuring that she was comfortable while her body healed and readjusted.

"Thanks," he said, his voice sounding like sandpaper over glass. Such a small word, but one with a mountain of gratitude within it.

Thankfully, Michael understood and nodded.

Kieran came through the door, the look on his face unreadable. Shane realized he hadn't seen much of him over the past several days. Then again, he hadn't been able to think about much of anything besides Lacie. His brothers, as always, had his back.

"How is Lacie?" Kieran asked immediately.

"Better than expected. Rebecca's with her now," Michael answered. "Where's Davidson?"

Kieran's eyes blazed with the signature blue flames they all had in common. "Dead. Fucker somehow managed to off himself with a blade he'd concealed. Messy as hell though."

"Saves us the trouble," Kane said, his eyes cold and deadly. It was true enough.

They hadn't reached a consensus on exactly what they were going to do with him once Lacie was safe. They would have preferred to handle it among themselves—Shane in particular—but back in Pine Ridge, the police were already involved, and it might have proven to be rather tricky. Davidson's suicide tied off more than a few loose ends, if nothing else.

Shane's eyes glowed with the fury of being denied his vengeance, but he had more important things to think about.

"You take care of it?" Kane asked.

Kieran nodded. Kane grunted in approval—the

closest he came to praise—and the youngest Callaghan beamed.

Rebecca had left a sandwich and some soup for him, but Shane couldn't stomach it, not when it was tied in so many knots. Yes, Lacie was here. Yes, she was safe. But he had come so close to losing her, and that left him badly shaken. Shaken and filled with a sense of rage so hot that it threatened to consume him from the inside out.

Shane sat at the kitchen table, feeling weary and angry and drained. He was vaguely aware of Michael's watchful gaze.

"We think we're so tough, so strong," Michael said eventually.

Kane, polishing his guns in the living area, paused momentarily in his stroke but didn't look up.

"We train hard, spend hours, days, weeks in places no man should have to go, enduring all kinds of shit because life is so fucked up and people can be unbelievably cruel to each other. And we're so smug because we're above all that and we're the best at what we do. The fucking good guys."

He paused and took a deep breath. "Then, we find someone. Not just anyone, but the one we're meant to spend the rest of our life with. The one we simply cannot live without. And then we know what real terror is. We feel the pain and hurt and suffering that we thought we understood before and realize we didn't have a fucking clue."

Shane looked up, knowing Michael was speaking

from his own experiences. Yet it applied to all of them. Kane's eyes never left the gun as he rubbed the same spot over and over again. He, too, knew the truth of Michael's words and was likely remembering scarier times when his wife had been brutally attacked in the shelter at which she volunteered.

"But somehow, we get through it. And it makes us stronger, and we're better men for it. Because now, we really and truly understand. We get it. And it makes each day so much better than the last."

No one spoke.

Michael rose from his seat and paused by Shane to place a hand on his shoulder, and then he proceeded out to the porch, probably to call his wife, Maggie.

Like Shane, Michael was generally quiet by nature. Extremely intelligent with a special gift for healing. He wasn't prone to offer unsolicited wisdom or truths, but maybe this was a form of healing too.

Shane sighed. Everything Michael had said was true. Would he be a better man for having walked through hell? He didn't know. He did know that Lacie made him a better man though. She filled a part of him he hadn't even realized was empty. To Shane, she was hope and love, comfort and home.

They would get through this. Somehow. Together. Because if there was one thing Shane knew for certain, it was that he never wanted to be without her again. He wanted to marry her, have a family with her, and spend the rest of their days getting the most out of life together. As long as they were together, they could handle anything life threw at them. Even this.

Was it a test? Or was it God's way of revealing the truth to them? Being raised as an Irish Catholic had certainly shaped a big part of his life. He might not be a regular at Sunday Mass, and he hadn't been to confession in many years, but he never doubted there was a higher power. Not once. Except maybe for a few brief seconds when Lacie had lain lifeless in that bedroom and Michael pounded on her chest and Shane breathed his life breath into her lungs. In those few moments when he had been afraid he had lost his *croie* and possibly a child they had created, he'd had thoughts he was now ashamed of.

They'd saved Lacie, and Michael had said that she would make a full recovery. Physically, it would be relatively quick. But emotionally, that would take longer and require a lot of patience and support.

There was no child to consider, not at this point. Had there been? Perhaps it was better if he didn't know. Jake had known. Taryn had been nearly three months along when she lost their first child. Shane knew not a day went by that Jake didn't think about his unborn son. Lacie wouldn't have been anywhere near that point, but ...

"She's resting," Rebecca said later, emerging from the side room where they'd taken Lacie. "Angus and Lily are watching over her."

Angus and Lily were the bear-sized canines Rebecca had adopted from the animal shelter. They had taken to Lacie instantly and appointed themselves her guardians. Since Lacie was okay with it, so was everyone else.

"Does she remember?" Shane couldn't contain the question any longer.

Given the shape Lacie had been in when they found her and the amount of drugs in her system, there was the distinct possibility that she might have been mercifully unaware for a good part of her captivity.

Rebecca's face, ever a vision of serenity, clouded over. "She's confused. She spoke of nightmares but is having trouble distinguishing them from reality." She paused. "I think she's in denial."

Shane felt as though someone had thrust a blade straight through his ribs and twisted. He had hoped she'd been too out of it to realize what was happening.

Rebecca's hand touched his arm. "But a woman always knows in her heart even if her head can't process it," she said softly.

He exhaled heavily.

"She's more worried about *you* right now," Rebecca continued, surprising him.

"Me? Why?"

Big, soft golden-brown eyes regarded him. "She feels stupid. Betrayed. Humiliated. I think she's afraid that you see her as responsible, for failing to see the signs, for not doing enough to prevent it from happening."

"Jesus, Rebecca." Shane was absolutely stunned. "How could she ever think that?"

"Because, Shane," she said slowly, "it is what *she* believes."

Shane stared at her in disbelief, but there was nothing but truth in her eyes. Truth and an unspoken request that he do something about it.

"Fuck. How do I fix this?"

"You can't," she said gently. "But you can be there for her. You can make her understand that no matter what, you always will be. That when she looks in your eyes, she won't see her own horror reflecting back at her."

CHAPTER TWENTY-ONE

Kane and Rebecca told her she was welcome to stay for as long as she wanted, but Lacie declined. She thanked them, explaining that what she needed more than anything else was to be back in her own private space, surrounded by her own things. Rebecca said she understood.

"Can I call you?" Lacie asked quietly as she hugged Rebecca good-bye. "I love my sister, but I'm not sure I'll be able to talk to her about this. Not all of it anyway."

"Yes," Rebecca assured her emphatically. "Please call me. Anytime. Kane and I are driving down next weekend. Maybe we can go out for lunch or coffee or something?"

Lacie nodded, relieved that she wouldn't have to place her burden on Corinne and thankful she would have something solid to look forward to and get her through the next week. It was going to be tough. She had no illusions about that.

"Maybe Taryn can come too," Lacie said.

Rebecca had told her that Taryn had been in a similar situation once and suggested that maybe Lacie could speak with her when she was ready.

"I think she'd like that," Rebecca said sincerely. "Having someone who truly understands can make all the difference in the world."

"Lacie," Rebecca said before stepping away. Her glance slid over to where Shane waited by the car. "Shane loves you, honey. Let him help you through this. He needs it as much as you do."

"I find that hard to believe," Lacie responded, summoning a tiny smile.

She felt so fragile, as if at any moment, she was going to shatter into a million pieces. And Shane was a rock. So solid. So strong. Unbroken.

"If you do," Rebecca said when Lacie told her how she felt, "Shane will pick them up and put you back together. Trust in him, Lacie. The love a Callaghan man has for his *croie* knows no bounds. There are no limits, no conditions. It just *is*, and it is everything."

The ride home was relatively quiet, but it was a nice silence. Neither Shane nor Lacie felt the need to fill the time and space with senseless platitudes or polite conversation. Something much deeper, much more profound passed between them on that trip down the mountain and back into Pine Ridge. Lacie sat next to him, holding his hand, grateful for the warmth it generated deep in her soul.

She had been so worried about what he would

think of her and of what had happened, but when he looked at her, she only saw love. It was in every word, every touch. When he held her, she swore she could actually feel his love pouring into her, infinite and unconditional. It was what had gotten her through those first couple of days.

"I love you, Shane," she said as they crossed over the final ridge that would take them down into the valley. "Be patient with me, okay?"

He squeezed her hand. "Always and forever," he promised.

Lacie thanked God once again for bringing him into her life. He was her rock, solid and warm, anchoring her to everything that was good and decent in this world, and she loved him so much. She hoped beyond hope that once the dust settled, he would still be there.

∼

LACIE'S HOMECOMING was nothing more or less than he had expected. Shane wished he could have made it easier on her, but there was little he could do. Lacie needed her family. Her parents had been worried sick; they'd cut their cruise short and made arrangements to fly home the moment they'd received Corinne's call. They rushed out of their house even as Shane pulled into the driveway.

Without letting him out of her sight, Lacie held herself together pretty well in front of them as they hugged and cried and hugged again. None of them knew the details, of course. Lacie didn't want them to. But one look in her haunted eyes, and they could probably guess.

The next few hours were tough. The police came out to the house. With Shane watching over her protectively and giving counsel, she made her statement. There was no reason to go into specifics. She kept her answers concise and truthful, based on what she had endured while she was conscious.

There was no point, Shane had advised her, in speaking of what she believed had happened while she was drugged. Davidson was gone, unable to hurt her or anyone else ever again, and no one needed to know the grisly details. Lacie was relieved that she could spare her family that at least. They were still reeling from the realization of how far gone Craig had been. News of his death was met with the numb acceptance that accompanied a major shock.

Lacie was afraid that news crews would be pulling up to the house all afternoon, but Shane assured her that his family had a couple of contacts in the media and that everything would be kept quiet.

The school year was officially over, so Lacie didn't have to worry about facing her coworkers and dealing with hushed whispers, curious glances, and all the questions they surely had. She felt bad about missing the year-end carnival and seeing her kids once more before they officially became "graders" but agreed that it was probably for the best. This way, she had the whole summer to concentrate on taking those first few steps toward healing.

Lacie moved back into her parents' house for the time being. Corinne took care of retrieving whatever she needed. Shane and his brothers made a complete sweep of her apartment and Davidson's, ensuring Davidson's surveillance equipment was removed and properly disposed of. Lacie was unaware that Craig had been spying on her, and Shane saw no reason to tell her. If she asked, he wouldn't lie, but it was not information he would volunteer. At this point, it would do nothing but provide more fodder for her nightmares, and she had enough of those as it was.

Corinne kept Shane apprised of Lacie's progress. She told him that Lacie woke up most nights in a cold sweat, shivering and crying. Shane ached to be the one who was there for her, holding her through the terrors, but knew Lacie needed her family too. He spent every evening with her, sitting quietly, talking, and going for brief walks while she recovered.

Two weeks after their return to Pine Ridge, when Shane was certain Lacie would be fine without him for a little while, he told her he had to go out of town with his brothers for a few days but that he had something special planned for when he got back. He refused to say any more than that, but he promised her that she was going to like the surprise.

It was harder than she ever would have thought to let him go. Those few hours spent with him each day had become the center of her universe. She looked forward to it, reveled in it, and then ached when he left her with nothing more than a chaste kiss.

She understood that he was giving her the time and space she needed, and she was grateful for that. The intimacy they shared went far beyond the sexual. She craved everything about him—his scent, the warmth of his hand as he held hers, his luminous blue eyes, deep voice, and clever wit. The world made sense when she was with him; the rest of the time, she was lost.

"Come back to me," she whispered, clinging to him as he was about to leave.

The way he looked at her then, his eyes reaching deep into her very soul, reinforced his words. "I will always come back to you, *mo chroie beloved*."

∽

Brian McCain flinched when he heard the heavy door leading into their underground cell creaking open and mentally prepared himself. He and what remained of his team had been left alone for so long; he prayed his captors might have finally given up, realized they weren't going to get any useful information out of them, and moved on.

He quickly hid the tiny six-inch-long piece of bone that was their last chance of escape, the only remaining piece of the poor bastard who had occupied this hellhole before him. Progress was slow, but he wasn't giving up. He would get them out of here, or he would die trying.

What would it be today? he wondered grimly. More torture? Or perhaps another few slices of that moldy shit they kept shoving at them along with some rancid water.

His stomach cramped, just thinking about it. But as bad as it was, they would eat it. He wasn't going to give the bastards the satisfaction of starving to death.

Then, he heard it. A string of vile curses—*in English*! He shook his head, sure that he'd misheard. But no, there it was again! Every swear word he'd ever heard rang through the air like the most beautiful music, barked in deep, masculine American voices.

Brian forced himself to his knees and gripped the bars, afraid to breathe. Lights. He saw lights and heard heavy footsteps approaching double-time along the narrow passageway. The beam of a powerful flashlight flicked over the interior, into his cage. His arms flew up to protect his eyes.

"McCain?" a deep voice asked.

He wanted to weep with the pure joy of it, but he simply gave a jerky nod instead.

"How many with you, soldier?"

Brian lowered his arms and opened his eyes slowly, getting his first look at the men filing into the cave. Seven of them. Huge fuckers. Black shadows in the darkness, making no sound but for the spoken words.

"Two. Who are you?"

Brilliant white teeth flashed.

"We're the ones who are going to take you home, Brian."

Relief washed over him like a tidal wave, intense and powerful. As it ebbed away, it carried the last of his strength with it, and he collapsed.

He thought he was dreaming, finally having succumbed to the inhumane conditions they'd been forced to endure. But when he opened his eyes again, he was on a stretcher and being moved. He floated in and out of consciousness for a while, had vague recollections of being washed and bandaged.

When he woke up again, it was to see a man sitting beside his cot, holding out an honest-to-God, ice-cold Coca-Cola for him.

"The beer and burgers come later," the man told him with a knowing smile. "Mick says your stomach can't handle the real stuff yet."

Brian greedily grabbed it.

"Easy now. Just sips, yeah?"

Brian had never tasted anything so heavenly. He looked at the man, certain that he was one of the ones who had saved him and what was left of his team. A brief glance to the right showed one of his men sitting up, giving him a thumbs-up. The other was still prone, but he appeared to be awake and talking to someone.

Brian turned his attention back to the man beside him. His jet-black hair was too long for standard military. He wore black cargo pants, a skintight black tee, and sported a Celtic tat with the scales of justice on a substantial bicep. But it was his eyes that really drew Brian's focus. They were a unique shade of blue, at once fiery and cold.

He looked around again. The guy talking to his buddy on the other side of the room had the same outfit, the same build. So did the one talking on a SAT phone, his fingers flying over the keys of a notebook computer. And the two standing guard at the door, looking more like archangels than men.

"My brothers," the man beside him said quietly, catching his gaze. "Your extraction team."

"Who *are* you?" Brian's voice was rough, unused for so long and permanently damaged by the screams he hadn't always been able to contain.

"Shane Callaghan," the man answered.

Callaghan. Brian knew that name. It was the name of a family from Pine Ridge. *From home.*

"How'd you find us?"

"Your sister," Shane said, smiling, and Brian knew in that moment from the look in the guy's eyes that he was more than a mere acquaintance.

"Lacie ..." It could have been Corinne, but Brian knew with certainty it was Lacie who had found him. Moisture pooled in his eyes. He should have known she would never give up on him.

Shane nodded, confirming his thoughts. "She said she knew you were out there, waiting for someone to come get you." He grinned. "Sorry we're a little late."

"No problem," Brian answered roughly. He had all

but given up hope of ever being rescued alive. "Better late than never, right?"

"Right."

"So ..."

"So," Shane echoed.

"My sister."

"Yeah."

"Do I need to shoot you, man? 'Cause I have to tell you, I don't want to."

Shane chuckled. "Only if you don't want to be invited to the wedding."

CHAPTER TWENTY-TWO

"Lacie, it's good to see you again." The multihued blonde offered a warm smile as she wiped down the bar and pulled out two bottles.

It was only then that Lacie realized her feet had carried her into Jake's Irish Pub. Shane had been gone more than a week. Lacie supposed her subconscious had led her here, needing to be close to him.

Lacie nodded, accepting the light beer. Her eyes were drawn once again to the eyes of the dragon tattoo that seemed to stare at her over Taryn's shoulder. "You, too, Taryn. Missing Jake?"

"Guilty as charged," Taryn answered.

Lacie looked closer. Taryn's violet eyes captured and fractured the lights hypnotically.

"Are those contacts?" she asked before she could stop herself.

"Nope." Taryn grinned. "They're the real deal." She

leaned in close, so Lacie could get a better look. "They drive Jake wild." She winked.

Lacie couldn't help herself; she laughed for the first time since Shane had kissed her good-bye.

They sat in companionable silence for a few minutes, each on a different side of the bar. Taryn got up a few times to tend to a customer, but other than them, there were only a few guys watching the game being rebroadcast and shooting pool. Anyone stupid enough to eye Lacie with interest received a lethal, warning look from Taryn. Lacie realized Taryn was every bit as tough as the men.

"So," Taryn said finally, "you and I, we've got something in common."

Lacie bowed her head. She'd thought she was ready to talk about it, but now that the moment was here, she wasn't so sure.

At least until Taryn leaned closer and said quietly, "Thank God I'm not alone anymore."

Lacie's head snapped up as Taryn grabbed a set of keys from behind the register.

"Hey, Dad, you okay if Lacie and I make scarce for a bit?"

An older man on the far side of the bar smiled and stood. Lacie knew immediately she was looking at the patriarch of the Callaghan clan. His hair, now woven liberally with silver, still boasted a fair amount of blue-black. And there was no mistaking the trademark Callaghan eyes, now looking at her with fondness.

"So, this is the young lass who has stolen my boy's

heart," he said, smiling warmly. "I was wondering when I would get to meet you."

He held out his hand, and Lacie took it, expecting a handshake. Instead, he brought it to his lips in an old-fashioned gesture.

"Well, at least I know where Shane gets his gentlemanly charm," she said.

Jack Callaghan chuckled.

"Aye, you'll do just fine," he said, his blue eyes sparkling. He turned to Taryn. "Well, go on then. Be off with you. No need to hurry back."

Taryn grabbed Lacie by the hand and tugged. "Have you ever ridden a Harley before?" she asked.

Uncertainty flickered in Lacie's eyes. "Uh, no."

"Awesome. You're going to love it." Taryn fitted Lacie with a helmet and then showed her how to straddle the bike and hold on. "Hang on tight," Taryn advised, kick-starting the machine with one powerful downstroke.

Before Lacie could catch her breath, it was stolen from her completely.

"That was ... amazing!" Lacie said half an hour later, reaching absently for a French fry.

She and Taryn sat on a rock overhang high above the valley, digging into the bags of takeout they'd picked up at a drive-through on the way.

"I know, right?" Taryn agreed, grinning. "It's such a rush. Jake broke down and got me my own bike for my birthday," she told Lacie, "but I'm only allowed to ride it when he's not around. He says I make him nervous, if you can imagine that." She laughed and rolled her eyes.

Lacie felt a tiny bit of weight lift from her shoulders. It was hard to imagine Jake Callaghan being nervous about anything. A few minutes in his presence had been enough to convince Lacie that he was a force of nature.

They ate in silence, enjoying the beautiful view.

"It never goes away, you know," Taryn said finally, wiping at some ketchup on the side of her mouth. "Not completely. But you learn to live with it. You use it to make yourself stronger and to appreciate everything more because of it."

Was that why Taryn was so strong? Because she had been through hell and fought her way back?

"What happened to you?" Lacie asked. She didn't really expect an answer; the question was meant more to deflect the conversation from her own painfully recent experience than to pry into Taryn's personal history.

But Taryn told her everything, beginning with her life as the privileged daughter of an aspiring US senator with presidential hopes. Then through the horrific murder of her entire family. She talked about the six months of torture she'd endured at the hands of an obsessive psychopath, a man who had been like family to her, a man who had been trusted to look out for them. Taryn told of her dramatic escape and subsequent rescue by a saint of a man named Charlie, ending with her unplanned, fateful stop in Pine Ridge and the erasure of her previous identity.

Lacie was speechless.

"I've never told anyone the whole story before," Taryn admitted when she was finished. "Jake and the others, they know pieces of it. Even Nicki, who had it worse than I did. They think they know all of it, but they don't. They don't know just how deep the betrayal went." She looked at Lacie, her expression a combination of suffering and grim determination that Lacie understood all too well. "I think it would kill Jake if he knew everything."

Minutes ticked by, the only sounds the soft susurrus of the wind in the full leaves and the occasional squawk of a circling hawk spotting its next meal down below. Lacie didn't know what to say. She didn't think there was anything she *could* say. Instead, she reached over and covered Taryn's hand with her own.

Finally, Taryn took a deep breath and spoke again. "Thanks, Lacie. I'm sorry I spewed all over you like that. You don't know how long I've waited to tell someone."

Suddenly, Lacie's arms were around Taryn, and they just held each other. Taryn was the first to pull away, wiping a tear from her eye.

"If you tell anyone I cried, I'll have to kill you."

Lacie laughed through her own tears, swearing an oath of silence.

"Maybe someday, I can return the favor," Taryn offered.

"Maybe," Lacie said, sighing heavily. "I can't talk about it. Not yet. But this ... it helped."

"I understand," Taryn said, and Lacie had the feeling that she was one of the few people who really did. "Besides, there's no rush. We'll be sisters soon enough, and then you're stuck with me."

Lacie turned away, gazing back at the stunning view. "I don't know about that, Taryn. I'm having trouble accepting what happened, making my peace with it. How can I expect any more from Shane?" She drew her knees up to her chest and wrapped her arms around them. "For all I know, this sudden trip of his is his way to put some distance between us and reevaluate things. I can't blame him."

Taryn gasped. "Lacie, that's not what you really think, is it?"

Lacie shrugged, afraid that if she voiced her thoughts aloud, it would make them one step closer to being reality.

She remembered Shane's words from what seemed like a lifetime ago. *"Some things should never be spoken of."*

Did that include her fear that Shane was already having a change of heart but was too honorable to come right out and say so? That he was just biding his time until she got herself together enough to move on?

"Shane told you that you were his heart, didn't he?"

Lacie nodded. "But that was before ... everything."

Taryn vehemently shook her head. "Doesn't matter. If you believe this is something that will change, something that Shane—or you—can simply walk away from, then you really don't understand how this *croie* stuff works, girlfriend. That line about *for better or worse*? Honey, you have no idea."

Though Taryn's words filled her with hope, Lacie still had her doubts. She wanted Taryn to be right but was afraid to believe. With everything else that had happened, she couldn't bear to pin her future on a man who might—with great cause—believe that a serious relationship at this point just wasn't worth the hassle. If she did and she was wrong, it would destroy her, more than anything Craig Davidson had ever done. Losing Shane was something she would never completely recover from.

The trip back down the mountain was a lazy one. Lacie discovered she loved riding on the back of a motorcycle. As saying as much, Taryn agreed they should make it a regular thing, and even promised to teach Lacie how to drive one.

When they returned to the pub later that evening, they were surprised to see Jake and Ian there, talking to Jack. Taryn ran into Jake's arms; he held her as if he'd never held anything so precious.

"Shane's looking for you," Ian told Lacie. "He was headed over to your parents' house."

Lacie couldn't get there fast enough. Her feet

covered the fairly short distance quickly, and soon, she was sprinting up the steps and bursting through the door. What she saw stopped her dead in her tracks.

It couldn't be. And yet it was.

"Brian?! Oh my God, *Brian*?!" Lacie couldn't take another step forward, afraid that if she did, he would disappear.

He turned around, flashing her that familiar grin, and she held her breath. He was so much thinner than she remembered, a shell of the big, hulking mass he had once been, but there was no mistaking that smile or his favorite way to greet her.

"Hey, brat," he said.

Lacie flew into his arms, crying hysterically. He laughed and held her tightly, as if he had never thought he'd do so again.

"Missed me, huh?"

It was a long time before she allowed herself to step back, but she continued to hold on to his shirt. Tears coated her face, dripped onto her clothes and his.

"Only a little." She sniffed. "What happened, Bri?"

He wiped carefully at her tears. "Our location was compromised. The bastards took us by surprise. We never knew what hit us. How about you? You okay?"

She nodded, taking a deep breath. "I will be." And for the first time, she actually believed it.

"How did you do it?" Lacie asked later, sitting on the front porch swing with Shane, drinking a mug of decaf.

She wasn't sure she would ever be able to stomach another cup of tea.

He shrugged. "Your files gave us the starting point we needed," he answered. "Ian was able to figure out the rest."

"How?"

She'd felt like she'd been running around in circles for the past few years. Everyone she talked to said there was absolutely nothing that could be done. Yet within the span of a few weeks, Shane and his brothers had managed to locate and rescue Brian and what was left of his unit.

He winked. "Family secret. One I can't share with you yet."

"But you will someday?"

"Oh, yes."

"When?"

"As soon as you say yes."

Before the words could fully take root in her mind, Shane Callaghan was on his knee before her, holding a small box, opened to reveal a stunning diamond.

"Lacie McCain, *mo chroie beloved,* will you marry me?"

Lacie stopped breathing. Both hands flew up to her mouth as she sat, frozen, staring at the ring.

"This is where you say yes, brat," Brian said from the doorway.

Lacie's mother swatted him, her father cleared his throat, and Corinne giggled.

"Will you, Lacie?" Shane said, looking up at her

with so much love in his eyes that she thought she might start crying again. "Will you be my wife and fill my soul?"

"Yes," she whispered, even as the first tears fell.

She slid off the swing and into his arms.

It felt just like coming home.

EPILOGUE
THREE MONTHS LATER

Patrick Callaghan left his mother and father and aunt and uncle behind in the hallway, proudly taking the hand of his new teacher in one hand and his cousin, Riley's, in the other. Like a true Callaghan, he escorted both women into the room.

Riley dropped his grip the moment they entered, zeroing in on the life-sized princess dollhouse at the far end of the room. Lacie paused, looking around the room with a practiced eye. It looked just as she remembered, but so much had happened since she'd last been here. She wasn't the same person she had been then. The events of those few weeks had changed her forever.

Not all of it was bad though. She was now married to the most wonderful man in the world. Her brother, Brian, was home safe. She and Rinn were closer than ever. Not to mention, she now had several more women who had become like sisters too.

There was Taryn, of course. She was keeping her promise, teaching Lacie how to ride a motorcycle on the sly. And Lexi, Ian's wife, was patiently showing Lacie how to make all of Shane's favorite dishes. Maggie, whom she had known casually before, now invited Lacie up to her farm for coffee several times a week. Nicki, Sean's wife, and she were working on several new children's programs for the local shelter together. And Rebecca had been—and continued to be —so very kind.

"Don't be nervous," Patrick told her, his face holding the confidence and mischief of his father. Familiar blue eyes, far too deep and knowing for a five-year-old, glanced up at her.

Someday, when she and Shane decided the time was right, would their little boy or girl have the trademark Callaghan hair and eyes?

"Aren't you?" she asked.

"A little," he admitted quietly with a discreet glance toward his cousin, and Lacie knew the boy had entrusted her with his deepest secret. "But we have each other, right?"

"Right." She smiled, squeezing his hand.

Patrick's eyes grew wide as he and Riley helped her prepare the room for the first day of school, officially proclaiming that she had some of the coolest stuff *ever*. By the time the other students started arriving, Patrick was welcoming them in, excitedly tugging them over to show them around the room and pointing out some of the "wicked" things they had.

Lacie looked on. Patrick was a Callaghan all right. Already, the little girls were eyeing him appreciatively with his jet-black hair, blue eyes, and disarming smile. The boys flocked to him as well, instinctively drawn to him.

Riley, it seemed, had already made quite a few friends too. She was outgoing and friendly but had clearly inherited her mother's strong spirit. Lacie couldn't help but smile when she saw a couple of the girls giggling and pointing at Patrick, though Riley was much more interested in the toys than she was in her cousin.

Lacie let them get comfortable with their new surroundings while easing the fears of first-time parents and welcoming new students with a friendly smile.

"Good morning," Lacie said a bit later once everyone was seated and staring at her with rapt attention. She glanced over at the exquisite ruby crystal rose on her desk that had been waiting for her that morning. "My name is Mrs. Callaghan, and we are going to have a great year ..."

Having Faith (Kieran's story) is the next book in the Callaghan Brothers series. Read on for a preview ...

READY FOR KIERAN?

Check out this excerpt from *Having Faith*, book 7 in the **Callaghan Brothers** series...

∽

"Is that the kid you hired?" Kieran asked as he pulled the big pickup into the driveway and spotted the unfamiliar teen.

"No," answered Shane.

"He doesn't look familiar," Lacie added.

She'd convinced Shane to let her tag along and help with some general cleaning and tidying while he and Kieran took care of the heavy work and repairs. It hadn't taken much. The last couple of weeks had been especially difficult for her, and Lacie welcomed the opportunity to keep busy. It allowed her to work through things, she'd said, and Shane was more than willing to agree to anything that kept her by his side.

After nearly losing her, he was feeling extremely overprotective and hard-pressed to deny her anything.

As soon as he spotted them, the teen looked up from the ancient mower and stood tall, his posture wary but not aggressive. "Can I help you?" he called out as the two much larger men approached.

With the observation skills of the ops men they were, they took in everything about the boy in a matter of seconds. Tall and lean, the kid was going to be big by the time he finished growing; it was something they understood all too well. Rich brown hair extended beyond the rag he'd tied around his head to keep the sweat at bay; half-shuttered gray eyes displayed both curiosity and caution. The kid's stance was relatively casual, suggesting a confidence rarely seen in one so young.

Kieran liked him immediately.

"Shane Callaghan," said Shane, extending his hand. "My fiancée, Lacie. My brother, Kieran. Are you the new owner?"

The boy proudly puffed his chest out as he accepted Shane's hand with a surprisingly firm grip and then Kieran's, and he gave a respectful nod to Lacie. "Yeah. Matt O'Connell."

Kieran suppressed a knowing smile. It had been a long time since he'd been at that awkward phase when he wasn't really a kid anymore yet not quite a man, but some things a man never forgot. "We thought we'd ready the place up for you, but it looks like you arrived earlier than expected."

Matt gave a slight nod. "Got here last night."

"You stayed here?" Kieran asked, remembering the state the house had been in the prior afternoon.

"Yeah." There was no mistaking the pride in the kid's voice. He didn't seem bothered at all.

"Well, since we're here, would you like some help?"

Matt considered them, and then his eyes wandered over to the truck. The back of the pickup was loaded with equipment and supplies. "S'okay with me." He shrugged nonchalantly. "But we'd better check with my mom."

Matt pulled another rag from his back pocket and wiped the sweat from his face and neck. It was still pretty early in the day to work up a sweat like that. Kieran wondered how long the kid had been at it.

"Come on. She's inside."

The strong scents of bleach and wood soap assaulted them as they entered the house. A battery-operated radio played from the back, and a woman's voice could clearly be heard singing along, slightly off-key but with lots of heart.

They found her in the kitchen. Her knees were on the floor, the upper half of her body swallowed up by the double-doored cabinet beneath the sink. The lower half of her body, including her rear end, moved in rhythm to the song as she scrubbed and sang. Lacie put her hand over her mouth to stifle the giggle, but the men had better control and somehow managed to keep their smiles from extending beyond a few twitches at the corners.

"Mom," Matt called, looking slightly embarrassed. She didn't hear him. "Mom!" he called louder, startling her.

There was no mistaking the loud crack as she jumped, knocking her head on the underside of the sink basin. Everyone winced in sympathy.

"What?" the woman asked, extracting herself from beneath the sink, rubbing at the spot on the back of her head. She didn't seem nearly as angry as she might have been under the circumstances.

"Mom," Matt said, breaking into her obvious hallucination, "this is Shane Callaghan, his fiancée Lacie, and his brother, Kieran."

"Shane Callaghan. We spoke on the phone. The seller, right?"

Three male hands reached out to assist her, but it was Matt's she chose for a hand up.

"That's me," Shane said with a friendly smile.

"Hi." Faith returned Shane's smile with one of her own. Tugging off the heavy-duty rubber gloves, she took the hand he offered, then Lacie's, and then Kieran's. "I'm Faith."

Kieran prided himself on the complete and total control he had over his mind and body. But the moment Faith put her hand in his, he could scarcely recall his own name.

Part of it had to do with the sudden rush of sparks and tingles that radiated outward from the point of contact, making him feel as if he had just grabbed an electric fence. For as unexpected as it was, it was not unpleasant; rather, it felt as though some hidden, heretofore unused part of him had just jolted to life. The growing unease that had been accumulating in his chest, getting heavier and heavier over the past couple of days, simply vanished.

In addition to the strange physical reaction, Kieran was caught mentally unprepared as well, for the image of the single mother he had been envisioning was nothing like this woman. He had expected an older woman, late thirties maybe—an opinion that had been enforced after encountering Matt. But Faith was not old, not by any stretch of the imagination. Unless she had discovered the secret of perpetual youth, she was no older than he was. Younger, by the looks of it. She was small, sexy, and quite possibly the most beautiful woman he'd ever seen.

Damn didn't even come close to covering it.

"You've already met my son, Matt, I see."

Kieran felt like he was in the twilight zone. There was no way in hell she was the single mother of the teen currently towering protectively over her shoulder. He blinked at her words and was dimly aware of Shane clearing his throat and Faith attempting to reclaim her hand.

"Sorry," he murmured, stammering out an apology. He reluctantly released her hand. "I didn't expect you to be so ..."

Matt scowled, but Faith's features softened. He could tell he'd embarrassed her, given the shy way she averted her gaze and the pretty pink color blossoming in her cheeks, and he immediately felt bad. It wasn't like him to zone out like that.

"It's okay," she said kindly. "You're not the first." She pointedly scanned him from head to toe. "But you might just be the biggest."

Her smile was dazzling, and he found himself chuckling with the others as the awkwardness passed. "Fair enough."

CONNECT WITH ABBIE

Sign up for Abbie's newsletter today! You'll not only get advance notice of new releases, sales, giveaways, contests, fun facts, and other great things each month, you'll also get a free book just for signing up, access to exclusive bonus content not available anywhere else, *and* be automatically entered for a chance to win a gift card every month, simply for reading it!

SIGN ME UP!

~

Connect with Abbie on social media and your favorite book-centric sites:

Facebook
Zanders Clan Reader Group

Connect with Abbie

Instagram
Goodreads
BookBub

Callaghan World Timeline Reading Order

Can't get enough of those Callaghan boys? They appear in more than just their own series, you know. Here's a complete list of books in which they appear by the Callaghan world timeline. Sometimes it's just a cameo; other times, they play a pretty major role.

1. Celina (Connelly Cousins, Book 1)
2. Jamie (Connelly Cousins, Book 1.5)
3. Johnny (Connelly Cousins, Book 2)
4. Dangerous Secrets (Callaghan Brothers, Book 1)
5. Michael (Connelly Cousins, Book 3)
6. First & Only (Callaghan Brothers, Book 2)
7. House Calls (Callaghan Brothers, Book 3)
8. Seeking Vengeance (Callaghan Brothers, Book 4)
9. Guardian Angel (Callaghan Brothers, Book 5)
10. Beyond Affection (Callaghan Brothers, Book 6)
11. Having Faith (Callaghan Brothers, Book 7)
12. Bottom Line (Callaghan Brothers, Book 8)
13. Forever Mine (Callaghan Brothers, Book 9)
14. Two of a Kind (Callaghan Brothers, Book 10)
15. Spencer and Kayla's Wedding (short / subscriber bonus)

16. Protecting Sam (Sanctuary, Book 1)
17. Not Quite Broken (Callaghan Brothers, Book 11)
18. Danny's Happy Trails Ranch (short / subscriber bonus)
19. SEAL Out of Water (Silver SEALs)
20. Best Laid Plans (Sanctuary, Book 2)
21. Callaghans in Quarantine (short / subscriber bonus)
22. Shadow of Doubt (Sanctuary, Book 3)
23. Nick UnCaged (Sanctuary, Book 4)
24. The Proposal Plan (Sanctuary short / subscriber bonus)
25. Organically Yours (Sanctuary, Book 5)
26. Callaghans Down the Shore (short / subscriber bonus)
27. Finding Home (Long Road Home, Book 3)
28. Prodigal Son (Sanctuary, Book 6)
29. Cast in Shadow (Shadow SEALs)
30. Home Base (Long Road Home, Book 8)
31. Too Close to Home (The Long Road Home, Book 13)

ALSO BY ABBIE ZANDERS

Abbie Zanders Starter Set

For those who like a little bit of everything, this is a great intro to some of Abbie's series. Includes the first in series for the Cerasino Family Novellas, Callaghan Brothers, Mythic, Sanctuary, and a Timeless Love

Abbie Zanders First in Series Collection

~

Contemporary Romance – Callaghan Brothers

Plan your visit to Pine Ridge, Pennsylvania and fall in love with the Callaghans

Dangerous Secrets

First and Only

House Calls

Seeking Vengeance

Guardian Angel

Beyond Affection

Having Faith

Bottom Line

Forever Mine

Two of a Kind

Not Quite Broken

Callaghan Brothers Collection #1 (books 1-3)

Callaghan Brothers Collection #2 (books 4-6)

Callaghan Brothers Collection #3 (books 7-9)

∾

Contemporary Romance – Connelly Cousins

Drive across the river to Birch Falls and spend some time with the Connelly Cousins

Celina

Jamie (novella)

Johnny

Michael

Connelly Cousins Complete Series

Home Base (Connelly Cousins / The Long Road Home crossover)

∾

Contemporary Romance – Covendale Series

If you like humor and snark in your romance, add a stop in Covendale

Five Minute Man

All Night Woman

Seizing Mack

∽

Contemporary Romance – Sanctuary

More small town romance with former military heroes you can't help but love

Protecting Sam

Best Laid Plans

Shadow of Doubt

Nick UnCaged

Organically Yours

Finding Home (Sanctuary / The Long Road Home crossover)

Prodigal Son

Sanctuary Collection 1 (Books 1-3)

Sanctuary Collection 2 (Books 4-6)

∽

Cerasino Family Novellas

Short, sweet feel-good romance that'll leave you smiling

Just For Me

Just For Him

Just For Her

Just For Us

Cerasino Family Novellas Collection #1 (books 1-3)

~

More Contemporary Romance

Standalone & crossover titles

The Realist

Celestial Desire

Letting Go

SEAL Out of Water (Callaghan Brothers / Silver SEALs crossover)

Rockstar Romeo (Cocky Hero Club)

Finding Home (Sanctuary / The Long Road Home crossover)

Cast in Shadow (Shadow SEALs / Callaghan / Sanctuary crossover)

Home Base (Connelly Cousins / The Long Road Home crossover)

~

Time Travel Romance

Travel between present day NYC and 15th century Scotland in these stand-alone but related titles

Maiden in Manhattan

Raising Hell in the Highlands

A Timeless Love Box Set

∼

Paranormal Romance – Mythic Series

Welcome to Mythic, an idyllic community all kinds of Extraordinaries call home.

Faerie Godmother

Fallen Angel

The Oracle at Mythic

Wolf Out of Water

∼

Paranormal Romance – Beary Christmas Series

Sweet holiday romance with an ursine twist

A Very Beary Christmas

Going Polar

Bearly Festive

∼

More Paranormal Romance

Standalone, complete stories

Vampire, Unaware

Black Wolfe's Mate (written as Avelyn McCrae)

Going Nowhere

The Jewel

Close Encounters of the Sexy Kind

Rock Hard

Immortal Dreams

Rehabbing the Beast (written as Avelyn McCrae)

More Than Mortal

Falling for the Werewolf

∾

Historical/Medieval Romance

A Warrior's Heart (written as Avelyn McCrae)

ABOUT THE AUTHOR

Abbie Zanders is a USA Today Bestselling Author with more than 60 published romance novels to date. Her stories range from contemporary to paranormal and everything in between. She promises her readers two things: happily ever afters, always, and no cliffhangers, ever.

Born and raised in the mountains of Northeastern Pennsylvania, where she sets most of her stories, she's known for small town romance featuring golden-hearted alpha heroes and strong, relatable heroines. Besides being an avid reader and writer, she loves animals (especially big dogs), American muscle cars, and 80's hair bands.

Made in United States
Troutdale, OR
09/28/2025